WINGS
OF
FIRE

WINGS OF FIRE

THE FLAMES OF HOPE

by
TUI T. SUTHERLAND

SCHOLASTIC PRESS
NEW YORK

Library of Congress Cataloging-in-Publication Data available

ISBN 978-93-5471-181-7

10 9 8 7 6 5 4 3 2 1   22 23 24 25 26

First printing, April 2022
This reprint edition : September 2023

Book design by Phil Falco
Printed in India at Saurabh Printers Pvt. Ltd.

For Steve Malk, who
first said "What do you
think about dragons?" and
made all of this happen;
I am so grateful!

And for Sunshine —
I love you forever, Snuggles

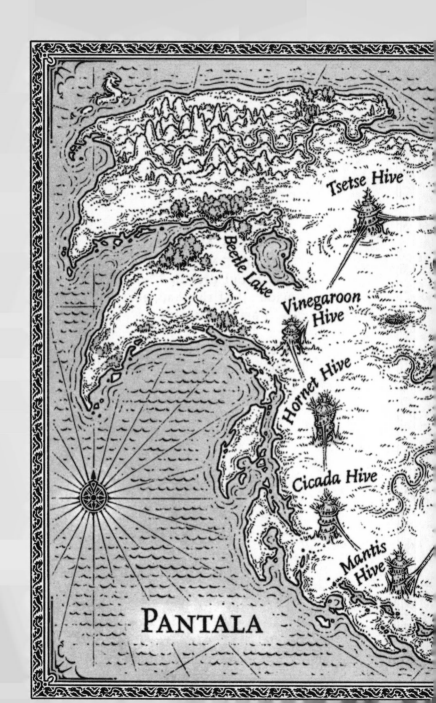

Tsetse Hive

Beetle Lake

Vinegaroon Hive

Hornet Hive

Cicada Hive

Mantis Hive

PANTALA

Tsetse Hive

Beet

A GUIDE TO THE
DRAGONS

Cicada Hive

Mantis
Hive

Yellowjacket
Hive

Wasp
Hive

OF PANTALA

Bloodworm
Hive

Scorpion

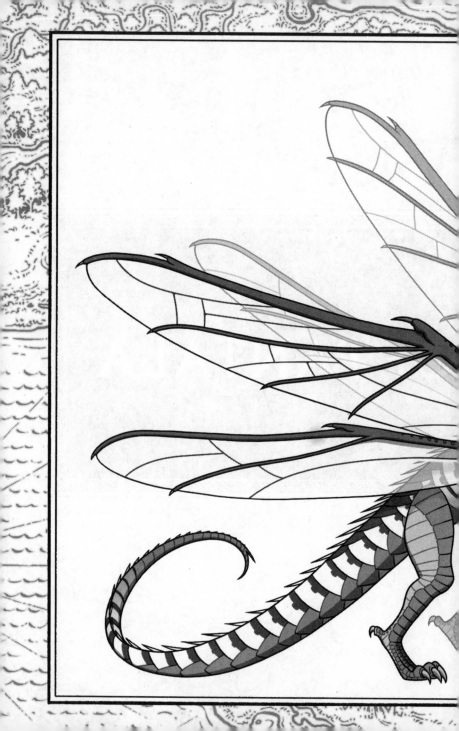

HIVEWINGS

Description: red, yellow, and/or orange, but always mixed with some black scales; four wings

Abilities: vary from dragon to dragon; examples include deadly stingers that can extend from their wrists to stab their enemies; venom in their teeth or claws; or a paralyzing toxin that can immobilize their prey; others can spray boiling acid from a stinger on their tails

Queen: Queen Wasp

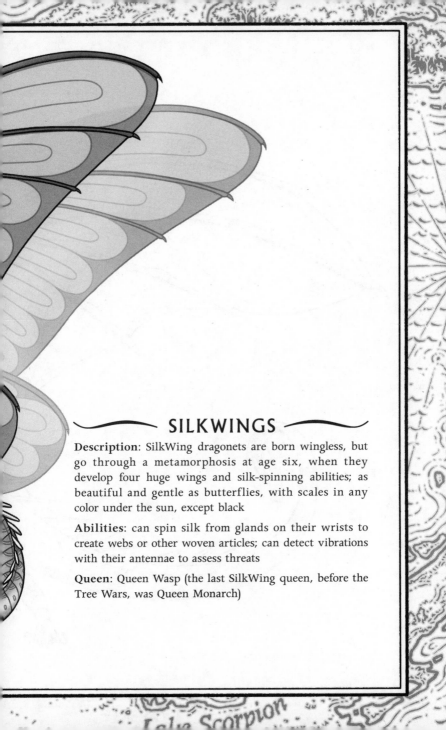

~ SILKWINGS ~

Description: SilkWing dragonets are born wingless, but go through a metamorphosis at age six, when they develop four huge wings and silk-spinning abilities; as beautiful and gentle as butterflies, with scales in any color under the sun, except black

Abilities: can spin silk from glands on their wrists to create webs or other woven articles; can detect vibrations with their antennae to assess threats

Queen: Queen Wasp (the last SilkWing queen, before the Tree Wars, was Queen Monarch)

Lake Scorpion

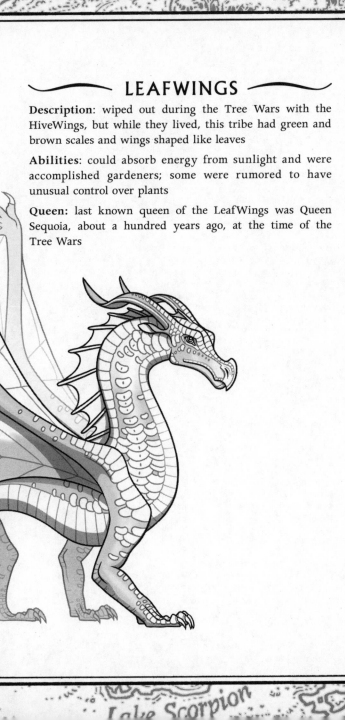

LEAFWINGS

Description: wiped out during the Tree Wars with the HiveWings, but while they lived, this tribe had green and brown scales and wings shaped like leaves

Abilities: could absorb energy from sunlight and were accomplished gardeners; some were rumored to have unusual control over plants

Queen: last known queen of the LeafWings was Queen Sequoia, about a hundred years ago, at the time of the Tree Wars

Lake Scorpion

Tsetse Hive
Beetle Lake
Vinegaroon Hive
Hornet Hive
Cicada Hive
Mantis Hive

THE
LOST CONTINENT
PROPHECY

Turn your eyes, your wings, your fire
To the land across the sea
Where dragons are poisoned and dragons are dying
And no one can ever be free.

A secret lurks inside their eggs.
A secret hides within their book.
A secret buried far below
May save those brave enough to look.

Open your hearts, your minds, your wings
To the dragons who flee from the Hive.
Face a great evil with talons united
Or none of the tribes will survive.

WINGS OF FIRE

── PROLOGUE ──

The problem with belonging to a village that worshipped a big ominous hole in the ground is that holes in the ground tended to be *very cryptic* about their mystical instructions.

Messages from the deep didn't arrive all that often, luckily, and they arrived even less often once the Leaders decided to abandon the Guardian of the Abyss. After all, if no one ever visited him and there were no more ceremonies, how could he (or the abyss, if you believed that part of it) demand anything?

Instead: pretend it's not there, forbid any mention of it, ignore the whispers in the shadows, and maybe everyone would eventually forget about the big ominous hole that had ruled the village for centuries. That was the Leaders' plan.

In principle, Raven agreed with the Leaders. She agreed that the abyss was creepy and that it was weird to worship a giant hole in the ground and that it wasn't great to let that hole take a person to keep for itself every ten years. *But it's tradition!* was not a good enough reason to go along with it, even after thousands of years; maybe *especially* after thousands of years.

If it had really been that long, that meant hundreds

of humans had been swallowed up by the abyss. The great and wonderful ancestor who had agreed to this in the first place was long, long gone, and maybe he hadn't ever done the math on how much sacrifice would be involved.

(That still felt a little blasphemous. Their ancestor had saved them all; he was perfect and could do no wrong! But maybe he could have made a better deal with the abyss, was all Raven was suggesting.)

So yes, she agreed with the Leaders. It was time to stop feeding the abyss. It was definitely time to stop giving it new Guardians. Vole could be the last one ever.

But abandoning the abyss and the whole practice of Abyss Worship was one thing; abandoning Vole himself was too hard and too sad. Once upon a time, Vole had been a normal person. He'd been Mole's silly big brother: funny, charming, really good at climbing sheer rock faces. It wasn't his fault that a green tentacle had reached out of the abyss and dragged him in during the Guardian Ceremony four years ago. No one could ever predict who the abyss would choose.

If *Raven* were a sinister chasm looking for someone's brain to steal, she would have picked Quartz, who played ball-kicking games all day long and was extremely boring. Quartz could have become Guardian and sat beside the abyss all day staring into space, and it wouldn't be all that different from how he was before.

Raven could have gone on with her life just fine if everyone decided to give up on Quartz. (She thought. Probably. Even that idea made her feel a little sick inside.)

But Vole . . . if there were a tiny part of him that was still *himself* in there, she didn't want him to be alone. She didn't want him to think she'd left him, like everyone else.

Mole was the only one still allowed to visit him, to bring him food; the Leaders couldn't condemn Vole to starving to death. But no one else was supposed to go near him. At first, a few had tried to talk him into leaving the abyss and coming back to the village, and that had gone very poorly. The Leaders didn't want anyone else to risk getting thrown into the chasm, so when Raven visited Vole, she had to do it in secret.

Which meant she had absolutely no one to tell when the Guardian gave her his terrifying instructions.

"Find the dragon. Bring it here. Or everyone you know will die."

So, all right, first question: WHAT dragon? ANY dragon? Was Raven supposed to somehow find a specific particular dragon somewhere, deduce that that was the one the abyss wanted, and then . . . what, tie it up and haul it all the way down to the abyss? Did the abyss think she had superpowers?

How was a human supposed to *make* a dragon go anywhere?

And again: What dragon?! Saying "THE dragon" sounded nastily specific. The abyss wasn't like, "Bring me A dragon," as in, "any one will do."

But if it did want a particular dragon, it needed to give her something to work with. A color, for starters, would be great. How many wings? Big or small? Alive or dead?

Ha ha ha, as if Raven could kill a dragon, whether the abyss wanted her to or not.

In any case, the abyss had not deigned to answer any of these questions. Vole had continued to stare intently over the edge into darkness, ignoring her.

So after days of useless thinking and a few unsuccessful experiments, Raven had done the only possible thing: she'd dragged Mole into her problem.

She found him alone at one of the cave lakes, knocked him over, and sat on him before he could run away.

"Don't be mad," she started.

"Gah, nooooo." Mole gripped his face with his hands. "Raven! How about: don't do things that MAKE people mad!"

"I didn't do this!" she protested. "I swear! I mean." She squinted up at the ceiling. "That is, I did *a* thing that might make you mad, but the actual problem I have to tell you about is not my fault! Seriously!"

"Can you tell me one without telling me the other?" he asked.

She thought for a minute. Mole lay still on the stone floor underneath her, his fishing net dropped nearby, his arms propped behind his head. He was a little judgmental and too much of a rule follower, but he was smart and still usually the most agreeable person Raven knew.

"Hypothetically," she said, "if you really needed to get a dragon from one place to another, how would you do it?"

He stared into her eyes. Finally he said, "What."

"Imagine there's a dragon," she said, "and you need it to go somewhere pretty specific, and you would prefer to not get eaten on the way. What would you do? Specifically."

"Raven," he said. "When you say *somewhere pretty specific*, do you mean the abyss?"

"Who said anything about the abyss?" she flailed. "I didn't, why did you, nobody said — hey, wait. What happened to the rules?! You said abyss, not me! It wasn't me this time!"

(The rules:

Nobody mentions the abyss.

Nobody goes near the abyss.

Everyone pretends the abyss does not exist anymore.

Everyone acts like they hear absolutely zero whispers and feel zero weirdness coming from the creepy big dark hole.)

Mole rubbed his face again and gently pushed her off him. He sat up and buried his hands in his hair. "If you're talking about what I think you're talking about, Vole said the same thing to me."

"He did?" Raven poked him in the arm. "Why didn't you tell me?"

"Why would I? We're not supposed to talk about the abyss, remember? I'm not even allowed to mention Vole. How could I tell anyone he's given me a weird abyss message? You definitely shouldn't somehow know about it already!" He sighed. "Raven. How did you . . . ?" He trailed off.

"I visit him sometimes," she mumbled. She pulled one of the knives out of her boots and stabbed it into a crack in the floor. "I don't get too close. I just . . . sit nearby and talk to him."

When she looked up, she was startled by Mole's expression. It wasn't mad at all. He looked like he was about to burst into tears.

"Don't be weird about it!" she cried. "I feel bad for him! I know he's not really there anymore, but I still kind of keep waiting to see if he is. I can't help it. I'm an idiot; I know that."

"You are, but so am I," Mole admitted. "So he gave you the same message?"

"Find the dragon, bring it to the abyss?" Raven sighed as he nodded. "How can we possibly do that, Mole?"

"Do you think we have to? Could we ignore him?"

"My message ended on a pretty clear 'or everyone you know will die' note," she said. "Which also wasn't very specific, but I can imagine how a possessed Guardian and an abyss full of green tentacles might go about killing everyone."

"On the other hand, I don't want to make the dragons mad either," Mole said. "I'm guessing we need one from that big group that settled in the caves last month. But if we somehow did steal one of their dragons, wouldn't that make the rest all furious and vengeful? I don't know about you, but I don't love the idea of living in a cave system with hundreds of angry dragons. That sounds even worse than an angry abyss."

"So we have to be clever about it," Raven suggested. "I was thinking we skip over the problem of *which* dragon it wants, and see whether we can get *any* dragon there. My first thought was to let one of them see me and hope it's hungry enough to chase me to the abyss."

"Oh, wow," Mole said. "Terrible, terrible plan. I hate it very much."

"More terrible than you realize," she said. "Only, like, two or three of the dragons in that group are hunters. I can't get *any* of the colorful four-wing ones to chase me."

"You've tried?" he said, looking at her aghast.

"Of course I've tried," she said. "I've tried lots of things! I wouldn't bother you without trying everything

I could think of first. The colorful dragons are not interested in me at *all*. I can dance under their noses, and the worst they'll do is sniff me. I could get the big green dopey one to chase me, but that's risky. He's really determined. I don't want him to accidentally find the village."

"Right," he said. "We should definitely avoid that."

"What have you tried so far?" she asked.

"Um," he said. "Worrying? I've tried every variety of worrying."

"That's my best friend," she said, punching his shoulder affectionately. "Doing the hard stuff so I don't have to."

"Ha ha. What have you done besides volunteer as dragon snack?"

She made a face. "I looked for treasure. Dragons like shiny things, right? That's what the storybooks say. I thought maybe if I made, like, a trail of diamonds, some dragon might follow it all the way to the abyss."

"That's . . . a lot of diamonds."

"I know! There's no way I can surreptitiously gather that much treasure. I tried prying ONE teeny-tiny diamond out of the wall in the Salvation Tunnel and Mom caught me and I got in SO MUCH TROUBLE. You have no idea."

"The week I didn't see you?" he guessed, and she shrugged. He knew her parents; solitary confinement was their usual punishment for everything.

"So what else can we do? Any ideas?" she asked. "There's that flower juice the doctors use to make people sleep during surgeries . . . what if I somehow got a *lot* of that and gave it to a dragon?"

"*Maybe* you could trick a dragon into eating something so it fell asleep," Mole said pensively. "But then you'd have to figure out how to MOVE A GIANT SLEEPING DRAGON, Raven."

"Yes, all right, that's where the plan fell apart in my head, too," she said. "Unless . . . wheelbarrows? Pulleys? Hypnotize the whole village and have them carry it for me? OK, fine, too hard."

"What about some kind of message for the dragons?" he suggested. "Like a drawing — a map to the abyss — with a picture of a big pile of treasure IN the abyss?"

Raven laughed despite herself. "We might end up luring the dumbest dragon in the history of the world," she said. "La la la, what's this lying here on the floor? A map! To treasure! This doesn't seem suspicious at all! Off I go, dum de dum, along this trail to get my pile of diamonds. This is completely normal."

"Your imaginary dragon sounds way too human," Mole protested. "I'd be more worried that dragons wouldn't know what a map is, let alone how to follow one."

"You don't watch them enough," Raven pointed out. "They are definitely smart enough to read maps, and too smart to fall for a fake one."

"Next you'll be telling me they have feelings like us, too," he said. "As though there are dragons who care about their brothers or something." He glanced sideways at her. "Or dragons who would do anything for their best friends."

Her hand stilled on her knife. *Wait . . . dragons with feelings . . .*

If any dragons had feelings, it was probably those rainbow-colored butterfly-looking ones. Maybe they did care about one another like humans did, more or less, and if so, maybe she could use that.

Maybe this was how they could trick a dragon — by finding its most human weakness.

"Raven," Mole said as she tucked her knife back into her boot. She met his eyes and smiled ruefully at him. He was wearing his "rules are rules and what am I going to do with you" face, which usually meant a lecture was coming.

But then he said, "I know I should be mad you broke the rules to see Vole, but . . . Raven, I'm so glad I finally have someone I can talk to about this."

She felt little cracks spreading across her heart. Mole had been all alone with this secret, just like she had. He'd thought the fate of the village and everyone's lives rested entirely on his own thin shoulders. Poor Mole, when he already had so much to deal with, between being Vole's sole caretaker and the only remaining son and heir of the Leaders.

She put one arm around him, and he rested his head against hers. "We'll figure this out together," she promised. "You don't have to do it alone. I have a new idea."

"Uh-oh," he said, and they both laughed. He reached across her and took her free hand in both of his.

"Raven — why do you think the abyss is asking for a dragon now, after all this time?"

"I don't know," she said. "That seems like the dragon's problem, not mine."

"It's one of the things I've been worrying about," he said. "Like . . . if the abyss is angry, is it a *good* idea to give it a dragon? What is it going to do to the dragon?"

And if dragons have feelings like humans, Raven thought, *well . . . I wouldn't want to be given to a sinister abyss.*

"Is this any better than the Guardian Ceremony?" Mole said quietly.

"Do we have a choice?" Raven asked. "Won't the whole village be in danger if we don't do what Vole says?"

Mole frowned, and Raven instinctively reached to rub his temple the way his brother used to.

"Listen, whatever's going on with the abyss and the dragons, maybe this will fix it," she said. "Maybe this will make the abyss focus on the dragons and leave us alone. Maybe —" Her breath caught in her throat for a moment. "Maybe if we give it a dragon, it will give us back Vole, the way he used to be."

Mole sat up with a gasp and stared at her. "Do you think so?"

"I don't know. Don't get your hopes up. But we can ask, can't we?"

He nodded, his eyes drifting toward the lake. "Right. And it's only one dragon." He let out a long breath. "I hope we're doing the right thing."

Tsetse Hive

Beetle Lake

Vinegaroon Hive

Hornet Hive

Cicada Hive

Mantis Hive

PART ONE

THE LAND ACROSS THE SEA

CHAPTER 1

Luna wanted to change the world.

She knew what it should be like; she knew it *could* be more just and more beautiful and more safe and more kind. A world where dragons loved whoever they wanted to love, where they created art and took care of one another and were happy instead of hurtful.

Surely everyone wanted that world, so why couldn't it exist already?

Luna knew exactly what she wanted to change and why. She just wasn't quite sure *how* yet.

She wished the world was more like a weaving, where she could tear out the bits that were knotted wrong or colors twisted in the wrong places, then reweave it all again, better and mended and perfect. She knew how to fix a messed-up tapestry; she had no idea where to start fixing a broken world.

The problem was, there were so *many* things wrong and they *all* needed fixing. And the other problem was how many dragons didn't seem to see that. A lot of dragons thought everything was fine! Even some of Luna's very favorite most-loved dragons didn't seem to care about all the wrong, bad things!

This had been baffling her all her life. She had started noticing the problems with her world from the first moment her mothers had walked her through Cicada Hive, and even more clearly during her earliest days of school at Silkworm Hall. How could anyone else miss them?

For instance: It was wrong that the HiveWings had cut down all the trees, and it was very, very, *very wrong* that the HiveWings had wiped out all the LeafWings. It was wrong that a SilkWing couldn't choose her own life partner, her job, or where she lived. It was awful that Luna's father had been taken away before she even hatched, and it was unfair that Queen Wasp got to decide everything that happened to the SilkWings, and they couldn't say anything about it.

A lot of dragons might argue that those things were fine because Queen Wasp was the dragon in charge and she said so, and also something something war and something something danger, so that was how the world had to be. But even if you accepted all of that (which Luna didn't), it was still obviously wrong, all wrong, that HiveWings could treat SilkWings like tiny bugs under their talons.

SilkWings were dragons, too, just like them. SilkWings didn't deserve to be stepped on, sneered at, poked without permission, punished for no reason, or ignored. It made no sense. Why would a different wing shape, or a slightly different scale color, or antennae, make one dragon superior and another dragon worth nothing?

But how did you *fix* that? How could one dragon, even a dragon who cared *very much*, make a whole tribe change how they thought and behaved? How could she get into the heads of all those sneering HiveWings and shake their brains around until they stopped being awful?

She wanted them to see the better world she could picture. She wanted to stuff it into their eyeballs until every HiveWing went, "YES! That world is WAY BETTER than this one! Let's be like that instead!"

Luna wished she had magic. Magic would be so *useful* for problems like this! Even if it was a magic like Clearsight's, seeing the future — well, she'd find a way to make it useful! But proper magic, like spells and enchantments and brain changers, like in the old dragon fairy tales, that's what she really wanted. Something to go, "POOF! Now you are all fair and kind and incapable of cruelty or injustice!" That's what she needed, but apparently it didn't exist — or if it had existed, once, in the Distant Kingdoms, now it didn't work anymore.

She traced her claw through the sand with a sigh. The sun was rising behind her, casting golden ripples across the ocean like trails of flamesilk. On the other side of that ocean was Pantala: her home, her mothers, her tribe, Blue, and Swordtail, and they were all in trouble, and it was all a mess, and she didn't know how to begin untangling it.

Before her Metamorphosis, Luna had dreamed of flying.

She dreamed of scattering the clouds with her new pale green wings, and she imagined sunshine pouring through her scales the higher she flew. She planned to weave tapestries with secret Chrysalis messages in them. She imagined herself and Swordtail at clandestine Chrysalis meetings, whispering with other SilkWings about how to change things together.

But as it turned out, she couldn't simply be Luna, an ordinary SilkWing quietly changing the world alongside other SilkWings. Now she had to be LUNA THE FLAMESILK! Luna, who spun FIRE from her wrists! A flamesilk, RAREST OF ALL SILKWINGS! Chosen to save everyone somehow!

To Queen Wasp, a flamesilk was a valuable tool to be locked up and controlled.

To the Chrysalis and the LeafWings, flamesilk was power — a weapon they could use to fight back.

Luna didn't particularly like thinking of herself as a tool *or* a weapon. She had planned on changing the world in a SilkWing way, not in a "setting your enemies on fire" way. Setting your enemies on fire *sounded* fun, but it was actually extremely scary, once you had a real dragon in front of you who would really burn if you wanted them to.

Not to mention, the first time she tried, her flamesilk got caught in a hurricane that then blew her to a whole other continent. So that wasn't the most auspicious start for the Great and Glorious Flamesilk Savior Luna.

But she had to use this power now that she had it, didn't she? She'd been chosen by the universe to be a dragon who could throw flaming lassos. She couldn't exactly be like, *Oh, no, thank you, someone else go set Queen Wasp on fire instead of me, please.*

This was fine. She just had to rethink her plans to change the world, now that she was a little bit scarier than she used to be. Now that she had a Destiny and maybe had to save the world all by herself with fire.

I'm not all alone, though. Even though I feel that way, without Blue and Swordtail.

Today she was returning to Pantala with nine other dragons, a human, and a mission.

One of those dragons went galloping past, charging into the water and plunging his head below the surface. His human stopped near the edge of the waves, crossed her arms, and sighed.

"Did you see one?" the RainWing called from the air, swooping overhead.

"No, of course he didn't," Wren called back.

Sky's head shot out of the water again, and he shook himself vigorously, then stood with his snout tilted as though he was waiting for water to drain out of his ears. "False alarm! Not a dolphin!" he called to the RainWing. "Just a confused jellyfish!"

Pineapple, Luna reminded herself. *Pineapple the RainWing.* She was great at remembering faces because they were kind of like tapestries on dragon snouts, but usually she had trouble with names. This time, though, she was determined to memorize all the names of her traveling companions.

It would help if Pineapple could pick *one color* and *stay that color*, because her trick of picturing him in a tapestry holding a pineapple didn't work if he kept looking completely different all the time.

Not that I'm complaining. Having all these dragons to figure out is much better than sitting on this beach by myself, staring wistfully at an ocean that's entirely too big.

"Are you still here?" a voice demanded behind her.

Luna smiled over her shoulder at Jerboa. "We're leaving as soon as the IceWing arrives," she said reassuringly. "Soon this beach will be so quiet and you'll miss us so much."

"That sounds GREAT," Jerboa grumbled, clomping up to sit beside Luna and scattering sand everywhere. "I haven't talked to this many dragons in *literally centuries*, and now I remember why."

Jerboa always moved in an odd way, which at first Luna had thought was how all two-winged dragons walked. But now that she'd met a bunch more, she was pretty sure there was something different about Jerboa . . . as though she was secretly in pain, or her bones didn't fit together quite right.

"I, um — I made you something," Luna said tentatively. She handed Jerboa the leaf-wrapped packet beside her.

The SandWing furrowed her brow at it, as though every present she'd ever been given before had bitten her.

"It's just a little thing. It's terrible," Luna said in a rush. "I don't have a loom here, so I couldn't weave you the tapestry I was imagining in my head, and then I thought, maybe I can create a new kind of art with my fire, so I've been trying to carve pictures into wood with bits of flamesilk, and it's harder than you'd think! So this is the best I was able to do so far, but it is still pretty awful and you don't have to keep it if you don't want to. I just wanted to give you something to say thank you."

"Thank you for what?" Jerboa asked.

"For helping me get better and for putting up with all of us in your space. You didn't have to come find me when I crashed here," Luna said. "I know you could have stayed in your hut and kept out of all of this."

Jerboa didn't say very much about herself or her past, but she had clearly lived alone for a long time, and Luna got the sense that the SandWing both really wanted to connect with someone and also got very overwhelmed very quickly by normal dragon interactions. That was a guess; Jerboa was not in the business of discussing her feelings or making facial expressions. She mostly looked either bored or mildly annoyed.

But Luna was familiar with the "no feelings here" face. Her own was more of a "see, I'm smiling, I'm not causing any problems, everything is totally fine" face, but it was still in the same genre of face.

"It's no problem," the SandWing said brusquely. "I figured I might as well do something useful."

Jerboa gingerly peeled the leaves off the gift, revealing the soft white curve of driftwood underneath. Luna had burned the shape of two little dragons into it, each sitting on their own continent on either side of the ocean. One had four wings, and the other had two. They were looking toward each other and waving. Well, they were supposed to be. The one with four wings looked like she was about to fall over backward, and the other one's face had come out all wrong, so she looked like she was sneezing.

"Never mind," Luna said, trying to grab it out of Jerboa's talons. "It's an awful, weird-looking art fail, sorry."

"Stop that," Jerboa said, batting her away. "This is *my* weird-looking art fail; get your claws off it."

"When the world is all fixed, I'll make you a tapestry," Luna said. "It'll be much better than this, I promise."

Jerboa squinted at the dark clouds that were huddled like suspicious HiveWing guards on the far horizon. "When the world is all fixed," she echoed. "Hrm. Don't get your hopes up. Every time you think you've fixed something, something else always goes wrong."

"That's the spirit," Qibli, the other SandWing, said, popping up behind her. "Hey, I have an idea: let's stop fixing things, and then maybe nothing else will go wrong."

Jerboa frowned at him.

"Uh-oh," Qibli said to Luna. "I think I'm about to be called a preposterous whippersnapper."

"Tell your continent they can keep this one," Jerboa said, flicking her tail at Qibli.

Qibli grinned at her, then turned to Luna again. "Tsunami wants to show you something important, if you have a minute." He pointed up the beach to where the blue SeaWing was sitting with Cricket.

"Oh — sure, thanks," Luna said. Her scales always gave an odd little shiver when she saw Cricket from a distance. Even though her brain knew *this* HiveWing was safe and had helped them, her body still sent her an instinctive "eep! run! hide! set it on fire!" reaction to the yellow-and-black dragon's face. There was a difference between *knowing* she should trust this dragon and *feeling* like she could.

She knew Blue trusted her, but she'd only seen Cricket and Blue together for a moment before Luna was blown out to sea. And to be honest, Blue wasn't the *most* reliable truster-of-dragons. He would probably trust a giant hissing scorpion wielding knives if it said something sympathetic.

Also, there was a small part of Luna that was *really angry* that Blue and Swordtail had fallen into Wasp's mind-control clutches, but Cricket hadn't. After all that, why should this blissfully lucky HiveWing get to escape yet again, but the dragons Luna loved didn't?

It wasn't fair.

She couldn't say that out loud.

But it really wasn't.

"Luna," Tsunami said, beckoning her closer as she approached. "I'm going to share another Pyrrhian secret with you. Because I think it will help and I think it's important and, you know what, it's *my* thing — well, the Jade Mountain Academy's thing — and I'm the headmaster, basically, and so I don't need any queens' permission is what I've decided, so there."

"Um," Luna said. "OK."

Tsunami held out a star-shaped sapphire that fit neatly in her cupped front talons. "This is a dreamvisitor," she said. "One of those animus-touched magic objects you heard about."

Luna's heart sped up. Magic! "What does it do?" she blurted. *Please say it'll save my tribe.* She glanced sideways at Cricket, who was unusually silent. Normally the HiveWing would have been the first one asking questions, but she was staring down at her claws, half-buried in the sand. She looked as though someone had set all her favorite books on fire.

"I've already let Cricket use it," Tsunami explained.

Why?! Luna thought mutinously. *Why her first and not me? How is that fair, when she's one of the bad guys?*

No, no, don't let anyone see you think that. I'm smiling, I'm not causing problems, everything is fine.

Tsunami went on. "A dreamvisitor lets you step into the dreams of a sleeping dragon, no matter where they are, so long as it's someone you've seen before. I figured it's probably still nighttime in Pantala . . . and maybe there's someone there you want to check on?"

She carefully placed the sapphire in Luna's talons. Luna's mind was spinning. She could actually see one of them again? Right now? It wasn't tribe-saving magic, but it was still amazing. Who should she pick—Swordtail or Blue? Blue or Swordtail? And then she realized —

"Did you visit Blue?" she asked Cricket.

The HiveWing nodded. "I tried," she said quietly. "He couldn't really hear me, though. He was having a nightmare."

"About what?" Luna asked sharply. That was *her* little brother. *She* should be the one worrying about his nightmares.

"A room full of SilkWings," Cricket said. "Plants growing out of the walls, strangling them. It can't be real. Can it?"

she appealed to Tsunami. "I mean, was I seeing something he actually saw?"

Tsunami spread her wings. "*I* don't know. We have dreams about real things and not-real things and both mixed together all the time."

Cricket sighed, took off her glasses, and rubbed her eyes.

"I'll visit Swordtail," Luna said. "What do I have to do?"

"Hold it up to your forehead," Tsunami said. "Close your eyes and concentrate on him. If it doesn't work, he might not be asleep right now — or if he's having a nightmare, like Blue, you might see him but he might not hear you. But if he's having a normal dream, you might be able to communicate with him."

Luna's claws were trembling as she pressed the dream-visitor to her forehead. It wasn't magic that could make all HiveWings disappear, which would have been nice. But the chance to talk to Swordtail, after all this time, was a magic she hadn't dared hope for. They'd never gone this long without talking to each other, not since the day they first met five years ago.

"Swordtail," she whispered, closing her eyes. She pictured his unexpectedly sweet face. Other dragons saw his mischief, his loud jokes, and his reckless arguments with guards or teachers. They might notice that he was strong and brave, too. But hardly anyone seemed to see the true Swordtail under all his noisy silliness.

It was like the red leaf, the secret Chrysalis symbol hidden in the Metamorphosis tapestries. You had to look for it; you had to know to care about it.

Swordtail understood about all the things Luna saw that were wrong. Even if he hadn't noticed them before, he understood immediately when she pointed them out. He was the absolute best at going from vaguely interested to completely outraged in the span of a conversation.

Swordtail looked back into her eyes, and his whole face lit up.

Three moons. She was really — somewhere; somewhere that wasn't a sunrise-lit beach in the Distant Kingdoms. Somewhere dark, although a single bright light shone over Swordtail's head. He was standing up on a pedestal, his wings spread behind him, his front talons outstretched.

"Swordtail!" she cried.

He didn't respond. His claws twitched like he wanted to reach for her, but he didn't move.

Oh. She knew where they were now. This was Misbehaver's Way — the place troublemakers like Swordtail were sent to be punished whenever they disobeyed HiveWings.

She walked up to the base of the pedestal and touched the letters carved in the stone. They looked like real words until she tried to read them, and then they went wobbly and slipped away from her brain.

Like in a dream.

"Swordtail," she said. "This isn't real. You're not on Misbehaver's Way. This isn't even what it really looks like." She turned to look behind her. There were no other pedestals, no other prisoners. The stone paths rolled away into darkness, and the darkness hummed like it was full of bees.

The light over Swordtail's head was wrong, too; it was too bright, and she couldn't see a fixture or a ceiling — just the light blazing down on him.

"Swordtail, get down from there right now," she said. "I don't know why you're dreaming about this."

"This is where I'm supposed to be," he said suddenly, sounding resigned and reasonable, which was not a very Swordtail way to sound. "I'm always here. Remember? You come and sit with me. You should weave a hammock and live here because I'll probably be here more and more as we get older."

Luna felt like she was about to cry. The three times he'd been punished like this before, she'd found a way to go sit with him for as long as she could. On Misbehaver's Way, the prisoners were temporarily paralyzed with a HiveWing nerve toxin so they couldn't move or speak — but they could still hear and see, so she'd read to him, or sing, or tell him about the day he'd missed.

"You're not going to end up here again," Luna said. "I'm coming to set you free, Swordtail."

"No, no," he said. "I'm coming to rescue *you*. I'm helpful! That's what . . . Wait, didn't I already . . ." He trailed off, looking confused.

"You did," she said. "Swordtail, this is a dream, but *I'm* real. You can get off that pedestal. Get off it right now and come hug me."

He thought for a moment. "I like that idea much better than standing here." He furrowed his brow, concentrating.

"Moving is tricky, though. Not sure if everyone knows that. Hey, who's the boss of me? Are these my muscles or what? Don't I tell them what to do? Look at them, arguing back, not listening to me. Hey, do what *I* say, stupid talons." He glared at his claws, but they stayed frozen in place. "All right, hang on. I'll fix this. I AM the boss of me! Nobody else tells my talons what to do! Let's all not look at me for a minute while I yell at myself. Luna, talk about you instead. What do you mean, you're real?"

"I'm in the Distant Kingdoms, using magic to talk to you." Luna spread her wings and flew up to him. This pedestal was also higher than the real ones on Misbehaver's Way. But it was only a dream, so she did not feel guilty about shoving him off.

"YARRGH!" he yelped, flapping around to break his fall. "Hey! My wings can move! Check me out! Guess those ants-for-brains guards didn't stab me the right way this time!"

"Swordtail!" Luna took one of his talons and tugged him down to the ground. He settled his wings behind him and looked down at their intertwined claws. A thread of silvery-gray silk spun out of his wrist and wrapped around hers.

Now she was crying. She wondered if she was crying in the real world, too, sitting on that beach with Tsunami. She let a thread of harmless flamesilk — the kind that shimmered gold but didn't burn — spin out and wrap around his talons, twining through his own silk.

"Listen," she said. "I'm in the Distant Kingdoms, but I'm coming for you. I'm coming with Sundew and Cricket and some other dragons and we're going to save you, OK? Do you know where you are? I mean, really in real life, not in this dream?"

"Cicada Hive," he said, blinking. "Guarding SilkWings until Wasp has enough of her plant to infect them." He tried to laugh. "Very boring job, actually. It's a bit like guarding a flower shop to make sure the orchids don't make a run for it. I can see why the HiveWing guards were always so excited when I gave them something to chase."

"Wasp sent you back to our own Hive?" Luna asked. "So the SilkWings you're guarding —"

"Yeah, everyone we know," he said with an awkward shrug. "Your moms are here. They're all right."

"What about Blue?" she asked.

"Here, too," he said in a quieter voice. "But not really, you know? It's like he's gone into a Blue cocoon somewhere inside himself. I kind of wish I could do that, too. I mean, I want to *fight* something, but I *can't*. I can't do *anything* with these stupid traitor talons." He looked down at their intertwined claws and took a deep breath. "She — *we* captured Io. So she's here, too. She can't even look at me."

"It's not you," Luna said fiercely. "Whatever Queen Wasp is making you do, it's not *you*, Swordtail. Don't forget that. You're still in there, and we're going to get you away from her, I promise."

"I wish I were really talking to you," he said. "These dreams always end with you being dragged away in chains made of lightning."

"You *are* really talking to me, you lummox," Luna said, shaking his talons. She wrapped her wings around him and pulled him closer. With a sigh, he rested his head on her shoulder. "Swordtail, there's a dragon on this continent who's like Clearsight. She told us this prophecy about Pantala and a buried secret, so we're coming to look for an abyss that we think is connected to the mind control. We're going to fly into the abyss, find a big obnoxious plant with a grudge, and then Sundew's going to kill it a lot until it's really, really dead, and then the mind control won't work anymore and you'll be free. All right? Isn't that a great plan?"

"I . . . feel like I missed something," Swordtail said.

"Me too. It's very confusing," Luna agreed. "But it's going to work! We're leaving the Distant Kingdoms today! So pay attention, and in a few days, you'll be like, *Oh wow, they did it! The mind control doesn't work anymore! Let's go stab Queen Wasp in the face! And then find Luna and hug her forever!*"

He laughed, shaking his head to clear the tears from his eyes. "You do sound like real Luna. Where will I find you after you save us?"

"The Mosaic Garden," Luna said off the top of her head. "That hill where you finally confessed your desperate love for me and said you couldn't live without me."

"Um, I believe my exact words were: 'Hey, Luna, want to be my girlfriend?'" he said with a grin.

"Yes. You're very lucky I can translate Swordtail," she retorted.

"And let's see — I believe *your* romantic response was 'Swordtail, did you sit on this box of honey drops? Why are they all squashed?' and then I was like, 'LUNA, pay attention to ME, I am TRYING to make us an official couple,' and *you* were like, 'Yes, all right, obviously that's fine, now go get us some more honey drops and DON'T sit on them this time.'"

"You do have a weird habit of squashing any candy you get your talons on," she pointed out. "Or your butt on, more accurately."

"I don't sit on candy on PURPOSE!" he objected.

"I certainly hope not," she said. "That would be weird, Swordtail." She nudged his snout with hers. "But it's all right. I love you anyway."

"I love you, too." He squeezed her talons. "I think I'm about to wake up."

"Oh no," she said, starting to panic. "Already? Wait —"

"I don't have a choice," he said. "She wants us for something. Luna — I'm all right, but — if you could come quickly, it would — it would be better."

"I will, I promise. Tell Blue we'll be there soon," she said. More silk was spinning out of her, wrapping around his wrists, trying to keep him with her. "Just hold on, Swordtail. We're coming, we'll —"

But he was gone.

Luna was back on the beach, early morning light brushing the clouds pink overhead. Tears were rolling down her snout, and her talons held a cold sapphire instead of Swordtail's warm claws.

~ CHAPTER 2 ~

Part of Luna wanted to dive to the bottom of the ocean and bury herself so deep that she would fall asleep and never have to feel anything ever again. And part of Luna wanted to throw the whole abyss mission out the window and fly straight to Cicada Hive and set everything on fire until she found Swordtail.

But by day three of their trip, *all* of Luna was focused on not screaming at her companions to fly faster. She did not think it had taken *her* this long to cross the ocean between the continents! Granted, she had been unconscious and dragged along by a hurricane, but they could try a *little* harder!

She tried to focus on the plan in her head: find Pantalan humans, follow them to the abyss, do . . . something . . . all right, most likely watch Sundew do something, and then the important part: all the HiveWings giving up and turning on Queen Wasp, Blue rescued from his nightmares, and Luna getting to hug Swordtail for real. And freedom for all the SilkWings!

There were some wobbly bits in the plan. Luna was trying not to think about the wobbly bits.

Think about the happy ending instead.

Think about how we're going to change everything.

Think about the tapestries you'll be able to weave when this is all over.

Luna did a twist-roll in the air to catch a quick view of everyone: ten dragons altogether, flying through the bright blue sky. Dragons from *ten different tribes.* Not too long ago, she'd thought there were only two living tribes in the whole world.

This is the kind of art I want to make, she thought. *A tapestry of all of us flying together. A tapestry that says: Look how much bigger the world is than you thought it was. Look at how different we are, but we're all still dragons. Look at how dragons we don't even know will fly across an ocean to help save us. Don't you want to be like these dragons? Don't you want to reach for different claws, fly alongside different wings? Don't you want to do something brave and kind because someone has to?*

I'll call it Talons United, from the prophecy.

After all of this is over.

If we survive.

Black wings fluttered in the corner of her eye, and Luna sighed. The good news: she was bringing a mini Clearsight back to Pantala with her. The bad news: Moon didn't have *quite* the personality Luna would have expected from a powerful seer.

Luna had imagined more trances, more mystical declarations, and plenty of dramatic swooping about. If *she* were a seer, Luna would get out of every boring conversation by suddenly closing her eyes and announcing a need for silence! the future is speaking! and so forth.

But on the plus side, Moon *looked* all cool and eerie, especially from a distance, and especially when she wasn't talking. She looked a lot like Clearsight did in the paintings. So that was a good start.

Luna liked to imagine a scene where they all flew into a Hive, pointed at Moon, and yelled: "BEHOLD THE SECOND COMING OF CLEARSIGHT! SHE SAYS ACTUALLY QUEEN WASP IS A JERK AND SILKWINGS ARE GREAT AND SHOULD HAVE THEIR OWN QUEEN! SO THERE!" And then all the HiveWings would cry, "Oh no! We have been so wretched and wrong! Tell us how to be better dragons, Luna!"

Unfortunately, Moon was too nervous and twitchy to be a convincing prophet. The NightWing would have to manage a much more Imposing and Inscrutable Face if she wanted any HiveWings to fall over at her talons and renounce their horrible ways.

In fact, after spending a few days with them, Luna had discovered that *all* the dragons who'd been chosen for the heroic quest of fulfilling Moon's prophecy were . . . significantly less terrifying than she would have preferred. (Apart from Sundew, who was impeccably terrifying at all times.)

Luna tilted her head up and sideways to study them each as they flew, one by one.

Lynx the IceWing, gleaming silver and blue like diamonds slicing through the air: too smiley.

Qibli the SandWing, playing tag with a seagull to make Moon laugh: too hilarious, nowhere near serious enough.

Moon the intimidating NightWing herself: too shy, lots of stammering, kind of spacey at weird moments.

Cricket . . . too easily distracted, not a fighter. Plus also a HiveWing, and that still felt weird. She kept trying to fly next to Luna, as though she wanted to talk about something, but Luna could usually find a reason to fly with Pineapple or Sky or Lynx instead.

Bullfrog the MudWing was big and strong-looking, but he never said *anything*, not even when Qibli was off hunting and there was a chance for other dragons to get a word in edgewise. If he had a personality, or any sort of passion for anything, it was buried *very* deep, like a fossil.

And Luna's favorite new Pyrrhia friend, Pineapple the RainWing, was literally falling asleep while flying. *Again.*

"Pineapple," Luna called, flying up behind him and nudging his wing. He was iridescent gold and rose and cyan all over today, which was almost too pretty to look at straight on.

"Very up!" he said, startling awake and tipping sideways. "Definitely awake!"

"It's the middle of the day!" Luna pointed out. "And we got so much sleep last night. *How* can you be tired?"

He shrugged, not at all embarrassed. "This is when RainWings usually have our suntime naps. And there's so much sun out here! The confusing part is how all of *you* are still awake." He yawned and then grinned at Luna as she stifled a contagious yawn in response.

"There's an island coming up," Qibli said. He pulled out the map and consulted it, tipping it to align with the ocean below. "We could rest for a bit."

Arrrrgh, arrrrgh, arrrrgh. Luna didn't want to rest anymore. She'd spent FOREVER "resting" on Jerboa's beach, waiting for Moon and Qibli to make a plan, waiting for the SeaWings to swim to Pantala and back, waiting for the fleeing dragons from Pantala to get organized and figure out their next step. She couldn't wait one second longer. Swordtail needed her *now*. She wanted to get to Blue and Swordtail and save them at ONCE.

"A *short* rest, maybe," Tsunami said, soaring up beside Qibli. "I want to make it to this island by nightfall." She pointed to another island, three farther along the chain they were following, and Qibli nodded. Luna exhaled with relief.

Tsunami was a pretty fierce and noisy SeaWing. Bigger than Sundew, and maybe even scarier sometimes. She'd probably be useful against the HiveWings, Luna thought.

But the last dragon in their group was her direct opposite: Sky, the affable pale orange SkyWing with the human pet. Luna wished he had his tiny human's personality. Wren could probably take down a Hive all by herself if she had fire and talons. Sky was more likely to bump into a Hive and then apologize to its walls.

He reminded her a little bit of her brother, Blue, although

Blue spent most of his time trying to imagine how other dragons felt and Sky seemed mostly interested in how snails felt, or turtles, or dolphins.

He was really sweet. They were all very lovely and funny and kind, and if Luna were organizing a dinner party, they'd be the perfect dragons to invite.

But this wasn't a dinner party; it was an *epic life-or-death battle with an evil queen and her evil tribe* and also a *vitally important rescue mission* with her own entire tribe's future at stake. How could ten sweet dragons (or, all right, eight sweet dragons and two reasonably ferocious dragons) defeat the scariest queen and the scariest tribe in the whole world?

Blue and Swordtail were counting on her, and this was the army she'd brought to save them?

Luna fidgeted with her talons and glanced back over her shoulder. The Distant Kingdoms were so far behind them now that there was nothing to see but sky and ocean. Maybe they should go back and ask for real armies again, though. Armies with lots of soldiers and weapons; *that* would be useful.

A *magic* army would be even better. Luna imagined that tapestry for a moment: the whole top third covered in wings, dragons swarming down surrounded by lightning bolts and enchanted swords, with Queen Wasp alone at the bottom, making an "uh-oh, very doomed" face. Landing in Pantala with a magical army sounded like a much smarter idea than flapping in with a talonful of cuddly dragons and a human.

"Don't worry," Moon said from her left. "Some of us are more useful than we look."

Luna pivoted to squint at her. Moon said things like that a lot — things that sounded like she was talking back to the thoughts in Luna's head. Why would she suddenly swoop up and say something like that now, out of nowhere?

"Not me!" Moon said quickly. "I meant, like, Qibli, just for one example." She looked a little less nervous for a second, as her eyes tracked the SandWing soaring down to the water, scooping up a floating coconut, and tossing it to Sky, who fumbled it through his talons and dropped it back in the ocean. "He's actually kind of great at saving the world."

Qibli is her Swordtail, Luna realized. She'd sort of guessed, from the way they looked at each other, and the way they slept side by side every night.

"Why are you telling me this?" Luna asked Moon. "Did you have a vision of what's going to happen to us in Pantala?" She wished *she* could have a vision of the future. Imagine knowing the whole plan: how everything should turn out and how to get there! The whole tapestry of the future, spread out in her mind. That would be amazing.

"S-sorry," Moon stammered. She pointed back the way Luna had been looking. "I just — you looked like you were wishing you'd brought someone else. Or like maybe you want to go back?" She took a deep breath. "Sorry, never mind."

"No, no, I'm totally fine! Not worried at all!" Luna blurted before Moon could swoop away. *Still smiling, not causing problems!* "It's only that the closer we get, the more I remember how terrifying Wasp is, and the more I think, you know, wouldn't it be great if we had something big and stabby. Or magic. Or both! Big stabby magic for stabbing HiveWings with."

"I know," Moon said sympathetically. "But remember, we're not going to confront Wasp. Our mission is to find out what's in the abyss that Queen Snowfall saw with her vision from the ring. And hopefully it'll be a way to save your friends without needing any magic or, um . . . stabbing."

The other dragons, especially Qibli and Moon, were convinced that this abyss would solve all their problems. But frankly, Luna had some concerns about what one might find AT THE BOTTOM OF A DARK OMINOUS ABYSS. The word *abyss* kind of sounded like it came with guaranteed death and creepiness. She couldn't imagine anything abyss-related that *wouldn't* require magic or stabbing to defeat.

"You haven't had any more specific visions?" she asked Moon hopefully. "Clues about what's down there? Hints about what we're supposed to do? Maybe the tiniest flash of me dancing on Wasp's grave?"

"Nothing helpful," Moon said with a rueful face.

But then, she always looks like that, Luna thought grumpily. *Moon has resting rueful face. Like a permanent "oh, I'm soooo sorry I can't help you even with alllllll my amaaaaaazing magic, I guess it only works on* my *problems" expression.*

She glanced over at Moon again and caught the little black dragon flinching, as though something had jabbed her in the snout.

"We do have a little magic," Lynx interjected from above

and to her right. She pointed to the silver bracelets on Sundew's wrists. "When should we start using those?"

The wristbands gave Sundew the power to turn any or all of them invisible, including herself. It was a small gift of magic from the IceWing queen, who was a flipping terrifying dragon, if you asked Luna. Snowfall could probably have defeated the HiveWings just by staring coldly at them.

"We're still at least two days from the coast of Pantala, by my estimate," Tsunami said. She glanced at Qibli's map again. "Cricket? Do you agree?"

"Me?" the bespectacled HiveWing said, startled. "Oh, me, yes — um, sorry, I was a little distracted when we left Pantala. And we were coming from farther north, but we don't want to aim for the Poison Jungle this time, right? We're thinking Dragonfly Bay? Also, we're moving faster now than we were with all the little and old LeafWings . . . but yes, right, two days, that sounds about right to me, too," she added quickly as Tsunami frowned at her.

The tiny human yelled something from Sky's back, but the wind whipped her itty-bitty voice away.

"Wren says maybe we should start using them now, then!" Sky offered cheerfully. "She says better safe than super dead! What? Oh, sorry." He cleared his throat and said in a much deeper, growlier voice: "Danger could be lurking around every cloud. We could be murdered by zombie bug dragons at any moment." Then he spoiled the effect by bursting into helpless giggles.

Pineapple grinned at him. Most of the Pyrrhian dragons seemed sort of flummoxed by Sky — "the least SkyWingish SkyWing ever," Tsunami had called him. But Pineapple found Sky delightful, which made Luna like the RainWing even more.

"She's not wrong," Sundew pointed out.

"I like the idea of using the magic now!" Luna said. "It won't run out, will it? We can use it as much as we want?"

"That's right," Lynx said, nodding. "Maybe we could start using it after our next rest stop, then."

"I'm not sure how much use it will be, though," Qibli said seriously. "I mean, even if we're all invisible, I'm pretty sure Bullfrog's nonstop chatter is going to give us away."

The silent MudWing swung his head ponderously around to give Qibli a puzzled look.

"Eh?" he said.

"Yeah, that's what I'm talking about," Qibli said. "That nonstop yip-yapping, Bullfrog. They're going to hear you coming from miles away."

Sky snorted a laugh that nearly knocked Wren off his back.

Bullfrog considered Qibli for a moment.

"Don't think so," he said after a while.

"I know it's going to be tough," Qibli said. "But I'm afraid you'll have to be way quieter."

Bullfrog turned his furrowed brow toward the others. "I'm confused."

"Qibli is being ridiculous," Moon explained. "He's trying to find someone to argue with him, since Winter's not here to do it."

"*Do* I talk too much?" Bullfrog asked Pineapple, who was flying beside him. "Do . . . *I* talk too much?"

"I think that was the most words I've ever heard you say," Pineapple admitted.

"I'm sorry, Bullfrog," Qibli said, nudging his wing. "I'm just kidding. You're the stealthiest dragon we have. I think you're awesome."

"Really?" Bullfrog said, looking confused all over again.

Qibli was not very much like Blue in most ways, but sometimes Luna saw little things in the SandWing that reminded her of her brother. They both wanted to be liked so badly. They both wanted everyone they met to feel warm and comfortable and happy around them. Qibli did it with jokes and banter, while Blue let other dragons push him around in order to keep the peace.

That was something she loved about Blue that also drove her up a wall. Luna did not care two honey drops whether any HiveWings liked her. So what? They were mostly all terrible! The worst! Rude and superior and entitled and sneering! Why would she need any of them to think, *Ah, yes, that Luna, what a lovely quiet SilkWing*? No, no, no. She would MUCH rather they thought: *Uh-oh, here comes Luna! Aaaaack! She's probably going to set us all on fire again!*

(Especially if that meant she never had to *actually* set anyone on fire.)

But Blue was always friendly and polite to everyone, no matter how awful they were. That's why she'd never told him about the Chrysalis. She had a feeling he'd be thoroughly confused by the secret group of SilkWings who gathered to talk about fighting back against Queen Wasp. "Fighting back" wasn't in Blue's vocabulary — at least, not until Luna turned out to be a flamesilk.

He'd been different when she came out of her cocoon. She hadn't been with him long enough to really see how different, but from the stories Cricket and Sundew told her, Blue had been through a lot while Luna was in her Metamorphosis sleep.

Qibli was a little bit like Swordtail, too. Swordtail was funny like Qibli. He also talked a lot when he was nervous, like Qibli did. Swordtail didn't need to be liked by everybody, though. He was happy to be loved by Luna and Blue and his sister, Io; everybody else could stuff termites up their noses if they didn't like him, for all he cared.

Luna wished she could talk to him again. She wanted to tell him about the dragons she was traveling with. What would he think of Pineapple or Lynx or Sky? Would he be able to trust Cricket more than she did? Would he find Moon a little unsettling, or would he feel sorry for her and how shy she was?

She was pretty sure he would like Qibli. She could imagine them annoying HiveWing guards together.

Luna had borrowed the dreamvisitor from Tsunami whenever they'd stopped, but she hadn't been able to find Swordtail asleep again. She wondered what he was doing — or worse, what Wasp was making him do. She couldn't bear to think of

Wasp inside Swordtail's head or manipulating Blue's talons. She had to stop thinking about it, or she might have to dive into the ocean and scream for days, and the whales probably wouldn't like that.

"There's the island," Pineapple said, flicking his tail toward the small blur of a white-sand curve rising out of the ocean ahead of them. "Thank the moons! I'm so ready to lie down!" He grinned at Luna and swooped ahead of everyone.

Tsunami checked the position of the sun in the sky — well past midday, Luna knew from her internal clock — sighed, and sped up to fly after him, shouting, "Not for long, Pineapple! Don't you dare fall asleep!"

"I don't . . . *think* . . ." Bullfrog said slowly, "that I talk too much."

"You don't," Moon reassured him.

"Qibli's the one who talks too much," Lynx said helpfully.

"You know, I feel like I've heard that somewhere before," Qibli said, tapping his chin. "Race you to the beach, Bullfrog!" He took off without waiting for an answer, which was especially funny when Bullfrog just blinked after him in more confusion.

"Maybe tomorrow?" Cricket said out of the blue, as though she'd been working out a question in her head and missed the entire last half of the conversation. "Starting tomorrow morning, we go into invisible stealth mode. What do you guys think? That makes sense, doesn't it?"

"I agree," Moon said.

"Sure. I'll feel safer once we're invisible," Lynx said, nodding.

"Although, if we're all invisible, Pineapple *really* can't fall asleep while we're flying," Luna joked. "Or he'll drop into the ocean and we'll never find him."

Up ahead of them, a dragon's scream sliced through the sky.

CHAPTER 3

Luna froze in midair, her wings beating backward for a panicked moment. She turned instinctively toward Sundew and saw Lynx do the same.

But Moon cried, "Qibli!" and shot away toward the island, leaving the rest of them behind.

"What was that?" Sky yelped.

"I think it was Pineapple," Lynx said frantically as Sundew yelled, "Moon! Wait!"

The little black dragon was too far ahead already, and now Luna could hear roaring coming from the distant beach. More than one dragon roaring. More than two, more than four, a dozen unfamiliar voices; too many dragons, roaring in fury and rage and pain.

"It's Wasp," she said, her throat closing over the words. "She found us. She found us *already*."

"Everyone stay close!" Sundew shouted. She vaulted to a higher wind current, spread her wings, and held up the magic wristbands.

"What if we get separated while we're invisible?" Cricket

yelped, but Sundew was already touching the diamonds together.

There was no time to answer, no time to make a plan. What were they supposed to do if they lost the others? Go on to the next island or go back? There was only one map. If something happened to Sundew, or you got separated from the group, would you be an invisible dragon alone forever?

Luna reached out in panic and found Lynx's talon doing the same. They clasped claws just as they both disappeared.

It was *so eerie*, feeling a cold talon in hers when she couldn't see the dragon on the other end. It was *beyond* eerie to see empty air where her own wings and tail and claws should be.

Sundew, Sky and Wren, Bullfrog, and Cricket were all gone, too, leaving only blue sky around them. Luna twisted in the air to look for Moon, tugging Lynx along with her, but the NightWing was nowhere to be seen.

"I think I got Moon before she was too far away," Sundew's voice said breathlessly. Luna felt a thick wing bump hers and a mumbled "oops" that she thought might be Bullfrog.

"What about Tsunami and Qibli and Pineapple?" Cricket's voice asked. "Did you turn them invisible, too?"

"I couldn't — the magic can only cover dragons in my line of sight," Sundew answered. Her voice sounded like it was coming from the smoke-thin wisps of clouds above them.

"So let's go save them!" Luna said urgently. She wasn't sure if it was her own wings or Lynx's moving them toward the island and the roaring and the screaming, but everyone else seemed to be behind them. Hovering, discussing, waiting, losing time. "Come on, it must be HiveWings attacking! We have to do something!"

How? Do what? yelled the panicked thoughts flying around her brain.

"Right!" Sundew cried. "Yes! Let's fight them! Finally!"

"Won't they hear us, even if they can't see us?" Cricket asked.

"They can't hear us," Lynx answered Cricket, her voice startlingly close to Luna in the empty air. "Queen Snowfall said only dragons inside the invisibility bubble can hear one another."

"But shouldn't we make a plan before we go charging in?" Cricket said anxiously.

"There's no time for a plan!" Luna cried. "We have to fly over there and — and — and — invisibly smack all the HiveWings in the head!"

"YES!" Sundew agreed. "Push them into the ocean! Drop some sharks on them!"

"Save Pineapple and Qibli and Tsunami!" Luna added.

"And feed all the HiveWings TO FIRE ANTS!" Sundew yelled.

"Wait, wait, no —" Cricket said.

There was a whoosh of wind past Luna's scales, and then Sundew's voice called, "You'd better all be right behind me!"

"But they're not —"

"Everyone see that palm tree on the south end of the

island?" Lynx shouted, her voice drowning out Cricket's. "Regroup there if we get separated!"

Luna thought she could hear the human yippering something at Sky, but then she and Lynx were flying fast, wingbeats in sync, and she lost track of where the others were. The only one she was sure of was Lynx, her strange ridged claws holding tight. *Don't let go*, Luna thought. *Don't leave me alone up here.*

The island was about as wide as Cicada Hive and maybe twice as long, curved like a dragon tail with a pair of huge boulders off the shore on the north end. The beach facing them rose quickly into a tangle of trees and cliff, blocking the view of the other side of the island.

Lynx gasped softly, tightening her grip on Luna as they flew close enough to see the dragons battling on the beach.

HiveWings swarmed across the white sand, teeth and stingers flashing. There had to be at least twenty of them, giant and deadly as a horde of murder hornets.

Luna's mind took an instinctive mental picture of the scene, even though she knew she would never, never want to weave a tapestry this frightening.

Twenty HiveWings. What are they doing all the way out here?

"Queen Wasp must have sent them to follow the escaping LeafWings," she said aloud.

"That means she could be inside all those dragons right now," Cricket's voice said hopelessly from above her.

Tsunami's blue scales were easy to spot in the crowd, where the fighting was thickest. She roared and spun, slashing at the HiveWings around her and smacking others in the head with her powerful tail.

Close to her, Qibli was surrounded by five HiveWings. His venomous tail was curved up, stabbing at his attackers as they darted in toward him. Luna saw him pull out one of the blowguns the RainWings had given them, but before he could aim it, a HiveWing lunged at him and knocked it into the sand. They grappled with their front claws locked, their teeth snapping at the air between them, both tails feinting jabs at the other.

But someone had managed to use the blowguns. One HiveWing was lying on the beach, eyes closed, with a dart in his neck. Another one, near Tsunami, suddenly clapped one talon to his cheek, staggered back, and collapsed.

Luna squeezed Lynx's claws. "I think Pineapple did that!" she cried. She'd never seen a RainWing's camouflage power in action before. It was much more impressive than she'd expected. She couldn't see Pineapple anywhere, but a moment later, a third HiveWing stumbled and went down.

"Do we attack?" Lynx called. "Sundew? Orders?"

"First priority is keeping Sky and Wren safe!" Sundew answered. "Sky, where are you?"

There was no response. Luna looked around, her heart racing, even though she knew she wouldn't see anything.

"Sky?" Sundew shouted again. "Come *on*, you twigbrain, where are you?"

"Sky, if you can hear us, go hide!" Lynx shouted.

Luna could hear Sundew muttering curses, but no sound from Sky or Wren. Had they lost them so quickly?

What happens to the rest of the plan if we lose our little human? How will we find the abyss without her to help us talk to the Pantalan humans?

"Sundew, can't you make Tsunami and Qibli invisible now?" Cricket asked.

"I'd have to make us visible first," Sundew said. "And I don't want the HiveWings to know we're here. We can't risk them seeing Sky and Wren — or catching the rest of us and leaving those two alone."

Below them, a sudden burst of flame flared along the tail of the HiveWing in Qibli's claws. The red-and-black dragon shrieked and flung herself away from him, rolling and rolling in the sand to put it out.

Where did that come from? Moon? Luna wondered. *Or Bullfrog?* NightWings and MudWings could both breathe fire. Maybe they were already down there, fighting invisibly.

I have fire, too. She flexed her free claws, feeling the heat of the flamesilk in her wrists.

Should I use it?

This is my chance, right? To use the weapon I was given?

But . . . can I really set other dragons on fire?

During one of those long days of waiting on the beach in the Distant Kingdoms, while Luna was practicing making different kinds of flamesilk, Jerboa had touched one of the fiery threads, not realizing that it would burn her. She'd pretended that it didn't hurt very much, but Luna had felt guilty about it for days. She still felt haunted by the angry red mark on Jerboa's claw.

I could throw ropes of fire at the HiveWings — but what if I hit one of the invisible dragons? What if I hurt one of my friends?

The other HiveWings around Qibli were turning, shouting, searching the dunes for the source of the flames. Qibli bolted away from them and threw himself at an orange-speckled HiveWing who was circling around behind Tsunami. They slammed into a pile of seaweed and skidded sideways, clawing and roaring at each other.

"Bullfrog, get that dragon off Qibli!" Sundew yelled. "Lynx, get out your blowgun and hit as many as you can. I'll help Tsunami."

"What about me?" Luna asked, but her question was lost in a rush of wingbeats. Lynx squeezed her talon and let go. Luna felt momentarily dizzy, untethered in the sky.

"I think Sundew still doesn't quite believe that SilkWings and HiveWings can be helpful," Cricket said quietly from somewhere nearby.

"*I* can be, though!" Luna protested, holding up her glowing wrists before she remembered that no one could see them. "I could set a HiveWing on fire. I *could*," she added, although Cricket hadn't disagreed with her.

Could you hurt another dragon like that? Blue's voice whispered in her head.

"But don't kill them!" Cricket said, her voice rising with

alarm. "Remember they're being controlled! This isn't their choice!"

That was a pretty hard thought to keep in mind as two HiveWings slashed at Tsunami's wings, one of them drawing blood, and another one jabbed his spear into Qibli's tail. Luna swooped lower, trying to find a good angle, trying to work up the courage to throw her silk. She was terrified of hitting Tsunami or Qibli, too; they moved so fast as they fought.

She also remembered the last time she'd tried to use her flamesilk to fight HiveWings. It had spiraled out of her control, caught a storm, and ended up carrying her all the way to Pyrrhia.

What if it happens again? What if I get blown away while I'm invisible and can't find my way back to everyone?

She hesitated, pulling her front talons in close to her chest.

The HiveWing on top of Qibli suddenly lurched sideways as if something had rammed into his side. He yelled and slashed upward with his claws, and Luna saw blood droplets spray out from the empty air. Flames from nowhere engulfed the HiveWing's tail, and he staggered, screaming, into the sea.

Qibli was up again, running back into the crowd of dragons around Tsunami, breathing his own fire now. As he ran, the seaweed underfoot began to slither around the HiveWings' claws. Luna saw one yellow-and-black dragon trip and slam heavily into the sand. Another pair found themselves wound together with long, wet strands and began shoving each other furiously.

At the same time, Luna saw another HiveWing yelp and fall sideways into the waves beside him, clutching his neck.

Maybe we do have a chance, she thought with a rush of surprise. She landed on a tall boulder and looked down at the strange battle that covered the beach. *Maybe we can win without even using my flamesilk. Maybe I don't have to do anything. I mean, we have three dragons who can breathe fire. Sundew and her leafspeak. Invisibility. The tranquilizer darts. And a dragon who can see the future — although, snakes and silkworms, Moon, why didn't you see this coming?*

Maybe these kind, funny dragons can fight a bunch of scary HiveWings.

Something rustled in the trees above the beach, and a new dragon came gliding onto the sand. His talons touched down lightly and he narrowed his eyes.

"There's another dragon here," he hissed. **"One we cannot see. Possibly more."**

Luna's heart nearly stopped. The new dragon's wings were gold dappled with lavender and gray — and long, pale purple antennae were slowly unfurling from his head.

That wasn't a HiveWing. That was a *SilkWing*, looking all peaceful and harmless, while Queen Wasp's voice slithered malevolently from his mouth.

A shudder ran down Luna's spine. Sundew and Cricket had said that Wasp could control SilkWings now, but Luna had never seen it herself. She hadn't quite believed it until that moment.

The SilkWing on the beach twisted his neck around and then slowly back in the other direction.

"What's he doing?" Cricket whispered from the air above Luna. "Why are his eyes closed?"

"He's using his antennae," Luna realized. "They pick up movement and vibrations in the air."

"Like from invisible dragons?" Cricket said with alarm. "Or camouflaged RainWings?" Luna heard a small clattering sound. "We have to stop him. Three moons, loading invisible darts into an invisible blowgun is impossible! Luna, help me! We have to knock out that SilkWing!"

Luna fumbled for her own blowgun pouch, but before she could get it out, the SilkWing suddenly flew across the beach and launched himself at one of the sand dunes not far from her boulder. Two other HiveWings spun and attacked the same spot in unison.

They all moved in the creepy, synchronized way Cricket had told Luna about, but it was so much more horrifying to see it with her own eyes. They didn't seem like dragons anymore. They looked like knives that someone else was slashing through the air.

There was a shriek beneath their claws, and a bright green dragon with white wings suddenly appeared on the sand. It took Luna a moment to realize that it was Pineapple. She had never seen him in those colors before.

"Pineapple!" she cried.

He couldn't hear her. A moment later, one of the HiveWings

smacked a rock into the side of the RainWing's head. Pineapple went limp, his white-spotted wings splayed awkwardly under the talons of his attackers. Bloody claw marks were scored along his underbelly, but she could see his chest still rising and falling.

What do we do? How do we rescue him?

"There's someone else we can't see," said the SilkWing, lifting his head again. **"One with fire."** He paused, and then smiled a slow, malevolent smile. **"A lost flamesilk, perhaps? Luuuuuuna. Little flamesilk, are you here?"**

Luna felt a sick yawning pit open up in her stomach. It was bone-chilling to think that Wasp knew her name — to know that Wasp had spent time thinking about her at all. Even though she was invisible, Luna felt as though Wasp was glaring straight at her through the SilkWing's maggot-white eyes.

"Everyone freeze!" Sundew shouted from somewhere along the beach. "Cricket says that SilkWings can sense movement! Don't let him find you!"

Luna didn't need to be told twice. She wasn't sure she could move anyway. She kept her wings tight to her body, claws gripping the rock, hardly daring to breathe.

The SilkWing took a step toward her, antennae twitching. Beyond him, Qibli was sinking under the attack of three HiveWings, and Luna couldn't even see Tsunami in the wave of dragons around her.

Another step. Luna's eyes were riveted on the enemy's antennae as they tested the air, pivoting slowly in her direction like mesmerizing cobras.

He was going to find her. Wasp was going to catch her and take her mind and control her like these brainwashed dragons, and Luna would end up as an empty shell spinning flamesilk for a monster for the rest of her life.

A blast of fire suddenly hit the SilkWing's left side — or almost did; he whipped out of the way at the last moment and, in one liquid motion, whirled and pounced on a spot of empty air that was not so empty, after all.

"HERE!" the SilkWing commanded, and ten HiveWings descended at once.

Luna pressed her claws to her face to stop herself from screaming. Silvery threads were pouring from the SilkWing's wrists, winding around the empty air in the unmistakable shape of a struggling dragon.

Flames burst from the invisible dragon, searing the closest threads to ash. *But if they set all the silk on fire, it'll burn their scales, too*, Luna thought. *Can I — if I burn the SilkWing — I have to use my flamesilk to stop him* — but it was all happening so fast.

One of the HiveWings stepped forward, and long black stingers slid from under her claws. She stabbed them into the air where the dragon's neck should be.

The silvery threads sagged and went still. With a grim smile, the SilkWing spun more and more silk, until the invisible, unconscious dragon was wound up like a spider's lunch.

And from the size and the fire, now Luna could guess who it was.

The HiveWings had captured Moon.

CHAPTER 4

We can still beat them, Luna thought desperately. *It's not over.* But when she looked along the beach, she saw that Tsunami lay unconscious on the sand. Another HiveWing with long claw-stingers stood over her, toxin and blue SeaWing blood dripping from the sharp points.

Behind them, five HiveWings had finally managed to pin Qibli down. He thrashed furiously, but even his tail was trapped under heavy red talons. The HiveWing who'd paralyzed Tsunami stepped over and sank her stingers into his neck as well. Barely a moment later, he was still.

"Sundew —" Lynx's voice said from somewhere near Qibli.

"Shhh," Sundew answered as the SilkWing's head snapped up, the antennae quivering suspiciously.

Silence fell over the beach. All the HiveWings seemed to be frozen in place, forced motionless by the queen in their heads. Only the SilkWing moved, stepping carefully around the fallen dragons, avoiding the seaweed and studying the talonprints in the sand. To Luna he seemed like a hollow shell of a dragon: nothing but a weapon for Queen Wasp to use against them.

Who was he before? Which Hive did he live in? Was he in the Chrysalis?

Does he know what's happening to him now?

"What kind of dragons are these?" the SilkWing hissed. He walked slowly around Tsunami and Qibli, pausing to study Qibli's tail with an expression Luna couldn't read. "I remember dragons like this," he murmured in a voice that suddenly wasn't Wasp's anymore. It didn't seem like his own, though. His movements seemed even weirder and more unnatural, as though dragon wings didn't fit quite right on him. His head pivoted to glare at Pineapple. "And *those*," he spat. "The ones that change color. I remember *those*." He lifted one of his claws to tap the side of his snout, then shifted his narrow gaze to the Moon bundle. "I don't recall invisible dragons who stayed invisible when unconscious, though."

"Will I be able to control them?" Wasp's voice demanded. **"Will the breath of evil work on them?"** She paused, and then the SilkWing hissed softly. "There's one way to find out," he murmured in the other voice.

A soft moan came from one of the collapsed dragons. Red and black scales rippled as the HiveWing tried to sit up, shivering with pain from the burns on her tail. Luna guessed she was the one who'd been fighting Qibli.

The HiveWing pressed her front talons to her forehead for a long moment. Then she glanced at the dark scorch marks across her tail and winced.

"Where are we?" she asked the soldier closest to her. He stared into the distance with those white marble eyes, unmoving and unresponsive.

The HiveWing scanned the beach: HiveWing bodies lying half in and half out of the waves or collapsed on the sand; others standing frozen, at attention; three unconscious prisoners who looked nothing like any Pantalan dragon; one mystery dragon-shaped bundle of silk; and the ominous SilkWing, still stalking around the sand and muttering to himself.

And the island itself, so vastly different from the Hives or the savanna.

The HiveWing blinked, bewildered.

Luna wondered how long these HiveWings had been under Wasp's mind control, and if they had any memory of what they'd done for her. She wondered why Wasp had released this one now, but not any of the others.

"Are we in the Distant Kingdoms?" the HiveWing asked, but once again the soldier did not respond.

The SilkWing, however, came gliding across the sand to loom over her.

"Were there any other dragons here?" the SilkWing snapped, back in Wasp's voice.

The HiveWing looked confused — and Luna thought there was a flash of contempt on her face, too. *She's never had a SilkWing talk to her like that.*

"How would *I* know?" the HiveWing demanded.

The SilkWing gazed coldly down at her. **"What is your name?"**

"Earwig," the HiveWing answered sullenly.

"Earwig . . . ah, yes, of Tsetse Hive. I'm inside your brothers now. I could have them kill each other so easily. Or perhaps this one could rip off the other's ears. That would be entertaining. Perhaps if you ever want to see them again, you could try addressing your queen with more respect."

Earwig stared up at him, her wings slack with astonishment.

"Use your brain," hissed the SilkWing. "There were two dragons we could see and two we could not. Did you sense any others?"

Luna held her breath.

"N-no, Your Majesty," Earwig said. "I mean — I wasn't really in myself — and there was a lot, um, happening." The SilkWing made an impatient movement that scattered sand across Earwig's burns, and she winced again. "But I don't think so," she added quickly.

"Did you notice any flamesilk?" the SilkWing demanded. An odd, brief struggle seemed to cross his face, and then, in the other voice, he spat: "Or any plants acting strangely?"

"Plants acting strangely?" Earwig blinked several times and glanced at the palm trees up the beach. "Noooo?"

She didn't notice the seaweed, Luna thought with relief. *Queen Wasp must have been so busy controlling the SilkWing that she didn't notice it either.*

Or . . . there are two minds fighting inside the SilkWing . . . and maybe even if Queen Wasp did notice, she's decided not to tell the other one, for some reason.

The SilkWing peered up at the clouds and then around at the sand, radiating suspicion. "SUNDEW!" he yelled suddenly. "Sundew, are you here?"

Silence. The sun shone brightly in an empty blue sky. Luna could hear birds fluttering in the trees, but no dragons. Nothing but Earwig's labored breathing.

What if the others left, and I'm the only one still here? Her heart sped up and she tried to think calmer thoughts, but in the emptiness, it was hard to believe she hadn't been abandoned there, alone on her rock with enemies all around her.

"Sundew," the SilkWing said, almost charmingly, except that his face didn't even try to make an expression. "We're not finished with each other. I know it; you know it. Why not come on out and face me?"

Another long pause.

"Don't you want to see your mother again?" the SilkWing taunted the empty air. He smirked. "All right, perhaps not her. I don't blame you. I'd chop that branch off, too, if it was related to me. But what about your queen? Or that little blue SilkWing you went to so much trouble to steal from me?"

Blue, Luna's heart thudded. *Blue, Blue, Blue trapped in Wasp's talons.*

The SilkWing turned toward her, and Luna feared that she must have moved at the thought of Blue — that a flinch or indrawn breath had given her away.

But he crossed to the silk bundle and prodded it, frowning. "This isn't you. LeafWings don't breathe fire. And that wasn't flamesilk, so it's not my Luna either. But if they're not with Sundew, why are these dragons here now?"

Earwig looked around at the other frozen soldiers, then back at him. "A-are you asking me?"

He gave her a disgusted look. "Do you know the answer?"

"No," she said. "I don't know anything. I don't know who Sundew is, or why we fought these mystery mutant dragons. I'm not even sure where we are." She tried to stand up, but a look of agony crossed her face as her tail moved, and she collapsed to the sand again.

The SilkWing jabbed one of the unconscious HiveWings in the face with his claw. When that got no reaction, he leaned down and sniffed the air around the dragon's snout, then squinted until he spotted the tiny dart jutting out between their scales.

"Not dead, then," said Wasp's voice. **"But utterly useless to me like this."** The SilkWing straightened. **"The rest of you will have to carry our prisoners back to Wasp Hive."**

"All of them? Right now?" Earwig asked. "Shouldn't we rest? My wings feel like we've been flying for days. Is it a long way back? If they have to carry a whole dragon, even these tiny ones, even with three HiveWings to a prisoner, they're going to get tired fast."

"It is unpleasant to converse with a dragon who talks so much," Wasp remarked.

Earwig closed her mouth and rubbed her forehead again.

"You will stay here and wait for these dragons to

wake up," Wasp said, waving the SilkWing's talons at the four tranquilized HiveWings. **"Then you will all return to Wasp Hive."**

He snapped his tail, and the other HiveWings began to move in silent unison, splitting up to circle the prisoners and dragging vines from the trees.

"Wait," Earwig said. "I don't want to be stuck here alone. What if you're right and there are other dragons lurking about?" She shivered. "Can't you jump back into me so I can go with you? Just make me like them again." She pointed to the white-eyed dragons who were lashing long vines around Tsunami.

Luna would have gasped if she could have moved. Earwig was *asking* for Wasp to take over her mind. She was inviting the evil queen back into her head! *How can she* want *that?*

"No." Wasp didn't even turn the SilkWing to look at Earwig again. **"You are in too much pain. It will distract me from the many claws I am working with right now."**

"But I don't know how to get back! None of us do!" Earwig cried. "You can't fly us all the way out into the middle of the ocean and leave us to die!"

"This conversation is boring me," Wasp said. **"Let me be clear so it can be over. I do not care what happens to you."**

Luna noticed that Earwig looked lost, but not terribly surprised by this.

The SilkWing made a commanding gesture at the marble-eyed HiveWings, and they bent toward their captives. As

Qibli was lifted into his net of vines, his head lolled, and the pouch around his neck slid off into the sand with a soft *fwshh*.

A panicked cry tried to claw its way out of Luna's throat, and she had to tense every muscle in her body to keep it from escaping.

She'd forgotten that Qibli was the one carrying the map in his pouch.

The map she and Sundew and the others needed to get home to Pantala.

The map that could lead Wasp and her army to Pyrrhia.

The map that must *never ever* fall into Wasp's talons.

Don't find it, Luna prayed. *Leave it lying there. Don't even notice it.*

The SilkWing turned, with agonizing slowness, and stared down at the pouch.

── CHAPTER 5 ──

Please, Luna prayed. *Please ignore it. Please don't find the map.*

The SilkWing nudged the pouch with one claw. It lay flat on the sand, like a deflated leather sack.

He reached to pick it up.

"It had this in it," Earwig said out of the blue. She held up Qibli's blowgun, which had fallen near her talons. She shook it a few times, and one of the darts slid out. "I think he was trying to jab me." Her claw flicked the dart.

"**Aha,**" Wasp said through the SilkWing. "**The trick they used on your unconscious comrades, I assume.**" The SilkWing turned to Tsunami and yanked the SeaWing's pouch off her neck to peer inside. "**Yes, they all seem to have them. So it's a weapon they made, not a natural dragon power. Interesting.**" He shook Tsunami's pouch, and the dreamvisitor sapphire tumbled out along with the blowgun.

Luna's heart sank. She knew that it was better to lose the dreamvisitor than the map. Wasp could do much worse damage with the map — and yet, losing the only way to contact Swordtail felt like having all her favorite tapestries torn to shreds.

The SilkWing held it up to his nose and squinted at it. "Strange thing to carry around," he said in one voice, and then went on in Wasp's voice, **"A gift for me from the Distant Kingdoms. How thoughtful."** He tucked it back into Tsunami's pouch, which he draped over his own head, then beckoned the other dragons with his tail. **"Time to go."**

They flared open their wings in unison and lifted into the sky. Qibli, Tsunami, Pineapple, and invisible Moon hung between them, wrapped in vines, breathing but otherwise still.

Luna couldn't believe it. They'd been arguing and joking and laughing with her only moments ago, and now they were Wasp's prisoners.

It's all falling apart. We haven't even reached Pantala yet, and everything is already lost.

She watched helplessly as their wingbeats faded into the distance.

Earwig slumped on the beach, staring out at the ocean. She was alone with the four unconscious HiveWings. The sand all around her was churned up by the battle, grooved with claw marks, and splattered with blood.

I can move now, Luna thought, but it was hard to convince her petrified limbs. *The SilkWing is gone. Earwig won't notice me. I can go to the palm tree and hope to find the others there.*

Should she try to grab Qibli's pouch first? What if Earwig spotted it floating away?

Earwig sighed, long and tragic, and then, as if she'd heard Luna's thoughts, she dragged herself over to Qibli's pouch and picked it up.

No! Luna cried inside her head. *No, no, no* —

Earwig opened the pouch and peeked inside. With a barely curious expression, she slid out the map and unfolded it.

Her eyes went wide. She started to jump to her feet, let out a yelp of pain, and toppled over again.

"Wasp!" she shouted. "Come back! Your Majesty! I found —"

Thwip went the tiny sound of a dart zipping through the air. Earwig's eyes rolled back in her head, and she flopped over with a thud.

"Whew," said Lynx's voice, loud and clear in the silence.

"Nice shot." Bullfrog's deep voice came from the mess of sandy talonprints near where Pineapple had fallen, not far from Luna. She couldn't believe he'd been that close to her and so silent that whole time. Well, maybe she could believe the silent part.

"Are we all here?" Sundew asked from the far side of the battleground.

"I am," Cricket's voice answered.

"Yes," said Bullfrog, and "Here," said Lynx.

"Me too," Luna managed.

"What are we going to do?" Cricket asked, her voice overlapping with Lynx saying, "That was awful — I felt like I couldn't do anything!"

"Poor Pineapple," Luna said. She pressed her talons to her snout and took a deep breath to stop her tears. "I can't believe a SilkWing . . ." She trailed off.

"Was that terrifying? Me neither," Sundew growled. "WREN! SKY! Where ARE you?!"

"Will the mind control work on the Pyrrhian dragons?" Cricket asked. "That's the first thing Wasp will do, don't you think? Inject them with her hive-mind toxin?"

"No, because we're going to get them back before that happens," Sundew said firmly. "SKYYYYY!"

"Can we re-visible ourselves now?" Cricket asked.

"If I make us visible, Moon will be, too," Sundew said. "And then they'll know she's another Clearsight. But I might have to anyway, if we can't find Sky and Wren. SKY! WREN!"

"Yes, WHAT?" the little human's voice demanded as wingbeats descended from the clouds. Four talonprints appeared in a puff of sand, followed by a spray of more sand as Sky shook out his wings. "What are you shouting our names for? Ack, Sky, quit that; you're getting sand in my mouth."

"Where did you go?" Sundew said irritably. "We were worried about you! I mean, not me specifically, but somebody probably was!"

"We went to the palm tree to wait for you," Wren answered. "I told you I'm not sending Sky into any battles with creepy bug dragon zombies. No offense, Cricket."

"Why — I'm not —" Cricket started.

"But we could see most of what happened," Wren went on. "And it didn't look great!"

"It was *so horrible*," Sky's voice added mournfully. "I did not like those dragons. Is Pineapple all right? Where did they take them?"

"I thought we weren't going to fight any HiveWings," Wren added. "I thought our very specific plan was to stay far away from any dragons who might end up mind-controlling us or hurting Sky."

"Or stealing our friends!" Sky added.

"We didn't go *looking* for them!" Sundew barked. "They attacked us! We couldn't not fight back!"

"I know," Wren said. "Just . . . Sky's not that kind of dragon. Battles like that scare him."

"I *beg* your pardon," Sky said, ripples appearing in the sand from his ruffling wings. "I'm not scared! I mean, my heart is going really fast and my stomach is flippy-wobbly and I wish I had a giant turtle shell that I could crawl into and stay there and never see those dragons again, but *mostly* I am *worried about Pineapple* and our other friends."

"They're still alive," Luna reassured him. "They were all unconscious. They're being taken to Wasp Hive, where the queen lives."

"Wasp prefers capturing dragons to killing them," Cricket explained. "They're more useful to her as new soldiers to control than as corpses."

"Ack," Wren said. "I don't like those options! No, thank you!"

"We should follow them, shouldn't we?" Luna asked.

"A hundred million nos!" Wren cried. "*Follow* them?! What did I *just* say?"

"Of course we have to follow them," Sundew said. "We stay at a distance until we can tranquilizer-dart the SilkWing — maybe while they're sleeping. Then we can sneak in and rescue everyone."

"I'm not sure Wasp is going to let them sleep until they're inside her Hive," Cricket said slowly. "She can drive the dragons she's inside beyond the point of exhaustion. I think that's how she got them this far out here without the map. I don't think she could get them all the way to Pyrrhia, but she can probably fly them back to her Hive without letting them rest."

"So if we try to follow them," Lynx added, "we might end up over open water with nowhere to rest when *we* need to."

"So? What's the alternative?" Sundew cried. "We can't let them take four dragons from us!" From the plumes of sand around her voice, Luna guessed the invisible LeafWing was lashing her tail.

"They'd rescue *us* if they were here," Luna agreed. "You know Tsunami and Qibli wouldn't even stop to think."

"Um, I'm in favor of stopping to think before doing dangerous things," Lynx interjected.

"Me too," Cricket agreed. "And remember, our goal is to get to the abyss and fulfill Moon's prophecy. Don't we think that's the way to defeat Wasp and the othermind? So it's actually the best way to rescue our friends?"

"Better than throwing ourselves at an army of creepy bug dragons, yes!" Wren chimed in.

"But we can't fulfill the prophecy without them!" Luna protested. "Talons united — that means all ten of us! And Moon is the only one who can tell us what to do! We need to follow the prophecy exactly, and we're already failing!" *You can't make a tapestry with half your silk missing*, she thought anxiously.

"Actually," Bullfrog's voice said slowly, "Clay says prophecies aren't like instructions. And they aren't messages saying, 'This will definitely happen.' He says a prophecy can give you a hint in the right direction, but you have to choose what you do with it."

Everyone fell silent for a long moment. Luna was so startled by the length of Bullfrog's speech that it took her a moment to process the meaning of it.

"Wait — so prophecies *don't* tell the future?" she asked.

"Who's Clay?" Cricket asked at the same time.

"A MudWing who was in a prophecy not too long ago," Lynx explained. "He saved Pyrrhia."

"But *our* prophecies told us what would happen," Luna argued. "I mean, the ones in Clearsight's book. They *were* like instructions — they were exactly instructions!"

"Maybe," Cricket said. "We don't know for sure because we never lived in a time Clearsight actually predicted."

"All I'm saying," Bullfrog cut in, his voice deep and implacable, "is that we're the ones who make the prophecy happen, not the other way around."

"I'm confused," said Luna. "I still think we need all ten of us."

"I think I get it," Sundew said. "You're saying the future is up to us. Whatever happens next, it's because of what we decide to do, not because of some mystical force pointing us here or plopping us there."

"So we could *decide* to save our friends, couldn't we?" Luna said. "Shouldn't we?"

"Let's vote," Sundew said. "All in favor of chasing the HiveWings right now to rescue Moon and the others?"

"Me," Luna said.

"Me too," Sky said. "Ouch, Wren! No kicking! Bad pet human!"

"And me," Sundew said. "Who thinks we should stick with the original plan and go find the abyss?"

"Me," Cricket and Bullfrog said together.

"Arrrgh . . . me too," Lynx agreed.

"So it's a tie," Sundew said with a sigh.

"AHEM," said Wren's little human voice. "I'm here, too! And I vote for the original plan. I'd rather take Sky to a creepy abyss than into a swarm of creepy murder bug dragons. Arrrrgh, Sky, stop!" There was a thump, and a large dent appeared in the beach where Sky had apparently flung himself down, followed by a lot of sand flying and crabs scuttling about as he had a rolling tantrum.

Little human footprints landed on the sand and darted out of the way, then stopped again. Luna could easily picture Wren with her hands on her hips, glaring at the mess Sky was making.

"Well, this is very mature," Wren's voice said crossly.

"Sky, I know how you feel," Lynx said. "My heart says rescue them, too. But my head says we'll only get ourselves caught or worse, and the most logical way to save them is to get to the abyss. If we can defeat the othermind, Wasp won't have an army to control anymore. Right? That's our theory?"

"And we can't risk losing you or Wren," Cricket agreed.

"You're the only ones who can help us talk to the humans to find the abyss."

"No!" Sky cried. "Wren, you came to save me in the Kingdom of Sand even when it was dangerous! That's what we do for friends! And I finally have dragon friends! Dragon friends who need saving!"

"All right, this is what we're going to do," Sundew said with such authority that everyone went quiet, and Sky stopped invisibly thrashing around. "Lynx and I will go try to rescue them. If it seems impossible, we won't risk it, but we'll take as many darts as we can and see what we can do. Meanwhile, the rest of you keep following the map to Pantala and wait for us there. If we don't catch up with you in two days, go look for the abyss without us."

"Just us?" Luna said softly. Her, Cricket, Sky and Wren, and Bullfrog. No Tsunami or Sundew to do the fighting. No Moon to tell the future. No clever Qibli plans, no reassuring Lynx smiles or Pineapple cheerfulness.

"Don't worry," Sundew said. "We'll be there."

Luna wanted to believe that. But if anything went wrong, the five of them would have to face the abyss alone.

The last words of the prophecy echoed in her head.

Face a great evil with talons united . . . or none of the tribes will survive.

CHAPTER 6

Luna was not surprised that it was raining. It was the rainy season on Pantala; she was used to the drumming sound of raindrops on Hive walls and silk ceilings.

She was *not* used to the damp, chilly air spraying her no matter where she tried to sit, though. This cave was not designed for dragons to live in during storms, especially if those dragons had nothing to do except anxiously watch the sky outside for missing friends.

Of course, she knew those friends would be invisible, so she wouldn't see them coming. But she couldn't stop sitting near the mouth of the cave and staring out at the thunderstorm anyway.

I could make a tapestry of this, Luna thought. *Endless rain. An empty beach. A sky that's all clouds and no dragons. Or maybe I'd weave shapes way off in the distance, blurred by lines of silver silk raindrops, but still there, like faraway hope coming toward us.*

I would LOVE some hope, even faraway hope, right now.

"Luna?" Cricket's voice said, her talonprints approaching through the wet sand. "Are you there?"

For a moment, Luna considered pretending she wasn't. If she held really still and didn't breathe, maybe Cricket would walk away and Luna wouldn't have to muster the energy for a conversation. Or more importantly, for a conversation where she had to act like she trusted this HiveWing, like it was fine that Luna was stuck in a cave with her instead of with any of the dragons she really wanted to be with.

She would know, though. And Luna couldn't bring herself to hurt Cricket's feelings, especially when she remembered the way Blue looked at her.

"I'm here," Luna said. "Just . . . waiting." *Again. Stuck in one place, no idea what to do or how to help anyone.*

"Maybe they're hiding out from the rain," Cricket said, accidentally bumping one of her wings. "Maybe they're worried about the lightning and they'll be here as soon as the storm lets up."

"Maybe," Luna said, more to let Cricket know she was still there and listening than because she agreed.

Sundew and Lynx should have been there yesterday. They'd agreed to wait for them at the cave that connected to the flamesilk cavern, the one where Luna had been blown away by the storm. A whole extra day they'd been waiting, with no sign of the LeafWing or the IceWing.

Have they been captured, too? It would be so, so bad for Sundew to fall into the clutches of Queen Wasp. With Sundew's leafspeak power, the othermind could grow the breath of evil plant from one edge of the continent to the other in a matter of weeks.

Don't think about that.

She's fine. I'm sure she's all right. They'll be here soon.

Keep smiling, no problems here.

Except no one could see her face, so she didn't have to pretend smile . . . the one upside of being invisible.

Luna kind of wished she could spin herself another cocoon and go back into it for a while. This happened to her sometimes. It felt as though she had her own rainy seasons and sunny seasons inside her head: some days, she was full of light and endless energy and *knowing* what was right and ready to fix everything. But then, some days, a kind of fog wove through her thoughts, and she just wanted to crawl away from everyone and wrap herself in silk and not be a dragon for a while.

She thought she hid those days pretty well. She had a lot of practice at smiling through the fog so her mothers wouldn't worry. She didn't mean to add to all the troubles everyone had. Even Blue, who noticed so much and tried so hard to understand everyone, usually couldn't tell when she was having a rainy-season day.

There wasn't always a clear reason for the sad feelings. Or rather, in some ways there were always reasons. Teachers yelling at Luna and Blue in school. Swordtail in trouble again. Luna's mother Silverspot lying sadly in her hammock after another long day of cruelty from her HiveWing mistress. All of them too squashed flat by the meanness of others and too exhausted to weave or make beautiful things or dream of a better life.

But this time there was a very clear reason, and so the sadness felt even bigger, like she was letting down the whole world. Losing Pineapple, Moon, Qibli, and Tsunami — not knowing where Sundew and Lynx were — SilkWings under Queen Wasp's mind control — their mission failing before they'd even begun . . .

And Swordtail and Blue.

She really couldn't let herself think about Swordtail and Blue, and how much they needed her, and how much she was failing to rescue them. Or else the fog-cocoon might wrap her up forever, and then she'd be no use to anyone.

It also didn't help that she was still invisible. Each day that passed without seeing her own talons or her friends' faces made Luna feel more and more unreal. As though she didn't really exist, or maybe they didn't, or maybe nothing did. She felt like she could dissolve into the clouds and no one would notice or care.

Swordtail would. He would care so much. He needs me to be real so I can rescue him.

My whole tribe *needs me to rescue them.*

Come on, Luna. Sit up and keep going.

Luna pulled back her shoulders and fluffed her damp wings. At least being this cold and wet meant that she must still exist, right? Also, being invisible was useful for gathering food without being spotted by the patrols that were constantly overhead.

The patrols were still mostly HiveWings. Luna had been afraid that mind-controlled SilkWings would be everywhere when they reached Pantala, but she hadn't seen very many so far.

She knew some of them were in the Hives, imprisoned until Wasp had more breath of evil to infect them with.

With poor Blue and Swordtail forced to guard them.

Shouldn't I go to them? If this abyss plan is falling apart anyway, shouldn't I fly to Cicada Hive and try to save them?

How, though? I have all this fire, but I don't know what to do with it. Flamesilk can't get Wasp out of their heads. And what else do I have?

"Isn't it weird being invisible for this long?" Cricket said, her voice more subdued than usual. "When it's quiet, I have these moments where I suddenly feel all alone, as though everyone else is gone and I'm a ghost floating around with no body. Do you ever feel like that?"

"Um," Luna said reluctantly. "Maybe a little." She hesitated, but her curiosity won out. "What do you do, when you feel that way?"

"I come looking for you," Cricket's voice said wryly. "I mean, Sky and Bullfrog and Wren help, too. But you're the most real to me, for some reason. Maybe because we're both from here?"

"Hmm," Luna answered. She wasn't sure quite what to say to that. Cricket's disembodied voice was easier to talk to than Cricket's HiveWing face, but she didn't exactly find it comforting.

"And sometimes," Cricket went on, "I close my eyes and

try to focus on what I can feel. Like, my claws feel wet sand sifting around them. My wings lift in the wind from the sea. I'm still here, I really exist, I'm in this dragon body in this world. You know? Does that make sense?"

Luna took a deep breath and tried to inhabit her senses beyond sight. *My scales are real. My talons are real. I am still here.*

"That does help," she said after a moment. "Also, if I were a ghost, I hope I would pick a better place to haunt than this damp, fishy-smelling cave."

Cricket laughed. "I would haunt a library!" she said. "Although it would be very frustrating to only read books over other dragons' shoulders."

"I'd haunt an art museum," Luna said dreamily. If she weren't real, she could look at beautiful things all day long and avoid mean dragons without feeling guilty about all the dragons who needed her and all the tasks she should be accomplishing.

But I am real. I'm really Luna, and I can't let myself drift away.

"Do you think Earwig made it back to shore?" Cricket asked. Grooves in the sand appeared as she drew shapes with her claws. She'd had a fight with Sundew about the unconscious HiveWing soldiers, back on the island.

"We can help them," Cricket had argued. "Earwig is lost out here — all five of these HiveWings are. We could draw her a map on a leaf or something, just showing the safe island trail from here back to Pantala. It wouldn't be the whole map. Just enough to get her home."

"So that Queen Wasp can have five more dragons for her army if we run into them again?" Sundew had demanded. "Why not leave them stuck out here where they can't hurt us?"

"Because they're still dragons," Cricket pointed out. "They didn't choose to come here or attack us. They're going to wake up scared, wishing they could go home, and we could help them."

"Sundew, we have to go now or we'll lose the trail," Lynx had said, breathing little ice crystals into the air from above them. "We don't have time to argue."

"Fine — do what you like," Sundew had said to Cricket. "I think it's a mistake, but if you want to take the time, go ahead."

And then she and Lynx were gone, leaving the map with Luna.

Luna wasn't sure who was right. Her instinct was to trust Sundew. But Cricket said Blue would want to help the HiveWings, and that, unfortunately, was definitely true. Luna knew her little brother would never fly away and leave them lost like that.

So Luna had used her flamesilk to carefully burn a copy of the map onto a wide leaf — just the part of it that would get the HiveWings back home. She'd added Cricket's note:

This is the way back to Pantala. Good luck.

— Friends who want you to be free

Then they'd left it in the sand under one of Earwig's talons. Luna hoped they'd done the right thing. She hoped Earwig would remember that someone had tried to help her when Queen Wasp had left her to die.

Luna realized she'd been thinking for too long and hadn't answered Cricket's question. "I'm sure she did," she said. "Cricket, do you really think there are good HiveWings? Ones who would help us if they could?"

She was glad she couldn't see the look on Cricket's face. Luna had been thinking about this question for days and couldn't believe she'd actually blurted it out.

There was a long pause, and then Cricket said softly, "I hope so. There's Katydid, for one. And my dad, I think. I haven't met him yet, but Lady Scarab liked him. I hope he turns out to be good once he's free from Wasp's clutches. But I guess I can't promise what any of them will be like then. I only know which side I want to be on, and it's with you and Blue."

We need all the allies we can get, Luna reminded herself.

She never did anything to help us before. But she's only a dragonet, like us . . . Maybe this was her first chance.

Maybe she felt like me: like she wanted to change things but didn't know how.

"What if you had to choose between saving Blue or, like, all the HiveWings?" Luna asked. "Or your family?"

"Blue, in a heartbeat," Cricket said. "I promise, Luna. Blue is my favorite dragon in all the world. My very favorite. I didn't know dragons like him existed. If it seems like I don't miss him enough, it's because I'm trying so hard not to cry all the time. It feels like my wings have been cut off, but I know I have to keep going, even on whatever stumps are left, because I'm not going to let this happen to him."

Luna hadn't been quite ready for sharing *all* their feelings. She hadn't expected a HiveWing, of all dragons, to just open up her chest, pull out all the pieces of her heart, and scatter them around on the sand like that. She wanted to stuff them back in and wrap Cricket in silk so she'd have to act normal again and they could pretend nobody here was on the verge of crying.

To her enormous relief, scuffling noises came from farther back in the cave. Luna turned toward the sound and saw damp little human footprints come padding over the rocks.

"I think I found something," Wren's voice said breathlessly. "Maybe a way to find the humans here."

A flurry of sand and raindrops erupted from where Cricket was sitting. "Really?" the HiveWing cried. "Did you see them? What were they doing? Did they have books with them?"

"I didn't see any people yet," Wren said, "but I found a human-sized torch that was burned at one end. It's in this huge cave that has at least two passageways out of it that dragons wouldn't fit into. I figured I'd search them, but I wanted to let Sky know first."

"I think he's on the beach looking for turtles with Bullfrog," Luna said.

"Oh, *Sky*," Wren said with a laugh. "How did he bamboozle Bullfrog into that?"

While Wren went out into the rain to find the others,

Luna tried to focus on shaking off the fog in her head. They had something to *do*, finally, besides sit and wait. The group needed her *up* energy, the "let's do it, let's change things, let's make a difference" Luna.

Come on, I know I'm in there somewhere.

Invisible wings came into the cave shaking off waterfalls of wet droplets. Wren's voice squeaked indignantly and said something stern to Sky in their part-human, part-dragon language.

"I hope we see a human," Cricket said. "Sundew said she saw one down here once — I wonder if it was in the same cavern!"

Wren's footprints pattered over to the spot where they'd burned a fire the last two nights, and one of the long sticks floated up into the air. "Luna or Bullfrog, could you light this for me?"

"I'll do it," Luna said. She put one talon on the free end of the stick and let a coil of gold fire spiral out of her wrist to wind around the wood. The silk burned in a thin thread for a moment, and then it spread upward until the end of the torch was alight with orange flame.

"Thanks, Luna," Wren said. "All right, you can all follow me — but if we see any humans, don't scare them! I mean, I know they won't be able to see or hear us, but don't, like, set anything on fire or try to pick them up. Or, say, dump an ocean's worth of water on their heads by accident."

"*Do* you know what 'by accident' even means?" Sky

demanded. The torch moved away to the back of the cave and Sky's voice followed, the two of them arguing affectionately.

They sound like me and Swordtail, Luna thought. For three years now, she'd been part of a pair — Luna and Swordtail, Swordtail and Luna. She felt so strange and untethered without him, like threads of loose silk tied to a loom but left out of the tapestry.

The floating torch led them on a winding path deeper into the dark underground labyrinth, until finally it stopped near an archway where the tunnel opened into a bigger cave.

"All right, everyone, shhhh," Wren's voice said from the area of the torch.

"Why?" Sky demanded at full volume. "We are not-see-able and not-hearable, aren't we? LA LA LA, I could sing all day and it wouldn't bother anybody!"

"Except *us*," Wren said. "It would bother *me*! And shhh because I'm talking, that's why. This is the cave — I'm going to leave my torch here so the humans don't see us coming, just in case there are any in there now." The burning stick floated over to the wall, and Wren tucked the end into a notch in the rocks. "Make sure you don't disturb anything, in case they come back and notice and it scares them off."

"Are they really that smart?" Bullfrog's voice asked skeptically.

Luna could hear the frown in Wren's voice. "Bullfrog. You do remember that I'm one of them, right?" the little human retorted.

"Right, just — thought you were — different, sorry," he ended in a mumble.

"She *is* special, but it turns out humans *are* pretty smart," Sky said sunnily. "*Almost* as smart as turtles!"

"NOT HELPING, Sky."

Their voices had moved off into the cave, so Luna stepped forward cautiously, feeling the brush of Cricket's tail ahead of her. It was a vast space, larger than the cave that opened onto the beach, bigger even than the marketplace in Cicada Hive. Rock formations jutted from the floor and ceiling like dragon teeth, some of them spiraled together into twisting columns. Dim sunlight and trickles of rain spilled in from a few cracks in the roof, waterfalling down the craggy walls to a shallow pool on the far side.

Luna tucked the space into her memory the way she usually did, by imagining it as a tapestry. She pictured the silk colors she would use for the shades of gray shadows and golden spills of light, and how the sizes of the stalactites would give a sense of how far back the cave went.

She cupped her talons and poured flamesilk into them, choosing the kind that glowed without burning. Her father had told her about different kinds of flamesilk in the brief half day she'd had with him. He hadn't taught her very much, but she'd had way too much time to practice while she sat on the beach with Jerboa, and by now she could spin five different kinds of flamesilk thread.

The silk lit the area around her with a golden glow, so she could see more clearly into the shadows. It wasn't visible to the others, though, or to any humans in the cave — not unless she lit something else on fire.

"Here's the torch I found," Wren called from a ledge halfway up the wall to Luna's right. A stick with a charred end waved in the air. Frayed bits of black thread clung to the wood as though it had once had something wrapped around it to burn. "And see, it's near this opening, which leads to a tunnel. I'm going to go in and see what I can find. You all look for more clues out here."

"Is that a good idea?" Sky asked nervously. "Couldn't I come with you, if I squished?"

"You're not an octopus, you big worrywart," Wren said. "There's no way —"

Luna left them to their arguing and wandered deeper into the cave, peeking into all the dark corners. She could see why Wren was curious about this place. There were holes and possible tunnels everywhere, just the right size for the small, soft species. It would be easy for something Wren's size to vanish into the wall if a dragon came in.

What if the abyss is down a human-sized tunnel? Luna worried. *What if it's buried in stone too deep for dragons to reach?*

She'd come to the far back wall of the cave and was trying to peer into one of the little holes when she heard a faint rustling overhead.

Luna stepped back and held up her flamesilk, trying to see onto the shelf of rock above her. Farther up, near one of the slants of sunlight, something moved.

It felt like the sudden fright of finding a spider pressed into a crack you thought was just a line in the wall. Luna gasped and nearly stepped on her own tail as she tripped backward.

On a ledge way up by the light, lying flat against the rocks, was a pale, soft-looking creature with a thatch of dark fur on its head.

They had found their first Pantalan human.

CHAPTER 7

The invisible dragons were crowded so close around the strange human's ledge that Bullfrog kept stepping on Luna's talons.

"This is *amazing*," Cricket said for the nine hundredth time. "It's not running away or anything! We can watch it for as long as we want! Look at how cute it is. Isn't it SO cute? Don't worry, Wren, you're cute, too."

"I most certainly am not," Wren's voice said from up near the human. She'd ordered Sky to lift her onto an outcropping so she could study the stranger.

"What is it doing?" Cricket asked. "Is it reading? It's looking at something, isn't it?"

"Please try not to lose your mind when I tell you this," Wren said. "This human seems to be comparing a regular book to a dragon-sized book."

Cricket gave a muffled gasp, and Luna felt her wings fluttering in the air.

"Or reading both of them at the same time or something,

but I don't think that's possible," Wren said. "I mean, they're looking very closely at the pictures in the dragon book, but I don't think they can actually read it."

"Where did it *get* a dragon book?" Cricket burst out. "Which book is it? What's the human-sized book about?"

"I have no idea," Wren answered. A faraway sound came from beyond the rock wall, and the strange human suddenly sat up and turned toward it. The sound came again. With something that looked astonishingly like a dragon sigh, the human folded its books into a covered sort of parcel, tucked that safely between two dry rocks, and then darted through a small hole Luna hadn't even noticed.

"Oh no!" Cricket yelped. "Why did it leave?"

"I think someone was calling them," Wren said. "I'm going to follow and see where they go. Back soon!" There was a little thump as she leaped to the human's ledge, and then she was gone, too.

"Wren?" Sky called nervously, but she didn't respond. Luna heard snuffling noises up by the humans' tunnel, as though Sky was trying to squash his snout into it.

"Can we look at the books the human left behind?" Cricket asked.

"We shouldn't — we might damage them," Luna said. "Wren said not to touch anything in case they notice, remember?"

Cricket made a frustrated noise, but she said, "Aaaaargh, you're right. Maybe Wren can get them out for us when she comes back."

Wren was gone for a long, long time. Bullfrog eventually went out to find food for everyone, and Luna paced around the cavern until she knew every corner. She bumped into Sky several times; he appeared to be doing the same thing. Maybe Cricket was, too, but if so, she was better at dodging them.

It is so weird to think Blue might have found his someone, and she's a HiveWing who overshares and is obsessed with humans and books. Not exactly who I would have pictured him with.

How would I even make a wedding tapestry for them? Their colors would totally clash.

No, they wouldn't, she admitted. She couldn't lie to herself about weaving. *Azure blue, lavender-violet, orange-gold, and black. Fine, I bet they'd be really pretty.*

She suddenly had a startling thought. *What if we somehow save the world, but never find Sundew or the magic wristbands? What if we're stuck invisible forever?*

Blue and Swordtail would have to learn to live with invisible girlfriends.

That might be easier, actually. No one would judge Blue and Cricket for liking each other across tribes. And I wouldn't have to think "ack, HiveWing!" every time I saw her.

If I had met her as a voice and never saw her scales, would I like her better?

She thought about the day she'd met Swordtail. *I'd have fallen for him no matter what he looked like or which tribe he was from, wouldn't I?*

It had been her first day at Silkworm Hall, and it had started as a sunny-season morning in her mind. She'd been *so* excited to finally go to school, where she could learn to read and weave and how laws worked and why "things just have to be this way, Luna," and how to make big old mean dragons listen to you.

But everything started to go wrong at the entrance to the Hive, when the guards there had roughly clamped on her metal wrist cuff, inscribed with the name of the school. It had been so unexpectedly heavy that she'd yelped, and the HiveWing putting it on had sneered at her. "Too bad for Silkworm Hall, getting a whining little caterpillar like you," he'd hissed.

"I'm not whining," Luna had huffed, ignoring Blue when he nudged her in the side. "I don't think it's supposed to be this heavy!"

"It is," the HiveWing had snapped. "Move along."

Don't let the fog in, Luna had ordered herself. *Don't let one mean dragon ruin your day.*

But the dragons who ran Silkworm Hall weren't any kinder. Some of the teachers were SilkWings, but the administration was all HiveWings. There were prickly guards at the doors, and the walls were thick with no windows and no sunlight at all. Students crowded the narrow corridors, quiet and listless. She was separated from Blue and given a different schedule. Teachers snapped at her to sit, be quiet, stop asking questions, fold in her tail, eat silently, wait for permission to speak (which never came).

By recess, Luna was in the grip of one of the worst sadnesses she'd ever felt. She knew she couldn't let herself cry at school, and if she escaped out the front gates and ran back to the safety of the webs, she'd only be in worse trouble later. But her wrist hurt and her heart hurt and she didn't know how she would make it through the rest of the day.

"Recess" apparently meant standing or marching around an open balcony on the side of Cicada Hive. It was boring, but at least there was sunlight and wind. Luna tried to breathe in all the air she could fit into her lungs.

"Bit close to the edge there, aren't you?" an older voice growled. She turned and saw one of the HiveWing guards approaching a student who was looking out at the savanna. The little SilkWing was not all that close to the balcony railing, and he blinked up at the HiveWing in confusion.

"Me?" he squeaked. His scales were light pink and lime green, with hints of darker rose inside his wingbuds. Luna had math class with him — Glider, if she remembered right.

"Seems a little dangerous, worm." The HiveWing smirked, looming over the wingless dragonet. He inched back, and she stepped closer. The balcony edge was a few steps behind him now. "Without any wings, you could tip right over, and just *think* how far you'd have to fall. All that time to contemplate the giant *splat* you'll make at the end."

"I d-don't — I d-didn't mean to — Can I p-please go inside now?" Glider stammered. He risked a glance over his shoulder as she crowded him back. The balcony railing was only as high as the students' wingbuds. It looked like it had been built as an afterthought: *Oh, right, SilkWing dragonets have no wings. We should pretend we care about their safety, but don't waste too much treestuff on this since we don't really.* It would not be hard to fall over it . . . or be pushed over it.

"We lose at least one dragonet every year," the HiveWing said in a fake-sad voice. "Poor little brainless worms who aren't *careful* enough." She took another step, and Glider squeaked with fear.

"Stop that!" Luna said. She was startled to hear her own voice lancing through the silk-fog around her. It felt like bright little flames of anger were burning holes in her sadness. "Why are you being so mean? You're scaring him just to be awful!"

Most of the other SilkWing students stared at her with wide, terrified eyes. The HiveWing flicked her tail, where a dangerous-looking stinger gleamed, and turned her head slowly to glare at Luna.

"A worm with a voice," hissed the guard. "Gross. No one has ever taught you your place, have they?"

"Has anyone ever taught *you* basic decency?" Luna demanded. "How to be a dragon with a heart? Or were all your classes about acting like a pile of poisonous sludge to anyone smaller than you?"

There were audible gasps from the rest of the class, who started edging away as fast as they could sidle. The HiveWing stepped toward her and raised her tail menacingly. Glider slipped away from the railing and bolted back into the school, but the guard didn't notice.

"Mouthy little worms end up on Misbehaver's Way," the

HiveWing snarled. "But I get to paralyze you with my tail toxin first. I hear it's quite painful."

"Oh NOOOOOOO!" shouted a voice on the far side of the balcony. Everyone hustled out of the way as the guard whirled around.

The shouting dragonet was a little bit older than Luna. He was dark blue with several small white triangular scales and larger orange splotches. And he was *standing on the railing of the balcony.*

"I got too close to the edge!" he yelled. "I wasn't careful enough! I was just WANDERING around exactly like a worm with no brains and SUDDENLY I ENDED UP HERE ON THIS RAILING! Oh no! The horror! I'm probably going to go SPLAT! I'm such a brainless worm! Tragic day! Poor world, what are you going to do without Swordtail?"

The HiveWing guard goggled at him. Luna could not imagine what her own face was doing.

"If only someone had warned me about going splaaaaaaaaaaaat!" the dragonet howled. "If only some brilliant HiveWing had reminded me I have no wings and should be careful in tall places! Alas, alack, woe and despair!"

"Get down from there!" the HiveWing snapped furiously. "Get down *right now!*"

Luna saw a strange flare of something in the HiveWing's eyes, and she suddenly realized that the guard was never intending to push Glider over the edge. The HiveWing wanted to scare them and prove her power over them — but if any of them actually fell, she'd be in big trouble.

"Get *down* from here?" Swordtail echoed, looking thoroughly befuddled. "But *how*? Which way do I *go*? I'm MUCH too stupid to figure this out myself!" He took a wobbling step along the railing and flailed around as though he couldn't get his balance.

The HiveWing charged over and yanked him onto the safety of the floor.

"What are you playing at?" she snarled. "You're going straight to the headmaster — and you, too!" she barked, pointing at Luna. "I know *you* know the way," the HiveWing added, scowling at Swordtail.

"I do," Swordtail said cheerfully. He sauntered over and bumped Luna's side with a grin. "Come along, troublemaker."

Luna glanced around the balcony, but everyone else was studiously avoiding her gaze. Why hadn't any of them stuck up for Glider or tried to stop the guard's bullying? Were they *all* too scared?

The dark blue dragonet led the way into the school and down a couple of levels, then stopped in a deserted corridor and sat down, beaming at her.

"That was *wild*," he said. "You are *bonkers*."

"Me?!" Luna protested, but she couldn't help smiling back. "You're the one who nearly ended up a SilkWing pancake on the savanna! I'm surprised she didn't shove you over, the way you were carrying on."

"They're getting used to me," he said with a shrug. "Yelling at a guard on your first *day*, though! What's the plan for day two — drawing trees all over the walls? No, wait — announcing at lunch that you're starting a rebellion against Queen Wasp?"

He must have seen something in her face because he added quickly, "I'm just kidding; don't do that. I mean, save it for day five, at least."

Luna giggled and realized this was the lightest she'd felt since stepping into Silkworm Hall. "I'm pretty sure *announcing* your rebellion isn't the best way to start," she said. "Mine will be stealthier than that. In fact, I just recruited you and you didn't even notice."

"Really?" he said. "I'm leading a secret rebellion now?"

"No, no, *I'm* leading it," she said. "You're the comic relief."

He laughed. "That sounds about right. I'm Swordtail, by the way."

"Oh, I know," she said. "The one this poor world would miss so terribly. Very dramatic. I'm Luna."

"It is thrilling to meet you, Luna." Swordtail dipped his head. "I'm so excited there's finally someone here who might cause even half as much trouble as I do."

"Speaking of which, I guess we'd better get to the headmaster," Luna said with a sigh.

"Let's not and say we did," Swordtail suggested. "The guards never check if we actually make it there; they just want us out from under their own claws. Have you seen the art room yet?"

"The art room?" Luna echoed, her spirits floating up to the ceiling.

"It's the best part of the day," he said. "I thought you might like something to look forward to."

"Yes, *please*," she said. She followed him around the corner and through a wide doorway into a huge room that was covered in weavings. Looms were set up all over the space, most of them with partly finished projects waving little rainbow and white tendrils at her. There were still no windows, but one entire wall was covered with a giant woven skyscape, bright blue with golden clouds and sunlight and hundreds of dragons in flight — most of them SilkWings, Luna noticed.

She stepped closer to the skyscape, hardly able to breathe. *This* was what she wanted to do with her life: make things so beautiful they could fix a dragon's heart. She wanted to use her own talons and silk to weave tapestries as powerful as sunshine. She wanted her art to reach into other dragons and lift the clouds away, to give them a reason to spread their wings and keep flying.

This tapestry was the world as it could be. All these SilkWings were free — Luna knew it; she felt it all through her scales. Maybe the HiveWings couldn't tell when they looked at it, but Luna knew this was the world she dreamed of.

"Miss Clorinde did that," Swordtail said. "She's the art teacher — and a SilkWing, obviously."

"It's amazing," Luna said reverently.

"Almost as good as mine," Swordtail said, puffing up his chest and strutting over to a display, where a small blue-and-orange tapestry hung. It looked as though a spider had gotten tangled in the threads and run amok, leaving trails of white zigzags all over the blocky background.

"Oh, ah," Luna said. "Very. Um."

"Would you believe there are people who can't read this?" Swordtail said, poking the zigzags.

Luna squinted at it. "Those are letters?" she asked.

"It says SWORDTAIL," he declared indignantly. "VERY CLEARLY."

"Of course, yes, clearly," she agreed. She touched one of the empty looms, her claws yearning to strum the cords. "When can I start a weaving?"

"Probably today," he said. "It's one of our daily classes — apparently weaving is one of the few things we're good for, so we'd better learn how to do it well. Lucky for us, Miss Clorinde is great. Don't tell any HiveWings, or they'll probably take her away. Mustn't let those wingless dragonets have any fun or joy."

"I *hate* that," Luna burst out. "Why is it like that? Why do they want us to be miserable? Why can't we decide for ourselves where we go to school or what we study or who our teachers are or whether we have *windows* in our classrooms, by all the moons?"

"I don't know," he said, really looking at her. "Because it's always been that way?"

"Nope," she said. "Not before the Tree Wars, it wasn't."

"Whoa. Didn't you start school today?" he asked. "How do you already know more history stuff than I do?"

"I listen to my moms when they think I'm asleep," Luna said. "SilkWings used to have our own queen and our own cities in the webs between the trees."

"Huh," he said. "And then . . ."

"And then Queen Wasp said we couldn't, and knocked down all the trees, and killed all the LeafWings, and told us we had to come live in these sunless termite mounds and do everything the HiveWings say from now on, because of some stupid old book of prophecies."

"Ha!" Swordtail said. "You *are* going to be trouble, aren't you?"

"I don't care if I am," Luna said. "I think they need to know how awful they are and we need to figure out how to fix everything."

"All right," he said, coming to lean against her empty loom, his dark blue eyes shining.

"All right what?" she said.

"All right, I'm in," he said. "I'm with you. Sign me up for fixing everything."

Thinking about it now made Luna's heart feel like it was made of flamesilk, the brightest burning kind. Swordtail was on her side from the moment they met. He always threw himself into danger to protect her, deflecting the punishment onto himself whenever she made a HiveWing angry. His noise covered her tracks and kept their attention while she found the Chrysalis. That was why he'd ended up on Misbehaver's Way multiple times and she never had.

But he couldn't stand by her now. She was alone, and he was in danger.

And I don't have time to be sad. I can't be an extra problem when our problems are so big already.

Luna sighed.

She could tell by her internal clock that it was well into nighttime when they finally heard the patter of footsteps returning.

"Wren?" Sky cried. "Wren, Wren, Wren, are you all right?"

"Of course I am," she answered from the human's ledge. "What could happen to me? I'm invisible! Which also means it's going to be tough to ask these humans for help, but it makes spying on them pretty easy. Help me down."

Wren sketched a quick map with water on the floor for them, showing the path that went from behind the wall down through some tunnels to a central human cave village.

"There are a lot of people there," Wren said. "I think it's actually bigger than Talisman, the village where I grew up, although it's hard to tell because it's kind of like a rabbit warren. A bit like Valor, Sky."

"Oh dear," Sky said. "I hope the humans here are nicer than Ivy's dad."

Luna had no idea what they were talking about. "Did you see the abyss?" she asked.

"No," Wren answered ruefully, "and nobody mentioned one the whole time I was there either. These might not be the same humans Queen Snowfall saw in her vision."

"You mean . . . you think there are other humans in Pantala?" Cricket asked. "More cave villages?"

"Probably," Wren said. "We're kind of everywhere, if you look hard enough. I'll keep spying on these ones for now and see if they say anything about it. The one we saw is named

Axolotl." She said the name in Human; Luna wasn't sure what the Dragon translation would be.

"Is it a boy human or a girl human?" Sky asked.

"Neither? Both? We'd have to ask them," Wren said. "They use they and them pronouns. Like that traveling librarian we met, Sky, remember? Sage?"

"Oh, right," Sky said. "What's an *axolotl*?" He managed the human word better than Luna would have, but it still sounded very weird coming from a dragon's mouth.

"It's kind of a cave salamander," Wren said. "There were a few around the village." The creature she described didn't sound familiar to Luna, but after a moment of listening, Cricket said, "Oh! An *axolotl*," in Dragon. Luna still wasn't sure what that was, but Bullfrog made an "ah, yes" kind of noise.

"Did you figure out how Axolotl has a dragon book?" Cricket asked.

"No — I think it's a secret from the other humans," Wren guessed. "I'll follow them again tomorrow. Hopefully someone will mention an abyss eventually."

The others decided to sleep in the cavern, but Luna crept back out to the sea-facing cave and spent the night there, despite the cold and wet. She wanted to be there in case their friends arrived. If finding Axolotl and the cave village meant they were one step closer to the abyss, then they really needed Sundew and ideally Moon and Lynx and all the others, too.

She didn't sleep much. She kept jerking awake, thinking she'd heard Sundew's voice, but it was only ever the waves on the beach or rain dripping down the rocks.

The next day and the next, Wren went back into the tunnels to study the Pantalan humans. Axolotl returned to their ledge twice in that time. It was fascinating to watch the little human sitting for so long, peering at the dragon book. Cricket pointed out that Axolotl was writing in the other, human-sized book, as if they were taking notes.

"I think they're trying to translate the Dragon," she whispered to Luna. "Isn't that brilliant? I knew our Pantalan humans would be just as clever as the ones in the Distant Kingdoms! Do you think Axolotl snuck into one of the Hives to get that book? That would mean they're really brave, too. I wonder what they think of dragons. Do you think they'll like us?"

On the third day — still no sign of Sundew and Lynx — Axolotl arrived earlier than usual and sat down with a sigh, looking tired. At least, Luna thought so, although they didn't have wings to droop or a long, listless tail, which were the signs that might have tipped off Luna's friends about her own emotional state, if they'd been able to see her. At least invisibility meant she only had to keep her voice sounding happy.

Wren had been eating breakfast with them, but they all cautiously hid or wolfed down their food when they heard Axolotl coming. Sky lifted Wren up to crouch on the ledge beside the curious human. Axolotl pulled out the dragon book and flipped it open again, trailing one of their long, thin appendages (like a claw but not in the least bit dangerous) down the page.

"It looks like a book about trees," Wren called down. Axolotl turned the page, and she added, "Hang on — in this picture the trees are burning."

"Maybe it's a history of the Tree Wars?" Cricket guessed.

"Our histories didn't have illustrations!" Luna said grumpily. "Even our books couldn't have any pictures of trees in them." She edged as close as she could, craning to see, and felt Cricket and Sky doing the same on either side of her.

All at once she felt a weird tingling in her talons, as though one of the less flammable forms of flamesilk was pulsing through her palms. She glanced down to make sure she hadn't unleashed some flamesilk by accident — but no, her front claws were right there, propped against the stone column she was leaning against, looking perfectly normal and not glowy.

Wait.

HER CLAWS. SHE COULD SEE THEM!

Luna looked up into Cricket's startled eyes — Cricket's face! Right there in front of her!

And right at that moment, Axolotl raised their head and discovered Wren, suddenly crouching next to them out of nowhere, and four dragons crowded around the ledge, gazing straight at them.

Axolotl shrieked, leaped to their feet, tripped over Wren, bonked into the wall, pinwheeled backward, bounced off Bullfrog's nose, shrieked again, and made a run for the tunnels.

Bullfrog calmly lunged over the rock shelf and trapped the human under one big talon.

"Ack!" Wren shouted at the MudWing. "Stop that! Get off them!" She ran over and grabbed Bullfrog's massive front leg, trying to yank it up.

"It's fine," Bullfrog said impassively. "I'm not hurting it."

"That is a *lot* of yelling for someone who's not hurt," Sky said, covering his ears.

"Because they're scared!" Wren snapped. "Wouldn't you be, if a human and four dragons literally appeared out of thin air and then stepped on you?"

"I'm not stepping on it," Bullfrog observed. "I'm preventing it from leaving, that's all."

"Poor Axolotl — tell them we won't hurt them," Luna said to Wren. "That we're friendly dragons! Two of us are vegetarians!"

"I think that would be a lot more comforting without a giant carnivore standing on them, but I'll try," Wren said. She crouched next to Axolotl and said something in the human language.

It took a moment for Axolotl to hear her over their yelling, but finally they went quiet, and their expression went from panicked to panicked-but-also-curious. Wren kept talking rapidly, waving her hands at the dragons.

"OK, *now* get off them," she said to Bullfrog in Dragon, shoving at the MudWing's talons.

"But then it might escape," Bullfrog said placidly.

"If *they* still want to do that, we let them," Wren said. She threw her shoulder under one of Bullfrog's claws and lifted it as much as she could. Underneath, Axolotl tried to wiggle free. "Because you dragons are *not actually monsters* is the point I am *trying* to make, and you are *kind of making the opposite point right now.*"

Bullfrog wrinkled his snout skeptically (expressions! Luna hadn't realized how much she'd missed seeing facial expressions!), but he lifted his talons and stepped back down to the cave floor.

Axolotl sat up, feeling their limbs as though making sure everything was intact. They looked at Wren with wide, astonished eyes and burbled something.

"What did they say? What did they say?" Cricket asked eagerly.

"They can't believe I can talk to dragons," Wren said. "They've always wanted to do that. They want to know what you're saying."

Sky laughed and said something human-sounding. Axolotl gasped, pointed at him, turned to Wren, waved their hands around, and pointed to Sky again.

"NOW what did they say?" Cricket demanded.

"This is going to take a while," Wren observed, rubbing her forehead.

"Wait," Luna said. "Why are we suddenly not invisible anymore?"

"Maybe the magic wore off?" Cricket guessed.

"I thought Lynx said that wouldn't happen," Luna said. She jumped to her feet. "Maybe Sundew made us all visible because she's here! I'll go check!"

"Meanwhile, I will stay here and explain my entire life to

yet another strange human," Wren said, sitting down next to Axolotl.

Luna dashed back into the tunnels and raced through the winding rock corridors to the beach cave.

Outside, it was pouring again, curtains of rain billowing into the open space. Luna ran out into the storm and looked up at the sky, then whirled around, searching the beach.

No Sundew. No Lynx.

There was nobody there at all.

CHAPTER 8

"Axolotl says they've heard of a village that worships an abyss," Cricket said to Luna when she returned to the dragon-teeth cavern, wet, bedraggled, and disappointed.

Cricket's eyes were glowing behind her spectacles, and she was practically bouncing on her talons. "They said they can guide us there if we translate the dragon book for them! Luna, isn't this wonderful? They're willing to help us! Maybe they'll like us so much they'll want to be my best friend just like Sky and Wren, and then we can learn each other's language and hang out all the time. I mean, after we save the world and rescue Blue," she finished, her expression sobering.

"The human says we can head for the abyss tomorrow," Bullfrog added. He was sitting by the entrance to the cavern, as far from the humans as possible, with a mildly grumpy look on his face. Luna guessed he had been ordered over here by Wren so he wouldn't scare Axolotl any more than he already had. Over by the ledge, Sky and Wren and Axolotl were chatting away like SilkWings having a day-off picnic in the Mosaic Garden.

"Tomorrow?" Luna echoed. "But we can't — we have to wait for the others!"

Bullfrog furrowed his brow at her. "Sundew said not to wait."

"And they're days late," Cricket agreed. "I wonder if maybe making us visible again was Sundew trying to tell us we should go on without them. She did say we should look for the abyss if they didn't show up."

"But we won't have any idea what to do if we find it," Luna said. She tried to keep her voice light instead of letting the panic seep into it. She hoped her face looked reasonable rather than like a tapestry of worries. Other dragons, especially HiveWings, didn't like her panic voice or worry face, she'd noticed in her six years of life. Showing her nerves did not make them kinder to her. Too often it made them more irritable and impatient instead.

Not Swordtail; Swordtail is never impatient with me. And not Blue — I can't even imagine what an irritable Blue would look like.

If they were here, they'd understand why I'm so worried.

"You're right," Cricket said unexpectedly. She poked one claw into a crack in the rock floor and wiggled it back and forth. In fact, Luna would have to say *Cricket* definitely had a worry face on. She'd never seen a HiveWing with a worry face before. "I mean, I know exactly how you feel, Luna. I didn't think I'd have to do any decision making or fighting while we had Sundew and Tsunami and Moon with us. I wouldn't send *me* to save the world. We have no idea what we're going to find down there, and it's completely terrifying."

Bullfrog grunted, and they both turned to look at him. He paused for a long moment and then said: "Same."

How come Cricket doesn't mind spilling out all her worries and fears in front of dragons she hardly knows? That's not a HiveWing thing. Is this what Blue likes about her — that she shares all her feelings before he has to guess?

"Here's what I tell myself," Cricket went on, touching one of Luna's talons lightly. "We're going looking for the truth. That's something I can do. I can discover things. Whatever is down there, Moon and Snowfall think we need to know about it. So that's all we're doing, at least in my head. Flying into the abyss, finding answers, flying out again."

"What if the answers eat us?" Luna asked.

"Then we hope the next dragons do better," Cricket said. "Maybe we can leave a message for Sundew and Lynx so they know where to look for us. But we can't just sit here, not when Blue needs us. Right? When we have a next step that might take us to him, don't we have to take it, even if we can't see the end of the path yet?"

Luna covered her face with her talons. Cricket was right, which was very annoying because Luna would have preferred nearly any other dragon to pull her back into her "let's do this!" state.

But it was true: They couldn't stay here in this cave, watching the rain, waiting for someone more heroic to show up. Blue and Swordtail and all the other SilkWings needed them to keep going.

"All right," she said. "How do we leave a message?"

"Ooo, let's think," Cricket said, bouncing to her feet. She picked up a rock, put it back down, picked up another rock, tapped it on the floor, and scratched her head.

"What are you doing?" Luna asked.

"Thinking," Cricket said unselfconsciously. "It has to be something Sundew and Lynx will find, but nobody else. We don't want patrolling HiveWings to see it by accident."

"So we can't paint on the wall of the cave —" Luna said.

"Or carve a giant arrow pointing wherever we're going," Cricket added.

"Because then anyone might find it," Luna finished.

"What should the message even say?" Cricket wondered. "Find a human and follow it? I wonder if there's something more specific we can write. I'll tell Wren to ask Axolotl."

This was an obvious excuse for Cricket to talk to — or at least, near — Axolotl again, but Luna didn't stop her. She spun out a coil of glowing flamesilk and held it in her palms, drying some of the leftover raindrops and wondering if she could use it to hide a message somehow.

"They say it's not far from a giant lake in the south," Cricket said, bounding back to Luna with her spectacles askew. "Must be Lake Scorpion, right? We can put that in the message. Did you have any more ideas? I haven't yet. Let's think."

"Bit noisy for thinking," Bullfrog observed placidly.

"Sorry," Cricket said at once. "I'll shush."

They thought quietly for a long moment. *A code?* Luna thought. *A trail of scraps of flamesilk, like bread crumbs to follow?*

"Hmm," Bullfrog said after a long time. "LeafWings like . . . plants."

"They *do* like plants!" Luna cried, jumping to her feet. "And HiveWings barely notice them! We need a plant to help us!"

Bullfrog squinted at her. "A plant to what, now?"

"Sundew can talk to plants," Cricket explained, equally excited. "If there's an unexpected plant in the caves, she'll notice. Then we bury the message near its roots and hope the plant tells Sundew about it."

"The plant," Bullfrog said slowly. "Will . . . *tell* Sundew?"

"Something like that," Cricket said.

Bullfrog looked skeptical, but he followed them out into the rain and stood guard while they dug up a hardy-looking violet from the clifftop overhead. Cricket's talons were gentle as she extricated it and all its roots. She cradled dirt around the flower's tendrils as they flew down to the cave, and then they planted the little purple flower in the wet sand near the back wall.

"Poor thing," Cricket said. "This water is too salty for it. I don't think it's going to like it here."

"Sundew will move it somewhere safe when she finds it," Luna said. "She'll take care of it. Sorry, little flower." She touched one of the leaves lightly, and then she stepped back and brought forth a twist of burning flamesilk.

Sky and Wren had found a wide, flat piece of driftwood on the beach, and Luna burned their message into its smooth gray surface.

Gone to find the abyss near Lake Scorpion. Meet us there.

Then Cricket dug a hole near the flower's roots and buried the message.

Luna felt like there should be more to say — as though the others had been gone a thousand years and needed to be told about everything they'd missed. She wanted to tell them to hurry, to be careful, to avoid HiveWings and be kind to any humans they saw. But they knew all that. They would be here already, if they could.

The next morning, Axolotl unexpectedly appeared with another human. This one wore an outer wrapping that was almost entirely made of stolen dragon silk. Orange and silver strips wound around the newcomer's pale brown limbs, and more were tied into its long dark hair. Like Axolotl, this human looked like it rarely saw the sun; the glow of Luna's flamesilk made it blink rapidly and shield its eyes.

"This is Ocelot," Wren explained after some back-and-forth chatter in Human. "She's offered to keep watch for our missing dragons. If we burn another message, she says she'll give it to them."

"She *will*?" Cricket said. "Isn't that really brave of her? Has she been around dragons before?"

Wren repeated the question in Human, and Ocelot laughed. She held up her arms, draped in dragon silk, and twirled as she answered.

"She says she steals from dragons all the time," Wren translated, sounding amused. "And she's not scared of them. I like her."

"Still," Luna said. "Tell her to stay away from HiveWings — and SilkWings — anyone who looks like me or Cricket. Only show herself to a green dragon or a white dragon. Sundew and Lynx won't eat her."

"Tell her only trust dragons with two wings right now, not four," Cricket agreed.

"Aren't there some LeafWings under Wasp's control, too?" Wren asked.

"Oh . . . right." Luna's wings drooped. She'd forgotten about that. She'd forgotten that Wasp had her claws sunk deep into even the fiercest tribe on Pantala.

She felt a light pat on one of her claws and looked up to find Axolotl giving her what she thought might be a reassuring expression.

"Axolotl says it'll be all right," Wren said. "Ocelot is smart. She'll know which dragons are safe and who should get the message." Wren pointed to Sky's wings and Bullfrog's wings and explained something at length in the human language.

Luna burned the same message again on a new piece of driftwood and tried to take comfort in the idea that they'd left a backup message — that Sundew just had to find the flower or the human, the violet or Ocelot, and she'd be able to follow them.

But was it enough?

Sundew, where are you?

"It is very wet outside," Sky said, bending to peer at Axolotl's layers of wrapping. "Wren, this poor little human is going to get all slippery and slide off my back if we try to fly right now. And sick! Don't fluffy mammals get sick if you get them too wet? What do we do? Can we wrap you both in waterproof leaves or something?" He got a mischievous look in his eyes. "Fancy umbrella leaf hats?"

"You are a ridiculous dragon," Wren said sternly. "We're not going outside. Axolotl knows a way through the caves that will get us most of the way there, which is safer than trying to fly with dragons everywhere looking for us."

Sky looked disappointed, and maybe a little nervous, Luna thought. "We're going underground? Like . . . a lot farther underground?" he said.

"I'm afraid that *is* where most people keep their dark, scary abysses," Wren said with an affectionate grin.

On the one talon, it was a relief that they didn't have to try to fly in the rain. On the other, Luna had never felt more claustrophobic as she followed Axolotl through the underground tunnels.

She had figured out a way to wind glowing flamesilk threads around her horns. They cast a circle of light that illuminated the stone pressing in all around the dragons, which was both comforting and unsettling. Most of the tunnels were so narrow that her antennae kept brushing the ceiling and she couldn't unfold her wings all the way.

But Axolotl strode forward confidently, chatting with Wren; they seemed to know their way even without any flamesilk light or Wren's torch. They kept one paw outstretched, lightly brushing the walls, and occasionally stopped to consult the notebook they'd brought with them.

Cricket also had Axolotl's dragon book tucked in the pouch

with her blowgun darts. She'd promised to help translate it during their rest stops. Axolotl seemed like a human version of Cricket in some ways, as far as Luna could tell. They were obsessed with the idea that dragons could read and fascinated by what they might find in a dragon book, exactly the way Cricket had been obsessed with human books ever since she found out about them.

"It's not just a history of the Tree Wars," she said to Luna late on their third day of travel through the caves, as they navigated a slippery rockpile with a small chasm off to the left. A droplet of water splashed onto Cricket's glasses, and she paused for a moment to wipe them dry on her pouch. Luna waited with her, and behind them, Bullfrog stopped as well.

Cricket set the spectacles back on her snout. "It's a whole history of the *world*," she breathed. "Books like this all vanished from my school library, especially if I ever happened to find one. The HiveWing philosophy is that everything started with the Tree Wars, and you'd better not ask any questions about anything before that."

Luna could imagine that had been a hard rule for Cricket to follow. "Is there anything in there about SilkWing villages before the Tree Wars?" she asked as they kept walking.

"Lots," Cricket said. "With illustrations! They were beautiful."

"What about Pyrrhia?" Bullfrog asked. "Stuff about us?"

"Yes, although the book calls you the Distant Kingdoms, like we always have. But there's a whole chapter about Clearsight, and another that goes further back to the dragons that first came over here and the whole Legend of the Hive."

Luna shivered. The Legend of the Hive was her new least favorite story, and this shadowy cave was not a great place to be reminded of it. She could too easily imagine clouds of mind-controlled bats swarming their faces, or hordes of cave centipedes scuttling over their claws.

Up ahead, Sky and the two humans had made it past the chasm and were resting near a pool in the rocks. Strands of a weird sticky substance hung down from the ceiling, with a flying insect trapped in one of them, still flapping weakly. Luna gave the translucent goopy threads a wide berth as she approached the others.

"It's after dark," she said, sitting down beside Sky. "Should we all sleep soon? Are the humans tired?"

Sky twisted to stare around the cave with a befuddled expression, then looked back at her. "How do you know it's after dark?" he asked. "I can't tell if we've been down here for two minutes or nine days."

"Oh — it's a SilkWing thing," Luna said. "We always know what time of day it is." It had taken her internal clock a little while to adjust when she'd landed in Pyrrhia, and then to adjust back once they reached Pantala, but by now she felt properly synced up with the sky.

"Wow. Very cool," Sky said with a smile.

"We can go a little farther if you can," Wren said. "Axolotl says there's a drier cave where we can make a fire and spend the night."

"All right," Luna said, and Cricket and Bullfrog agreed. They set off again, squeezing into yet another tunnel that seemed just barely big enough for dragons. Luna could feel Cricket edging along behind her, and she turned her head slightly to see the HiveWing.

"What else is in that book?" she asked, hoping to distract herself from the tons of rock currently between her and the sky.

"Let's think . . . well, I haven't read this part yet, but there's a short section on something called the Scorching," Cricket answered.

Behind them, Bullfrog grunted. "Course there is," he said. "It's in every boring history book."

"Not ours," Cricket said. "I've never heard of it; have you, Luna?" Luna shook her head. "Oh my goodness, Bullfrog, tell me everything! What do your books say about it?"

"Not much," Bullfrog said. After a moment, he must have felt the waves of disapproval coming off Cricket because he added, "Um. It's how we got tribes and kingdoms and stuff."

"It *is*?" Cricket said. "What? How? Weren't there always kingdoms and tribes?"

Luna had reached the end of the tunnel and wiggled out onto a wider ledge that sloped down to a cave floor. She started to slide down it and bonked her head on a stalactite.

"Owwww," she muttered, rubbing her forehead as she skidded to a stop at the bottom.

Bullfrog and Cricket slid down next to her, and they started after the light of Wren's torch, already more than halfway across the cave.

"Bullfrog," Cricket prodded him. "Say more things."

"Um," he said, sounding more stumped than annoyed. "I don't remember much. Not my favorite subject, history."

"But," Cricket prompted, "you *do* remember . . . what?"

"I guess there were more scavengers back then?" he said. "Like . . . over five thousand years ago? And no tribes. Dragons lived mostly on their own. I think? And then a scavenger made a dragon real mad, so the dragon ate him, and then the dragon burned a bunch of stuff and got some other dragons to eat a bunch more scavengers and burn a bunch more stuff, and then they made a kingdom, and that was the Scorching." He thought for a moment, and then added, "Yup."

"Wow," Luna said. "Those poor humans."

Bullfrog scratched his head. "I mean," he said. "I think they started it?"

"*One* human, you said," Luna pointed out. "One human made a dragon mad, so the dragons ate and burned everybody else. That's kind of intense."

"I wonder what the human did?" Cricket said. "What could make a dragon *that* angry? Stealing treasure?"

"Scaring away prey?" Bullfrog guessed. "Like . . . really good prey. Probably cows."

"Maybe it killed someone the dragon cared about," Luna guessed.

"Hmm," Bullfrog said. "Pretty hard for a scavenger to kill a dragon." He paused for another moment, then added, "I guess one managed with Queen Oasis, though."

"What?" Cricket said avidly. "Who?"

"No," Bullfrog said, pointing at her. "No, no, no, not your

walking history book, me." He hurried away to catch up to Wren and Sky.

"Any idea?" Cricket asked Luna, then sighed when Luna shook her head. "Doesn't it drive you mad, all the things there are to know and how much we don't know and how hard it is to find things out?"

"I guess, on the scale of all our problems, that one doesn't bother me so much," Luna admitted.

They reached the bottom of a sheer cliff and spread their wings to fly up to the top of it, where Sky had already lifted the humans.

"It would be nice to find a book called *What's in the Abyss and What to Do About It*, though, wouldn't it?" Cricket said wistfully.

"Yes," Luna agreed. "And also *How to Free Your Mind-Controlled Friends*."

"*101 Ways to Kill an Evil Queen Without, Like, Having to Be All Mean or Violent About It*," Cricket suggested, and Luna was surprised into laughing.

"Do you worry about that, too?" she asked Cricket.

"How to defeat bad guys without *being* bad guys?" Cricket answered. "All the time."

Luna held out her talons. "How to use a gift like fire to win a war but without hurting anyone."

"How to care about all dragons the way Blue does," Cricket said as they landed, "but fight them the way Sundew would if they hurt someone."

This was so almost exactly the thought Luna had been having that she reached out and grabbed Cricket's arm.

Once, Luna and Swordtail had been talking about the Salvation Wall and he'd said the exact thing she'd been about to say. She'd gotten so excited that she had jumped on him, yelling, "*My* brain words! Words of my head!" That had been their joke ever since: Whenever they agreed about something, one of them would declare, "*My* brain words!" or "Words of my head!" and they'd both fall over laughing.

She came within a breath of shouting "*My* brain words!" at Cricket before remembering that was only for Swordtail.

And then she had to stand there for a moment, eyes closed, until she no longer felt like she'd been punched in the stomach.

"Are you all right?" Cricket asked.

"Yup," Luna said, letting go of her. *Still smiling. No problems here.* "Yes. Just, what you said, exactly. But mostly, how to save Blue and Swordtail." She turned her wrists up to the ceiling again to study the fire-gold dots below her scales. "I *will* set dragons on fire for them, if I have to."

"Me too!" Cricket said. "Well, all right, no, I can't. But I will . . . I will *throw books at anyone who's mean to them*, so there. Big *heavy* ones, so watch out, jerks."

All right, Luna thought, hiding a smile. And for the first time, she thought, *Maybe I* kind of *get what Blue sees in this HiveWing.*

"Between those superpowers, we'll definitely get them back," she said. Today, now, she mostly believed it; she could feel the rainy-season fog fading and little cracks of sunlight hope pushing through her brain. Ironic, considering she hadn't seen the actual sun in three days.

They had been walking along the cliff top for a while, under a vast ceiling studded with spires and glowworms, when Bullfrog suddenly stopped. Luna nearly stepped on his tail.

"Shhh," he said, staring at the inky blackness beyond the flamesilk glow.

Luna and Cricket froze. Ahead of them, Sky and the humans did the same.

Was that a flicker of wind in the silent cave?

Luna's antennae unfurled instinctively, checking for strange vibrations in the air.

wwwwwwwssssshhhh

shhhhwwwwww

wshhhwshhhh

There was . . . something. A very still, distant sound . . . like someone hidden in the spires overhead, just . . . breathing.

And then the hidden something shifted, leaned forward, and began to glide on silent wings toward them.

CHAPTER 9

"The humans!" Luna shouted, lunging past Bullfrog. "Sky! Protect the humans!"

There was a flurry of shrieks and wingbeats, and muffled cries from Wren and Axolotl as Sky threw himself on top of both of them, covering them with his wings. Bullfrog rose up on his hind legs, front claws slashing at the air, hissing.

A dark shape shot over their heads and smashed into Cricket. She was thrown back against the stone wall with an awful thud. Luna whirled and raced over to her. As the light of her flamesilk got closer, she realized the dark shape was a dragon — a LeafWing — a large, furious LeafWing, who now had Cricket pinned to the floor with his talons around her neck.

"Stop!" Luna yelled. "Don't hurt her! She's with us! We're friends! We're all on the same side! By all the silk, STOP IT!" She rammed her shoulder into the LeafWing's side, but he only lifted one wing to glance at her sternly.

"Have to make her unconscious," he said, a little out of breath as Cricket struggled and kicked at him. "To protect us."

"No, no," Luna said, understanding what was happening. "She doesn't have Queen Wasp inside her! She's the one HiveWing who isn't mind-controlled! Haven't you heard about her? This is Cricket — the one who stole the Book of Clearsight!"

"Hmm," he said. "Rings a bell." He glanced down at her without moving his talons. "Better safe than sorry, though."

"You'd really better stop now," Bullfrog said, looming up behind Luna. "Or I will have to do some hitting."

The LeafWing looked skeptical — he was about the same size as the MudWing — and then confused. He squinted at Bullfrog in the flamesilk light but didn't stop leaning on Cricket's throat. Her flailing was getting weaker, Luna noticed with a touch of panic.

"What are *you*?" the LeafWing asked Bullfrog.

"We're friends of Sundew!" Luna blurted.

"Oh. Really?" said the LeafWing, immediately releasing Cricket and taking a step back. Cricket rolled onto her side, gasping. "Should've mentioned that sooner," he said, looking down at the HiveWing reproachfully.

"Wh-when?" Cricket managed to croak.

The LeafWing rubbed his chin for a moment. "Hm," he said. "Should wear a sign, maybe."

"Listing all our friends?" Luna demanded. "Who are you anyway? How do we know *you* don't have Queen Wasp inside you?"

He stared at her and then sat down heavily. "So it's true," he said, closing his eyes.

The devastation on his face nearly sucked away all of Luna's anger at him. "That she can infect LeafWings now?" she said gently. "Yes. And SilkWings."

"Not us, though," Cricket said with a faint wave of her wing at the group of them. "Not just anyone. You have to be exposed to the breath of evil first."

He still looked confused, so Luna added, "Either by being stabbed with her tail venom or breathing in the smoke from this awful plant. It's a long story."

"Why are you down here?" Cricket asked. "Why aren't you with the other LeafWings?"

"Was on a mission," he said morosely. "Hid. Got stuck here." He pointed at Bullfrog. "What *is* that?"

Bullfrog looked as ruffled as Luna had ever seen him. "I'm not a *that*," he said. "I'm a MudWing."

"This is Bullfrog," Luna explained. "He came from the Distant Kingdoms to help us, and so did they." She pointed to where Sky was still lying flat on top of the humans. The noises coming from under his wings sounded decidedly grouchy now. "Sky, you can let them out!" she called. "He won't eat them. You won't eat them, will you?"

"Eat wha —" The LeafWing's eyes went as big as the moons as the two humans scrambled out from under Sky's wings. "You — you have an underground monkey! *Two* underground monkeys! Huh. Rather think you could spare *one*, don't you? Seems selfish not to share when we're so hungry." His teeth gleamed.

"They're not provisions!" Luna cried. "They're *not for eating!*"

"We're not monkeys either," Wren added in Dragon, sauntering up and putting her paws on her hips.

The LeafWing flapped his jaw for a while in a very gratifying way. "It — it — You taught it to talk!" he finally managed. "How did you *do* that? Uh — *why* did you do that?"

"Oh, it was quite hard," Sky said. "Years of training. They're very clever mimics, though. Watch this: Not funny, Sky!"

"Not funny, Sky!" Wren said at almost the exact same moment. She frowned at Sky, then at the LeafWing. "I'm not a parrot. I can speak Dragon. And you shouldn't eat any humans; we're just as smart as you are."

"Ha!" said the LeafWing. "Ha. Ahem. Huh. This is. Very odd. I think I should take you to Hemlock. He'll sort this out." He gave Axolotl a measuring look. "What about that one? You sure I can't eat that one?"

"You're thick, aren't you?" Wren said.

The LeafWing growled resentfully. "Doesn't seem fair," he said. "There's hardly anything I *can* eat down here. Now you're taking a whole species off the list? Rude, that is."

"I'm preeeeetty sure it's more rude to eat something that can talk to you," Wren said.

"NO EARRING! NO!" Axolotl suddenly shouted in Dragon, popping out from behind Sky's leg and then immediately ducking back. Sky collapsed in giggles, nearly landing on the small human, who looked affronted.

The LeafWing blinked at them. "Er. What?"

"They mean *no eating*," Wren said, clearly trying not

to laugh. "We're working on it. No *eating*," she growled at Axolotl.

"No *eating*," they growled back, in a pretty decent Dragon accent, Luna thought. She'd noticed that Axolotl picked up written language more quickly than things they heard. Cricket had been looking at the book with them each night, and Axolotl was already recognizing several letters and a few words. If they actually had more time to sit and study, Axolotl might be able to communicate with dragons in writing, more or less, within a month or so.

"Wait," Cricket said, struggling to her feet. "Did you say Hemlock? Sundew's dad? Are you with Bryony and the SilkWings that fled Bloodworm Hive?"

He blinked at her a few times. "How'd you know all that?"

"A dragon in the Distant Kingdoms had a vision about all of you," Cricket explained. "I . . . don't think she mentioned you, though."

The LeafWing drew himself up and looked annoyed. "I'm Pokeweed," he said. "I'm *essential* to the mission."

"Pokeweed," Cricket echoed. "Huh. Nope."

"We're heading for a human settlement near an abyss," Luna said. "This one is guiding us." She waved one wing at Axolotl, who was staying as close to Sky's side as possible and making little muttery dragonlike noises.

"A what near a what?" Pokeweed scratched his head.

"An abyss — a really big dark chasm," Cricket told him. "Have you seen one of those down here?"

Pokeweed waved his wings around. "S'all one big dark chasm, isn't it?"

"This one would be bigger and darker and more . . . down," Luna said. "Like, way down."

"Seems weird," Pokeweed said. "Weird thing to look for. Unless it's for hiding. Is that what it's for? Hiding from Wasp?"

"No," Cricket said. "I mean, we're not sure. We're hoping there's something in it that can stop her."

"Hm. Even more weird." Pokeweed shrugged and turned, waving one wing. "You explain it to Hemlock. He won't believe me if I try."

Wren and Axolotl chattered for a moment in Human, then climbed onto Sky's back, and they all flew after Pokeweed, through the vast open cave. It was a bit hazardous, dodging the stalactites, but it was a relief to be flying again after three days of walking and climbing and sliding. Luna stretched her wings as wide as she could and shook out her tail.

Pokeweed had evidently ventured a long way from the rest of the group in search of food; Luna felt like they were following him for hours. Half the time they could fly, but for much of the journey, they had to crawl through tunnels or climb through passageways in the rock. Pokeweed radiated a distinct air of "slow and unimaginative," but if he'd been willing to explore this far alone and memorize the way back, Luna thought he must be braver and smarter than he seemed.

He wasn't a very good listener, though, at least not to

SilkWings, HiveWings, or humans. Maybe he paid more attention when other LeafWings were talking.

As they dropped down a shaft into a damp tunnel, Luna's antennae picked up movement and murmuring vibrations ahead of them. From a distance, it sounded like wind in a forest, leaves brushing and whispering ahead of a storm.

They emerged from the tunnel into a cave that surrounded an underground lake. Odd crystalline shapes jutted from the walls, like tapestries made of translucent gems instead of silk. Glowworms dotted the ceiling like strange blue constellations, and a faint phosphorescent glow came from deep under the surface of the lake, but those were the only sources of light.

The murmurs resolved into dragon voices, hushed and flat and echoing in the cavernous space. She couldn't see them all, but Luna's antennae sensed there were over a hundred dragons in this cave alone, with more scattered in caves and tunnels that branched off this one.

I'd weave this place with black silk thread, a tapestry all dark from far away, but with little circles of light in gold silk. And up close, around each gold silk circle you'd find outlines of wings or tails or dragon faces, maybe in dark gray silk, hovering all around the lights.

A quartet of small SilkWing dragonets were sitting near the tunnel, on the shore of the lake, dabbling their talons listlessly in the water. They looked up as Pokeweed stepped into the cave, and then they saw Luna and their eyes went huge.

"Mommy!" the little pink one shouted, leaping to her feet. "Mommy! There's a dragon with fire on her head! MOMMY, MOMMY, SHE HAS A FIRE HAT!"

"I want a fire hat!" cried the small orange one beside her. "Nobody ever lets ME set a hat on fire and put it on MY head! NOT FAIR!"

"It's not a hat," the lime-green one barked imperiously. "It is *obviously* a *crown*. I bet she is a *fire queen*."

The fourth dragonet, who was lavender with speckles of dark blue and turquoise, bolted straight up to Luna's feet, sat down, and stared up at her. He looked a bit like her earliest memories of Blue, between the colors of his scales and his trusting expression.

"Um," Luna said. "Hello?"

"Hi," the dragonet said softly. The reflection of the flamesilk glowed in his awestruck eyes.

Luna realized more dragonets were cantering her way, all of them with similar bedazzled expressions. Behind them came several grown SilkWings, who looked more tired than anything else, but at least a few looked happy to see her, she thought.

"Thank the moons," said one of the older dragons, clasping her front talons together. "The last of the flamesilk we brought with us faded days ago."

"And it's been *so dark*," said the pink dragonet. "I do *not* like it so dark!"

"Yes, you do!" said the orange one. "You said yesterday that it wasn't so bad and you called me a fraidy-slug! *I'm* the one who doesn't like the dark! If anyone's getting a fire hat, it should be me because you're mean!"

"You were mean first!" shouted the pink dragonet. "Mommy, tell him he's the mean one!"

"The dark is whispery," breathed the dragonet at Luna's feet, inching a bit closer to her. She noticed that he had a little star-shaped white scar on his forehead, over his left eye, and another on his shoulder near his right wingbud. *Poor little dragon*, she thought. *What happened to you?*

He also wore two of the heavy wrist cuffs instead of just one. She gently lifted one of his talons to read the inscription on the cuff: *Weaver Hall* — that must be his school. The other said: *Construction Apprentice.*

Apprentice? He can't be more than two years old. How could a dragon this tiny be part of a construction crew already? She knew from Swordtail's stories that it was a dangerous, exhausting job, working with the treestuff on the Hives. Maybe that was how this little dragon had gotten his scars.

He gazed up at her hopefully as she set his talon down again.

"I've never met an actual flamesilk," said another dragon, who had wings but didn't look much older than Luna. "Did you really make that?"

"I did," Luna said. "Um, hi. I'm Luna."

"Luna?" A pale yellow dragon limped forward, and the others stepped back respectfully to let her through. "The one Swordtail and Blue were looking for?"

"Tau!" Cricket yelped. She bounded past Luna and threw

her wings around the startled yellow SilkWing. The closest dragons in the crowd saw her HiveWing scales and jumped back, hissing.

"Cricket?" Tau cried. "No way! How are you *here*?" She turned to the other SilkWings, putting one wing protectively around Cricket. "This is the HiveWing who found out the secret of the mind control. The one who told everyone the truth about the Book of Clearsight — remember the paint on the posters in Jewel Hive? She's been fighting Queen Wasp longer than most of you!"

Luna felt a weird little stab of guilt that this SilkWing was quicker to defend Cricket than she had ever been. Then again, it was reassuring to see that Blue wasn't the only SilkWing who liked and trusted Cricket.

"You've read the Book of Clearsight?" one of the SilkWings asked Cricket.

"Did you really see Queen Wasp stabbing eggs in the Hatchery?" asked another.

"She can't get inside your mind at all?"

"All this excitement about us," Luna said ruefully to Cricket, "and they haven't even seen the humans or the Pyrrhia dragons yet."

She looked down and saw that the dragonet at her feet had, in fact, noticed Sky and Bullfrog. He had edged close enough to her that he was almost sitting on her talon, and he was now staring past her at the other two dragons, who were hanging back in the shadows of the tunnel.

"What we really want to know is what's happening up

there," Tau said, taking one of Cricket's talons in her own. "Is anyone else alive? What happened to the LeafWings?"

"We have a lot to tell you," Cricket said. "Is there someone in charge of everyone here?"

"Depends on who you ask," Tau said, rolling her eyes. "The LeafWings think *they're* in charge; Morpho keeps insisting *he* should make all the decisions; the Bloodworm Hive SilkWings have their own Chrysalis, which it turns out was way bigger than ours; and Lady Jewel and Lady Scarab are here, too."

"But we don't have to listen to any HiveWings anymore," a green-gray dragon said mutinously. "Now that they don't have their white-eyed stinger-clawed goons to push us around."

"Lady Jewel is the reason we all escaped," Tau said stiffly. "She's not our queen, but we don't have to be rotten to her."

"Chrysalis?" Luna said hopefully. "I was going to join the Cicada Hive Chrysalis after my Metamorphosis — are any of them here?"

Tau shook her head. "Sorry, little dragon. No one from Cicada Hive, as far as I know."

Pokeweed suddenly appeared with two other LeafWings and a feather-gray SilkWing. Luna hadn't even realized he'd been gone.

"Oh, wow, hello!" said the smaller LeafWing. "Visitors from the outside world! Please tell us you come with good news. I'm Bryony, this is Grayling, and this grumpy face is Hemlock."

"*Stern* face," Hemlock corrected her. "Not grumpy. This is an *intimidating* face. Pokeweed says you know Sundew," he said, turning to Luna. "Is she all right?"

"She . . . was when we left her," Luna said honestly. "She was supposed to meet up with us a few days ago, but she didn't show. We left her a message — we're hoping she follows us here."

"We've been to the Distant Kingdoms," Cricket said. "We came back with dragons to help us, and underground monkeys who can talk, and a vision about an abyss that we have to find."

Tau looked too astonished to speak. Bryony and Hemlock exchanged bewildered glances.

"Let's sit," Bryony said, waving to a circle of boulders nearby. "We want to hear everything."

Luna started to turn toward Sky and Bullfrog, but the little dragonet suddenly jumped forward and wrapped his tiny claws around her leg. He pressed his face into her scales and whispered something.

"Oh, goodness," Luna said. "Um. Hey, cutie? Can I have my leg back?"

"Please let me stay with you," he mumbled. "I'll be really good, I promise. I won't be any trouble, and I won't complain about anything, I promise promise."

Luna felt a stab of sad, familiar sympathy. "Won't someone be looking for you?" she asked, touching the top of his head lightly.

The dragonet shook his head. "No. They're gone."

Luna wondered if that meant dead, or captured by HiveWings, or just out gathering food. It was hard to tell from the dragonet's quiet voice. She wondered if a dragonet with parents would have been forced onto a construction crew, though. *Poor little guy.*

"It's only me," he said in an even smaller voice. "Just Dusky. I can be really quiet, really. You won't even notice me. Please?" He hesitated, then added softly, "I don't want to be alone in the dark anymore. I'm afraid I'll get lost and no one will ever find me."

Luna thought about being a small dragon with no family, in a giant cave in the dark because your home burned to ashes in the sky, hiding from monsters who were suddenly even scarier than they'd already been your whole life because now you could be turned into one of them.

She curved one of her wings around him. "Of course you can stay with me," she said. "And it won't be dark; don't worry. I can make lots and lots of flamesilk. Here, look, I can make a kind that gives light but won't burn you. Hold out your talons."

Dusky warily held out one small talon, and she uncoiled a little thread of glowing silk into his palm. He brought it close to his eyes, took a deep breath, and then clutched it to his chest.

"Will it make the whispers stop?" he asked softly.

"The whispers?" Luna echoed.

"In the dark," Dusky said. "There are whispers all the time in the dark."

Luna felt a chill run all through her scales like trickles of icy water. "What — what do the whispers say?" she asked, although she wasn't sure she wanted to know.

Dusky tipped his head up to look at her with large dark eyes. His voice, when he finally spoke, was so faint that it seemed to come from the clustered shadows outside her light.

"They say: *You're mine now, little dragon.*"

CHAPTER 10

Luna slept poorly that night. In fact, she wasn't sure she slept properly at all, and in the morning, she didn't know if she'd really heard whispers all night long or if she'd dreamed them.

It probably didn't help to have a twitchy little dragonet curled up against her side, but she couldn't bring herself to send Dusky away. He'd looped the flamesilk she gave him around his wrist like a talisman, and he stayed so close to her that she'd tripped over him three times on her way to the lake and back to her sleeping spot. He didn't say very much, but he did jerk awake several times during the night, startling her out of any almost sleep she might have been in.

She had hoped that making so many coils of flamesilk would have tired her out enough to sleep through anything. They'd spent hours sitting with Bryony, Hemlock, Tau, Grayling, and Lady Jewel, explaining everything that had happened in the Poison Jungle and the Distant Kingdoms. The humans had fallen asleep before the end of the story, both of them tucked protectively under Sky's wing. And that whole time, Luna had burned off wrist cuffs and made flamesilk for the hidden SilkWings while Dusky sat on her tail.

She'd decided to name the five kinds she could make and give the dragons options. The simplest one she called gold silk, which was much like the silvery silk most of her tribe could make, except that hers shimmered with a golden color. But it didn't glow or burn, and it could be used in normal tapestries. It wouldn't be much use to these dragons except for adding another color to anything they were weaving.

The next kind she called firefly silk: it gave off a little bit of light, like holding a firefly in your talons, but it didn't burn.

Then there was glow silk, the kind she'd given to Dusky. It felt a little warm and it glowed brighter, closer to a normal fire, but anyone could hold it. When she demonstrated that kind, all the watching SilkWings asked for some. They delightedly wound it around their own horns; a few wove it into necklaces or bracelets.

As Luna was helping one little dragonet tie it around her ankle, she realized that Lady Jewel was hovering right over her shoulder, peering at it.

"I've never seen flamesilk like that," the HiveWing said. She held out one talon. "May I?"

Luna felt a little flare of anger. This was one of Wasp's relatives. Jewel had happily ruled her Hive with Wasp's power behind her, keeping SilkWings as servants and enforcing Wasp's terrible rules. She'd never tried to make anything better for SilkWings before, and the only reason she was here now was because she knew Wasp might try to mind-control her if she were caught.

Maybe Jewel saw some of that in Luna's face, because she added, more humbly, "Please?"

Tau says she helped all her SilkWings escape, Luna thought. *And that she's not as bad as other HiveWings. And that Queen Wasp took her children, too.*

Tau trusts her.

That doesn't mean I have to.

But she doesn't have to be my enemy either.

Luna gave her a small curl of the glow silk.

"Thank you," Jewel said, peering at it. "This is extraordinary. I thought there were only two kinds — one that neither glows nor burns, and one that burns like regular fire. But this kind would be so much safer for the lanterns. Can all flamesilks make this?"

"I don't know," Luna said. "Your cousin keeps them all imprisoned in a cavern where they spend their lives slaving to make her as much flamesilk as they can, so I haven't had much opportunity to get to know any others."

Jewel ducked her head, looking chastened. "Right," she said. "Of course. Sorry."

"But you can make the kind that burns, too?" Hemlock asked.

"I can make two burning kinds," Luna said. "I call this one blaze silk — I think it's what you'll find in most lanterns." She made a little curl of the thread that burned and glowed like a normal fire, and held it up over Dusky's head when he reached for it. "No, little one, this will hurt you."

Hemlock held out a stone jar, and Luna carefully slid the blaze silk into it.

"And this is the last kind," she said, "which I wouldn't use very often." The thread that came from her wrist was so bright that everyone near her shielded their eyes. It looked like a bolt of lightning sizzling in her palm. "I call it sun silk," she said. "I can only make a little bit at a time."

She shook her head as Hemlock produced another stone jar. "It can burn through that, too. I have to drown it." The dragons all moved aside, even Dusky, as she placed the silk lightly on a corner of her wing and carried it down to the lake, where she held it under the water until the fire went out.

"Blaze silk is more useful, if you're trying to start a normal fire," she said, returning to the circle of boulders. "Do you want some of that, or just glow silk?"

"Both, please," Bryony answered. "If we can start a fire and keep feeding it, it'll last beyond when the flamesilk fades."

"Should've thought of that when we had flamesilk before," Pokeweed muttered.

"We didn't think we'd be down here that long then," Bryony reminded him, which made all the faces of the dragons around them go very gloomy.

The SilkWings here were from Bloodworm Hive, Jewel Hive, and Mantis Hive. They knew Cinnabar had gone to warn the SilkWings in other Hives, but none of them had shown up in the caves. Nobody knew what that meant. Were they safely in hiding somewhere else? Or were they all captured by Queen Wasp?

They'd seen SilkWings flying in formation with HiveWings on a few foraging expeditions, so they knew at least some of them had been captured. They hadn't known about the breath of evil plant or the othermind, though. Luna could tell that several of them didn't really believe that there was another controlling malevolence out there. They thought it was still Queen Wasp, despite Cricket's strange story about the possessed LeafWing in the eye of the Poison Jungle.

Everyone was fascinated by Moon's prophecy, though. Luna saw a shiver of hope go through them, all these starving homeless dragons suddenly sitting taller and touching their glow silk or brushing their neighbor's wing. They'd lost their faith in the Book of Clearsight but not their belief in the magic of prophecies.

"I don't know about any abyss," Tau said. "But there is a colony of — what's the word you said? humans? — living not too far from here. I know a cave where they go to gather water."

"You DO?" Pokeweed huffed. "You never told ME about it!"

"Well, I was afraid you might eat them," Tau said in a reasonable voice.

"Yes, exactly!" Pokeweed snapped. "That was the whole point!"

"And if you had, you'd be feeling very horrified right now," Tau pointed out. "I would hope."

Pokeweed subsided, muttering, "Wouldn't be quite so hungry, though."

Several of the SilkWings gave him a disgusted look. Wren and Axolotl were lucky that the first giant crowd of dragons they'd met were mostly from Pantala's vegetarian tribe. None of the SilkWings had had any trouble accepting that humans were clever, could communicate, and shouldn't be eaten.

Of course, that was how they felt about zebras, wildebeests, lobsters, and meerkats, too, as Sky pointed out to Wren with immense glee.

Lady Jewel, on the other hand, had looked decidedly green around the gills when they introduced the humans. She kept staring at Wren and Axolotl like she hoped they would suddenly throw off their mammal skins and turn out to be dragons in disguise, after all.

"Can you take us there? To the human colony?" Cricket asked Tau.

Tau nodded. "Tomorrow," she said. "After you sleep."

"Are we near Lake Scorpion?" Luna asked. "Could you send some dragons to watch the sky there, in case Sundew and Lynx and the others come looking for us?"

"Yes," Hemlock said immediately. "I'll go myself. It's not far."

"We'll send some of the Bloodworm Hive Chrysalis with you," Grayling said. "It's a huge lake — you'll want dragons stationed all around it so you don't miss them."

Hemlock flicked a glance at Bryony, her green tail criss-crossed with Grayling's, and nodded.

Luna's flamesilk filled the caves with light and warmth, and a fire crackled in the center of the circle of boulders. It was noisier, too; the light seemed to bring the dragons back to life, and the caves were full of voices.

But were they all dragon voices?

Was Luna just imagining it, or could she hear the whisper that Dusky heard, threading underneath them all?

Come to me, little dragon.

You're mine.

Find me . . .

Around sunrise, Luna groggily opened her eyes and found a pale brown-and-gold SilkWing crouched beside her, looking at Dusky. The dragonet was finally truly asleep, flopped out in the curve of Luna's side, with his flamesilk bracelet still curled close to his chest.

"Sorry," the brown SilkWing whispered when he saw Luna's eyes. "I didn't mean to wake you. I'm Whitespeck. I just wanted to check on Dusky."

"Are you his family?" Luna asked.

He shook his head, his wings drooping. "They're all dead or missing," he said, even more softly. He hesitated, then said, "Dusky's mother was shipped off to Vinegaroon Hive before Dusky even came out of his egg. And then Dusky's father died in a treestuff construction accident a year ago, when Dusky was one."

"Oh no," Luna breathed. "But his wrist cuff said —"

Whitespeck sighed. "Bloodworm Hive's rules were very strict. One member of each household must be employed on Lady Bloodworm's pet projects — even if that household consists of only one small orphan. The day after his father died, they came and dragged him off to work on the same construction site. He has to split his time between there and school."

"That's awful," Luna whispered.

"It's why I joined the Chrysalis," he said. "Dusky's father was my friend, so I've been trying to watch out for Dusky ever since. But I don't have a partner or anyone else to help — I was sent to Bloodworm Hive from Tsetse Hive and left my whole family behind. And they won't let me adopt him, so I can't do as much as I would like to." He paused, took a deep breath, and added, "Sorry, too much information."

"No, I'm glad you told me," Luna said. "I was wondering about him, but I didn't want to make him talk about it if he didn't want to."

"I'll get you both something to eat," Whitespeck said, standing up.

"I'm all right," Luna said. She knew there wasn't much to go around, and these dragons had been hungry a lot longer than she had. "But if there's anything for Dusky, that would be great. Thank you."

As they prepared to follow Tau to the human colony, Luna tried to talk Dusky into staying behind, but he clung to her and wouldn't let go.

"I think it's all right," Wren said, patting the little dragon on the head. He shied away from her hand and buried his face in Luna's scales. The dragonet seemed to have no problem with any of the strange-looking newcomers or Cricket, but he was absolutely terrified of the humans. "We're just going to look at the cave and see if we can find any people. No abyss today. He can come along for this fact-finding part."

"Please, please let me come with you?" Dusky asked. He gave Luna giant sad eyes. "I won't be any trouble, I promise."

"All right," Luna relented. She lifted him onto her back. "But be really careful, OK?"

"I will be the best quietest dragon ever, I promise promise," he said, snuggling into her neck.

They found Axolotl surrounded by dragonets, who were arguing over who would get to keep the clever human as a pet.

"I saw them first!" said the pink one. "And look, they like me best!"

Axolotl held out their hand for her to sniff. Instead she seized their hand in her talons and yanked them down so she could climb onto their shoulders.

"Not fair!" bellowed the orange one. "DAAAAAAD! *I* want a pet human!! Nobody ever lets me adopt weird-looking cave mammals!"

"Um . . . no eating?" Axolotl said cautiously. They patted the tail of the little pink one where it draped across their collarbone.

"Eeee, look how clever they are!" the pink one cried, wrapping her arms around Axolotl's head. "And squishy! I just want to love them and cuddle them and SMOOSH them!"

"Oh dear," Wren said. "I didn't realize I'd have to teach Axolotl how to say *'no smooshing'* as well."

She waded into the pile of squabbling dragonets and firmly peeled them off Axolotl, who looked disheveled, bewildered, and a little enchanted. *Not* a pet," she scolded the little dragons. "Humans can be *friends* but *not pets*."

"Friend!" Axolotl cried in Dragon, latching on to one of the words they'd been practicing. They crouched and clasped one of the pink dragonet's talons. "Friend," Axolotl said again with a smile.

The pink dragonet beamed. "Dusky, look! This human likes me best of anyone!"

Dusky shivered and buried his nose in Luna's neck.

"Probably because I am not a BRAT like SOME DRAGONS." The pink dragonet stuck out her tongue at the orange one.

"Awwwwwwwwwwwwwww," the orange one grumbled to Wren. "But whyyyyyyyy? We want a fluffy human to play with! That one said *you* were *his* pet!" He pointed at Sky, who did an extremely terrible job of trying to look innocent.

"Sky!" Wren stamped her foot.

"Don't make that mad face!" he protested. "They would have tried to keep you otherwise! I wanted them to know we go together, you and me!"

"You could have said best friends," Wren suggested. "Or that I saved your life, like, *multiple* times. Or that nobody gets to keep any humans! By all the moons, I mean, *really*."

"No humans for you," Sky said sternly to the dragonets. "Oooo, but I bet you could find some really cute cave snails!" He lowered his voice and whispered, "They'd probably be better-behaved than she is anyway."

"You are so lucky you're cute," Wren said, shaking her head. She said something to Axolotl, then added in Dragon to Luna, "Dusky kind of reminds me of baby Sky. Totally different scales but the sweet face. And Sky had no family either."

"Except you," Sky said, poking her affectionately with his tail.

"Well, you lucked into me," Wren said with a grin.

Tau led them out of the main cave, and for a while, they climbed and walked through the winding rock passages. At one point in a high-ceilinged cave, Luna wondered why they weren't flying, and then she remembered noticing that one of Tau's wings looked different from the others. She wanted to ask how Tau had made it all the way here from Jewel Hive, but she wasn't sure if that was too nosy. Tau seemed like someone who was good at both solving her own problems and asking for help when she needed it.

They had to splash through a long river for a while. Pale, eyeless fish darted between their claws. Cricket and Bryony tried to catch one but failed, and then Bullfrog tried, succeeded, and snarfed it down with a very self-satisfied expression. The frigid water came up to Luna's wings, rippled around her stomach, and occasionally splashed up her nose.

Eventually the river narrowed and curved through a thin gap between two walls of rock. They squeezed through one by one: Tau, Sky with the humans, Luna with Dusky, Bryony, and Cricket. It took more wiggling and squishing to get Bullfrog through, but eventually he flopped into the shallow water on the other side with an *oof* of disgruntlement.

"This is it," Tau said. She flicked her tail at the cave below them. The river swept past their talons and over an edge, waterfalling down about the height of two dragons into a wide, rippling pool. Luna could see more pale fish flickering in the dark water, but she didn't see any humans.

Cricket splashed out of the water and crouched at the edge of the rock, peering down. "You've seen humans here?" she asked Tau.

"A couple of times," Tau answered. "Can't you smell them?"

Luna sniffed, but it was hard to separate out any new furry smells from the scents of Wren and Axolotl right beside her.

"There's something else." Tau turned to Bryony, who offered one of her wings to support Tau's shorter wing as they glided down to the cave below. Luna and the others followed as Tau stepped around the shore to the far side of the pool and reached into the water.

She pulled out a small contraption. It took Luna a moment to realize it was a sort of cage. It was designed so fish would swim in but couldn't swim back out, and it currently held three squirming fish.

"Whoa," Cricket breathed. She hurried over to study it, blinking behind her spectacles. "This — humans made this?"

"Wren can make things like that," Sky said, sounding hilariously defensive. "She can make anything! She catches fish with weird inventions all the time!"

"There are several of these," Tau said. She lowered it back into the water. "I believe the humans come from there," she added, pointing to a hole higher up the wall. Now that she was looking, Luna could see an odd sort of path descending from the hole to the shore of the lake, made of stairs chiseled into the stone.

"Maybe Axolotl and I should stay here for the rest of the day," Wren suggested. "So we can meet anyone who comes to the lake? Without a bunch of giant drooling dragon faces looming around to scare them off." Sky snorted huffily.

A small scuffing noise came from behind them.

Luna whirled around, accidentally splashing Dusky, and stared into the dark corners of the cave. The stalagmites cast long shadows in the light from her glow silk, and for a moment, she thought she saw movement . . . *there* — no, there! No . . . maybe it was nothing . . .

And then something glinted overhead, catching the light. She lifted her gaze and locked eyes with a gaunt, shaggy, eerie *thing*.

It saw her see it, but it stayed perfectly still, without a flicker of movement or muscle tension, as though it was not afraid of her at all. It was shaped like a human, she thought, but it held itself in a weird spiderlike way, knees and elbows bent at painful sharp angles. Its arms were as thin as her antennae, and when it crouched, as it did now, its matted hair and beard brushed the ground. Its skin was as pale as the eyeless fish but less natural, as though all the blood had been sucked out of it. And its eyes — they seemed to be covered in a green film like algae, but they also seemed to be staring straight into Luna's soul.

She couldn't help crying out in alarm and jumping back,

stumbling farther into the pool. The human still did not flinch, but a crack opened in its hairy face, then widened to reveal rotting teeth in something like a cruel imitation of a smile.

"What is it?" Bryony asked, splashing over next to her. Luna pointed, and all the dragons turned to look up at the strange creature on the ledge.

Wren held out her hands and said something calm and soothing in Human. When there was no reaction, she added in Dragon, "Do you understand this language instead? They won't hurt you."

The creature lunged to its feet suddenly, hissed at them, and bolted away through a crack in the wall.

CHAPTER 11

"That was so creepy," Bryony said, looking down at Wren and Axolotl with a shiver. "I didn't know humans could be that creepy."

"*Was* that a human?" Cricket asked. "For sure? Not some other weird thing we haven't discovered yet?"

"I think he was human," Wren said. "But I have no idea what was wrong with him." She said something to Axolotl, and they raised their hands, looking equally puzzled.

Dusky had his face buried in Luna's neck again, trembling. She rubbed her wings together uneasily, then reached up and tugged the dragonet into her arms, partly to comfort him and partly to comfort herself. She'd expected tiny Wrens and Daffodils and Axolotls and Ocelots — calm, smart little creatures. She'd never pictured an unsettling, dangerous-looking version of them.

She felt her hope shiver, like thin glass that could shatter at any moment. *Don't fall into the fog, Luna. Don't let the worry win.*

"Humans are scary," Dusky whispered in Luna's ear. His breath smelled like the wild carrots he'd eaten for breakfast.

"Not all of them," she whispered back. "Wren and Axolotl are friendly. And kind of cute, aren't they?"

"I have bad dreams about humans," he said, so quietly she could barely hear him.

"Wait till you get your wings," she said, patting his head. "You won't be scared of anything then. I've only had mine for a little while, and look how tough I am."

"It's all right to be scared, too," Cricket said unexpectedly. Luna hadn't even realized she was close enough to hear them. Cricket offered one of her talons to Dusky, and he touched his nose to it, blinking up at her. "Everyone gets scared sometimes," she said. "Or sad, or worried. That thing scared me, too, Dusky. You can always talk to one of us about it, whenever you feel that way."

What would that be like, Luna wondered, *telling someone anytime I felt sad? Is that normal, for other dragons?*

"Should we follow him?" Wren asked, starting toward the ledge.

"No *way*," Sky objected instantly. "I'm not letting you near that thing! It looked like it would eat you in a heartbeat." He made what he seemed to think was a stern, determined expression and glared down at her. "I'm also not leaving you here alone. That thing could come back and get you, and so I am staying here to guard you, no matter what you say."

Wren put her hands on her hips. "No one is going to approach me if they see you looming around pretending to be scary, Sky."

"Well, good," he said. "I AM scary! They should think about that!"

"What if all the abyss worshippers look like that?" Bryony asked, flicking her tail worriedly. "Maybe the abyss makes them creepy."

Sky lunged forward and cupped his front talons around Wren just as she was about to climb the wall to the ledge.

"*Wren,*" he said with desperate seriousness. "If the abyss can do that to humans, you *can't go there*. I won't *let* you turn into a scary hair monster."

She put one hand on his nearest claw and looked up at him for a long moment, like they were communicating entire libraries with their eyes.

Finally Wren said, "You'd better not. I like my hair the way it is."

"We could turn around," Sky said hopefully. "And go home?"

"You wanted to help, Sky," she reminded him with a gentle nudge. "Listen, you protect me from becoming a scary hair monster, and I'll protect you from becoming a white-eyed murder zombie. Deal?"

He sighed. "All right, but if there are any reckless heroics involved, it's my turn to do them."

As they talked, Cricket had flown up to the ledge where the hair creature had been hiding. She paced along it, touching the rock wall and studying the shadows. "There is a gap here that some of us might fit through," she said thoughtfully. "Let's think. Should we try? Just to look?"

"What if it leads to the abyss?" Bullfrog asked. "Then what do we do?"

"Turn around," Sky said promptly. "Go back to the cavern

with all those nice rainbow dragons and have another bonfire party. Let's spend the night telling each other whatever the opposite of ghost stories are. Like, 'Once there was a turtle and then it met another even cuter turtle and then they had the absolute most adorable turtle babies and they lived forever in a sunny place and no one ever thought about eating them even once their whole lives, the end.'"

"I'll fly into the abyss," Bryony said. "I'd do it right now! I want to know what's down there that's worth a whole prophecy."

Cricket rubbed her forehead and scrunched up her eyes. "We have to, don't we?" she said. *"A secret buried far below may save those brave enough to look.* It's right there in the prophecy. We have to go look."

"But . . . Sundew," Luna said. "And Tsunami and Moon and Lynx and Pineapple — how can we go without them? *Face a great evil with talons **united** —* that's in the prophecy, too, isn't it? If we only have half the tribes represented, aren't we doing it all wrong?"

"That's true," Sky said hopefully. "We could give them a couple more days to find us, couldn't we?"

"More sitting and waiting," Bullfrog grunted. "No, thanks."

"What if we *look*," Cricket suggested, "but we don't *face* anything yet. We scout it out carefully first. I'll just — go through this gap and peek around and come right back."

"I'll come with you," Luna heard herself say, to her own surprise.

"No, no, no," Dusky whispered. The dragonet was trembling so hard Luna could feel the vibrations echoing in her bones.

"You stay with Tau," she said, unwrapping him from her shoulders. "I'll come right back, all right?"

He made a sad little noise as she tucked him into Tau's arms, but he didn't argue with her.

I hope I can make a weaving for him one day, Luna thought. *Something comforting. Maybe of what he'll look like with wings, to remind him of what he has to look forward to. It would have Dusky in the center, flying, looking happy instead of frightened, with dragons he trusts behind him, keeping him safe. Maybe I could put Wren and Axolotl in it, waving from the ground, or flying with his friends, to remind him that some humans are safe and friendly.*

She felt her worry-sadness lift a little as she pictured the tapestry and imagined the possible colors and composition. It distracted her enough to get her onto the ledge with Cricket, and it helped squash down the fear enough so she could squeeze through the small gap, right behind the HiveWing.

Her flamesilk illuminated a long, dark tunnel stretching away in either direction. The roof was low enough that Cricket and Luna both had to crouch. There was no sign of the hairy, hissing creature.

"Which way?" Cricket whispered.

Something glinted off to the left, reflecting in the light of the flamesilk. Luna pointed and Cricket nodded, and they crept toward it, with Cricket in the lead.

The shiny thing turned out to be a diamond: several diamonds, in fact, plus a few rubies and emeralds, embedded in the wall in a design that framed the archway into a new tunnel.

Cricket brushed her claws over the design. "Do these look like vines to you?" she whispered to Luna.

Luna nodded: emerald vines, diamond flowers, dark and blood-red rubies throughout. "I guess the humans made this. I wonder if that means the village is close. I don't see any humans down here," she added softly. "But there's something on the wall in this tunnel."

They went through the archway. In the light of Luna's flamesilk, the stone walls came alive, shapes flickering across them like darting shadows. She nearly yelped, thinking the hair creature was running toward them, but after the first moment of panic, she realized it was only paintings. Paintings covered the tunnel walls on either side of them and the ceiling as well.

"Pictures," Cricket said in an awestruck voice, leaning closer to study them. "It's a story, I think? The humans must have done these, right? There's so many of them . . ."

The walls and ceiling were covered in little drawings of humans. It was strange to see a story with this many humans in it — and no words to help figure out what was going on. And no dragons at all, as far as Luna could see.

No, wait, there was one. A little farther along the passage, tucked up near the ceiling, there was a drawing of a dragon curled in a cave, smoke rising from its nostrils.

Luna followed the tunnel, watching the pictures as she went. The walls seemed to mirror each other and were covered mostly with humans doing odd little human things. But here was the dragon again, this time flying low over a group of crouching stick figures — and farther along, here again, back in its cave, but now with little bones scattered at its feet. Luna shuddered. The idea of eating any animals gave her the heebie-jeebies; eating animals that were smart and self-aware made it so much worse.

These dragons didn't know who they were eating, she told herself. But to see a story like this, where dragons like her were the scary, dangerous villains . . . it made her feel strange and inside out, like she didn't know who she really was.

The drawings got more unsettling as they continued along the passage. More dragons appeared, most of them chasing the tiny stick figures, and more bones filled the empty spaces on the wall. A few dragons had little human legs poking out of their mouths. Next came several small human houses on fire, and a few small humans on fire, too.

My art won't be like this, Luna thought, touching one of the paintings. *Other dragons can do these kinds of stories. I want my tapestries to make dragons happy. I'll show dragons and humans side by side, communicating and living in peace, and maybe if enough dragons see it in a tapestry, they'll want to live it for real, too.*

"These aren't Pantalan dragons," Cricket said softly. "Did you notice that? They all have two wings, and they're breathing fire."

"Oh," Luna said, studying the dragons more closely. She had to admit that was smart of Cricket to notice, and admitting that to herself made her realize she hadn't had any angry thoughts about Cricket in a while. Somewhere along the way, she'd become "Cricket" in Luna's mind, an individual dragon who was not so bad, instead of "a HiveWing," representative of her entire cruel tribe. "You're right. What does that mean? How can there be drawings here, on Pantala, of Pyrrhian dragons?"

"I think they're very old," Cricket said, brushing one claw lightly over a small drawing of a shrieking human. "Maybe they're from a time when the same dragons flew over both continents."

"Hmm," Luna said doubtfully. That didn't entirely make sense to her. If this continent used to have two-winged dragons who breathed fire, why weren't they here anymore?

More and more little squares on fire, trees on fire, painted flames covering wide swathes of the wall with only a circle peeking out here and there that might have been a screaming human face. Luna really didn't love this story, whatever was happening in it.

"Oh!" Cricket yelped. She grabbed Luna's talon and pointed to the fire paintings. "Luna! What if this is the thing Bullfrog was telling us about? The . . . Smoking? The Burning — the Scorching!"

Luna gasped. *Could that be it?* "And this is how the humans saw it!" she cried.

"Lots of burning and death," Cricket said. "Sounds kind of like how the dragons saw it, too, actually."

"But wasn't the Scorching *thousands* of years ago?" Luna asked.

"Maybe there have been humans down here all that time," Cricket said. "Maybe this is how some of them survived, by hiding in the caves and living underground."

"I wonder who this is," Luna said, pointing to a little figure all by himself in a space on the wall, with a circle of figures at a distance around him. He was slightly bigger than the others, with a halo of light drawn around his head, and he was pointing toward the far end of the tunnel, the direction they were walking.

A little ways on, she saw him again, standing alone on a small crescent on top of what looked like waves. Lots of other humans were behind him, following him, stuffed ten apiece in their own crescents. She could tell it was the same figure, even if he hadn't had the halo, because in both paintings, he was holding a green box and wearing thick black gloves — at least, she thought that's what it looked like; either that or he had giant paws.

"Crossing the ocean," Cricket murmured, darting along the wall. "Coming to Pantala. And look, way along here, they've reached land again and are going into a cave." She paused and touched the painting lightly, then turned to look at Luna with worried eyes. "Does it seem like there are a lot of plants painted around this cave?"

It did look very leafy. There were vines curling around the entrance and under the humans' feet as they followed their hero into the mouth of the cave. The leaves and vines were streaked red and green, with little white flowers scattered around them.

Luna nodded. "Lots of one particular plant," she said slowly.

Cricket let out a long breath. "That's not just any plant," she said. "I'm pretty sure that's the breath of evil."

"Luna!" a little voice screamed from the tunnel behind them. "Fire dragon! Luna!"

"I'm here!" Luna called, recognizing Dusky's voice with a jolt of alarm. She ran back along the painted tunnel. "Dusky! Stay there; I'm coming!"

"Luna!" he shrieked again.

She flew through the archway and around the corner into the first tunnel.

She saw Dusky's flamesilk bracelet first, glowing warmly in the dark passageway, moving away from her.

Then she saw the human holding Dusky.

And the thick, twisted net Dusky was caught in, his little claws pinned to his sides.

And the other human, standing between her and the captured dragonet, holding a torch and a sharp, gleaming knife.

Neither human was the hairy hissing creature, but they were not Wren or Axolotl either; these looked spiky and dangerous in their own way. The closer one had short, straight dark hair and black feathers woven into the leather of her outer wrappings. Her face was thinner and sharper than Wren's, and she had a tiny emerald embedded in the side of her nose.

She called something to her partner, who wrapped his arms more firmly around the net and Dusky and took off running.

"No!" Luna yelled. "What are you *doing*? Stop! Wren! Wren, help!"

She ran full tilt toward them, but the feathered human flung down her torch in a blaze of flames and darted after the other one.

They were gone, and they'd taken Dusky with them.

━━━ CHAPTER 12 ━━━

"Wren!" Luna shouted again as she reached the gap she'd squeezed through only a moment before. "Help! There were humans here, and they took Dusky!" She kicked aside the burning torch, flinching at the stab of pain in her foot.

Through the haze of panic around her, she heard Tau crying something like "He promised he would just *look*! Luna, I'm so sorry! They came out of nowhere!" and Bullfrog grunting, "It's too small! Can't get through!" and Bryony yelling, "Then *get out of the way*, you big thick crocodile!" and Sky shouting, "Wren, don't you dare! Wren, stop, it's not safe!"

And then Wren was there in the passageway with her, seeing the look on Luna's face, turning toward the sound of Dusky's shrieks still echoing along the stone, and running, and Luna ran with her.

She thought she heard Cricket's talonsteps behind them, maybe Bryony's, but she didn't look back, only forward at the distant light of Dusky's bracelet moving away from them.

She wished she could run faster, but the third time she ran headfirst into a stalactite she forced herself to slow down and watch the passage ahead. She'd be no use to Dusky if she knocked herself unconscious.

"What did the humans say?" Wren asked as they ran. "Why did they take him?"

"I have no idea!" Luna cried. "They said *erplecheepsqueak* and threw a net over him and ran away!"

"Erple . . . cheep . . ." Wren muttered.

"Not literally!" Luna interrupted. "I don't know, it just sounded like squeaking to me, I'm sorry!"

"I think one of them said *abyss*," Cricket panted behind them. Luna remembered that the HiveWing had been trying to study Human with Axolotl, Wren, and Sky during their rest stops. Luna had been too tired to pay attention. She *should* have paid attention; she could at least have learned the word "abyss"! Or maybe something actually useful, like how to say "Stop!" or "Don't you dare take that dragonet!" or "I will give up vegetarianism just to eat you if you hurt that dragonet!"

"It is weird," Wren said breathlessly, "that they would grab a baby dragon with a big dragon right there. I mean, if they assume you're his mom, they should guess you'll chase them, and probably eat them, and so if they were smart, they would drop him and then they'd have a better chance of escaping. So it's . . . weird, is all."

The tunnel zigged and zagged, and the humans kept turning off into other branches, and a few times they nearly lost sight of Dusky's light at places where the path split, but then it would always appear again.

"If the humans know these caves well, they should

have been able to lose us by now," Wren pointed out, pausing to rest one hand against the wall, clutching her side. "Sorry — ow — I'll catch up."

Luna crouched beside her. "I'll carry you. If I catch them, I need you to communicate with them."

Wren clambered onto Luna's back without arguing, and they set off running again.

The ground kept slanting downward, and each turn took them lower and lower into the earth. Luna wondered for a moment how they would ever get back to the others. Sky was going to kill her for taking Wren off to get lost in this underground labyrinth.

Suddenly Luna realized there was a faint green glow coming from up ahead . . . and maybe the sound of distant whispers, too? It was hard to hear for sure over her running footsteps. But the glow became brighter as she ran closer, until she emerged into a sepulchral, echoing cavern and found herself on a plateau scattered with boulders.

The plateau overlooked a jagged slash in the heart of the planet: a stab wound in the stone that plunged down and down and down so far it hurt Luna's eyes to look at it.

The abyss.

They'd found it.

Luna had no doubt. There couldn't be anyplace deeper or creepier in the whole world; there couldn't be anywhere else where someone might stand and say, "Oh, THIS is much more of an abyss than that one." It felt like a place a prophecy would point to. It felt like it had been carved out of generations of dragons' nightmares.

And the humans were there, standing near the edge with Dusky. As Luna spotted them, she realized the feathered one was crouching beside the baby dragon and sawing through the net with her knife.

"Don't hurt him!" Luna cried, skidding to a stop.

The one with the knife looked at her, then yelled something at the other one, who shook his head.

"She told him to run," Wren murmured to Luna. "But he won't leave her. Luna, I think Dusky was bait. I think this is a trap."

Luna jerked her head around, but there was no one else nearby. The glow from the abyss and the light from her flamesilk illuminated the plateau. No other humans, not even the hairy creature. No hidden nets or anything that looked like it might trap her.

If Cricket and Bryony had been behind her, they hadn't caught up yet.

"It doesn't matter," she said. "We have to get Dusky back." It made her sick with nerves to see him so close to that awful hole, knowing he had no wings if the worst happened and he fell in.

Wren slid off Luna's back and stepped toward the humans, holding her hands with palms out. She called to them in Human, and both humans froze, staring at her.

"Here we go," Wren said with a sigh. "Luna, look as fierce

as you can. I'm going to try talking them down, but it'll help if you could look a bit more threatening."

She took another step toward the humans and said something else, and the one in black feathers responded.

Look fierce and scary. Luna fluffed up her wings, hoping that would make her look bigger, and frowned. *She* always found frowning dragons a little scary anyhow. What else could she do?

Oh, right. My terrifying superpower. As the humans said bristly-sounding things back and forth, Luna lifted one talon and let a smoking thread of blaze silk spill into her palm. It wound into a ball, and she cupped the fire between her claws. She'd never tried throwing flamesilk before, but maybe holding it menacingly would be enough.

The feathered human looked around the plateau and shouted something. Her partner shook his head and responded in a quiet, sad voice.

"What's happening?" Luna asked Wren. "Why aren't they giving Dusky back?"

"They're waiting for someone," Wren said. "They called him 'the Guardian of the Abyss,' but his name must be Vole because that's what that one just shouted. I think her name is Raven. She says the Guardian told them to bring the abyss a dragon — or the abyss told them, speaking through the Guardian — something like that." She listened to the conversation the other humans were having for a moment. "Apparently he's always here. It's creepy that he's missing. He's never left before; they didn't even think he could."

Luna felt a horrible chill, like arctic spiders tiptoeing down her spine. "The abyss talks to them?" she said. "It . . . asks for things? Do they know what's down there?"

Wren spoke to the humans, and the one without feathers answered her.

"They don't know," Wren relayed to Luna. "Only the Guardian can go into the abyss; I'm not sure how. But they get instructions through him." Wren shook her head. "I'd say it's all a made-up cult thing, but since it's in your prophecy, then I guess there really might be something down there."

The breath of evil, Luna thought. *The source of the other-mind. It has to be, doesn't it?*

"Well, it can't have Dusky," she said firmly. "Tell them no. Tell them I will set them on fire *right now* if they don't give him back."

Wren put her hands on her hips, and whatever she said in Human, it sounded very commanding to Luna.

Raven and the other human looked at each other for a long moment, and then Raven sighed, knelt down, and cut the rest of the net off Dusky.

"Luna!" he yelped as soon as his snout was free. He wriggled away from the ropes as the humans stepped back, and pelted across the plateau toward her.

"Dusky!" Luna cried with relief. "It's all right. We're here." She set down her ball of flamesilk and stepped forward, talons outstretched to catch him.

But he was still a few steps away when something dropped from the ceiling. Something that had been hiding among the

stalactites overhead, waiting to pounce like a vicious preda-
tory insect. Something hairy and leggy and hissing, giving
off a stench almost as bad as Lady Scarab's weapon as it fell.

The Guardian of the Abyss landed on Dusky, knocking
the dragonet flat. He seized the little SilkWing in his spindly
arms and sprinted sideways, darting away from Luna while
her brain was still screaming: "Ack, creepy things falling
from the sky!"

And then, before anyone could blink or scream or move,
the terrifying human hurled himself and the wingless dragonet over the edge into the abyss.

Tsetse Hive
Beetle Lake
Vinegaroon Hive
Hornet Hive
Cicada Hive
Mantis Hive

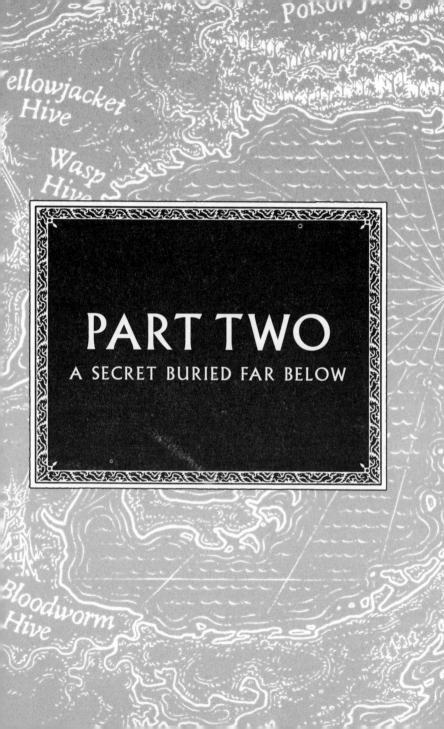

PART TWO

A SECRET BURIED FAR BELOW

CHAPTER 13

"Dusky!" Luna shrieked. *No, no, no, no, no,* this couldn't be happening; the little dragon couldn't be *gone* just like that. The abyss COULD NOT HAVE HIM.

She didn't stop to think. She ran to the edge and threw herself after them.

I can catch them. I can save Dusky before they hit the bottom. I can get him back.

Below her she could see the tiny dark silhouette of the Guardian falling, framed against the weird glow. Behind her, she heard Wren shouting, but she couldn't make out anything the human was saying.

I guess I am a dragon who can fly into the danger when I have to, she thought as she plummeted. *I never knew for sure. Swordtail always did it for me, before I ever could.*

Please be OK, Dusky.

The flailing stick figure below her looked as far away as before, and the fall felt endless. Luna tried pumping her wings to descend faster, but it didn't seem to help.

Why would the Guardian do this? Why would he take Dusky?

Why would the abyss want a baby dragon?

The light was getting brighter, bright enough to dazzle her eyes, and suddenly she couldn't see the human and Dusky anymore. They were swallowed by the green glow, which filled her field of vision, shimmering folds of eerie light consuming everything else and blinding her so she didn't know how much farther she had to fall —

— and then all at once she was there.

Luna had to swerve at the last moment to avoid landing in the morass of vines that carpeted the abyss floor. They were thick and wound together like an angry nest of eels, and she thought the whole tangle might be dragons deep.

The phosphorescent light came from the leaves and from a moist mossy coating on all the walls around her. It was bright enough here that she wouldn't have needed the glow silk on her horns — but she was glad she had it and its warm golden light.

There was no sign of Dusky or the wretched human.

"Dusky!" Luna cried. "Dusky!"

Maybe the vines had cushioned their fall — but then where were they now? How could they have vanished so quickly?

Wait — there! There was a section of the tangle that looked partly crushed; this had to be where they had landed. Luna hovered as close as she dared and peered at it. She didn't want to land on or touch the vines. She could too easily imagine long tendrils wrapping around her ankles, dragging her down so the plants could dissolve her into bone mulch.

And she was pretty sure this was the breath of evil. She'd

never seen it in real life before, but it looked like the plant in the cave paintings and it matched the description from Cricket and Sundew's stories.

"Luna!" Dusky's voice shrieked.

Luna whipped around. There was a trail across the vines if she squinted — the path of a small creature running full tilt, leaping from tangle to tangle like a fearless squirrel. And it led in the direction of Dusky's cry for help.

She shot over the vines, swooping around the curves of the abyss. Maybe the abyss monster could fall faster than she could catch him, but he couldn't outrun her wings, especially while carrying a baby dragon.

As it turned out, though, he hadn't had to run far. The vines and the trail converged on a cave in the wall of the abyss — or rather, the vines seemed to be exploding from it, swarming out in both directions. The cave entrance was full of plants, but there was a gap near the top where a small dragon — or a human and a tiny dragon — could fit through.

Luna held her breath and dove toward the opening. Her wings and talons brushed the vines as she glided through, and she felt the tendrils shiver, as if a million gleefully venomous wasps were waking up somewhere nearby.

On the other side, there was a room.

That is, it still felt like a cave — stone walls, chilly, dark — but it was the size and shape of a throne room: square, with four matching columns, and *corners*, and most importantly, a throne on the far end, up against a perfectly smooth, flat wall.

The vines were coming from the thing on the throne.

Luna tried to make the scene into a picture in her memory instinctively, the way she always did, but she couldn't . . . she couldn't figure it out . . . she couldn't get her brain to fit around what her eyes could see.

Her first thought was *This would be such a disturbing tapestry.*

Her mind desperately *wanted* to see it as a tapestry instead — as a picture, not real, not really right in front of her.

She'd expected a plant, and yes, there was a plant. A stem as thick as the columns rose from the earth below the throne, winding around the pedestal.

But on the throne was a man.

And sitting on his knees, captured between the thick black gloves on the human's hands, was a young dragon.

For a horrible moment, Luna thought it was Dusky — but as she flew closer, her light reflected off green and orange scales, and she saw that this dragonet had wings.

It also could not possibly be alive. The plant was growing *straight through the dragon's skull*, emerging horrifyingly from a split at the top of its head, and then continuing on through the human's skull. Behind the human's head, the vines divided and cascaded away like a parody of Ocelot's hair, like tentacles exploding outward. Some of them swarmed toward the cave opening, while hundreds of others clambered up the walls and disappeared into cracks overhead.

"What . . ." Luna breathed.

At the foot of the throne, on the vines that covered the floor, a hairy shape twisted around to glare at her. In his arms, Dusky flailed, whimpering.

"Dusky," Luna said, starting forward.

"*Stay back,*" hissed a voice in Dragon. The voice came from the Guardian's mouth, but sounded like the possessed SilkWing on the island where they'd been attacked.

Luna froze. Who *is talking to me? The othermind?*

"Who are you?" Luna said. She focused her gaze on the throne, on the grotesque tableau of the dragonet, man, and plant fused together. Their blank staring eyes seemed to be fixed on her. Both the human and the dragon had a white film covering their eyeballs, with a shimmer of mossy green overlaying it.

But they *couldn't* still be alive. They just *absolutely could not be.*

"I am the emperor of the world."

"You're so not," Luna said. "How can you be emperor if no one even knows you exist?"

Hissing filled the room, coming from the throne and the shivering plants and the Guardian of the Abyss all at the same time.

"They *will* know," said the voice. "They will all know soon. I am the ruler of everything. All of it is mine, all —"

"OK, you're deranged and sinister, got it," Luna interrupted. "But who is talking right now? What is *that*?" She pointed to the throne. "What happened to that little dragon?"

There was an offended silence for a heartbeat, two,

three, and then, with a rustling, the voice finally answered, "Give yourself to the vines, and we'll show you the whole story."

"Ha," Luna said. "No. Easy no. I will never let you take my mind."

"It's inevitable now," the voice said calmly. "As soon as you entered this chamber. Eventually your wings will tire and you'll drop from the air with exhaustion, and then my vines will have you."

"Pfft," Luna scoffed. "I can leave whenever —" She turned toward the cave entrance.

It was entirely barricaded with vines.

Luna shot over to the tangle that now blocked the exit. She nearly grabbed one of the vines to rip it away, but she pulled her talons back at the sight of wicked thorns bristling along the edges. If they scratched her, would she instantly be lost to the othermind? Or would it happen if she touched the sticky sap — or the jagged leaves? How did this work? Was it more dangerous here, this close to the roots, to its origin?

"How did you do this?" Luna demanded. "I thought you needed a dragon with leafspeak to move the vines."

"Oh, I have one."

Luna's gaze went to the mystery dragonet on the throne. Was it a LeafWing? But the orange scales — it didn't look like any tribe she'd seen so far.

"Unfortunately, my lizard is not strong enough for everything we want to do. Her leafspeak works for the vines close to us, in the abyss, but not in the overworld. Which is why this fool was supposed to bring me SUNDEW," the voice suddenly roared.

At the foot of the throne, the Guardian cowered, baring his teeth. He whined something in Human and shook poor little Dusky.

"That is OBVIOUSLY NOT THE DRAGON I NEED —"

The voice abruptly cut off. There was an odd strangled sound, and then it returned, suddenly soft and whispery. *"But it's the dragon I want."*

A few of the vines slithered toward Dusky like curious snakes. The Guardian took a step away from them and snarled something else.

"Pathetic," the voice said, back to its previous cadence. "You're not much use to me either, SilkWing. But I'll keep you, just for fun. Maybe Sundew will come looking for you. That would be convenient."

"I'm not afraid of you," Luna said. She turned her wrists upward and gestured at the vines all around. "I'm a flamesilk. All I have to do is burn my way out."

Maybe this is the reason I'm a flamesilk. Maybe I'm supposed to use my sun silk to burn all these vines to ashes. Maybe this is always where I was supposed to end up.

"Ohhhh," said the voice gleefully. "Oh nooo. No, don't. Anything but that."

Luna hesitated. Why did it sound so delighted?

"That would be just TERRIBLE," the voice went on. "You FIENDISH MONSTER."

Because . . . wait . . . because burning it would release

the same smoke that got the SilkWings and LeafWings at the Snarling River. It would be toxic; it would go straight into my brain, and if I burned too much, the smoke could rise and get the others beyond the abyss as well.

She clasped her front talons together, suddenly terrified. "CRICKET!" Luna shouted at the blocked exit. "WREN! BRYONY!"

"Oh yes, please doooooo bring them closer," the voice chuckled. "I would like allll those pretty dragons to play with, and the sparky humans, too. This Guardian is THE WORST!" it suddenly roared again. "I DEMAND ANOTHER AND NOBODY LISTENS! MY WORSHIPPERS HAVE BETRAYED ME!"

The Guardian shrieked, dropped Dusky, and threw his hairy arms over his head.

Dusky scrambled away from him and pelted across the vines that covered the floor. He stopped below Luna and reached up toward her with a heartbreaking look on his face.

"Luna, help me!" he wailed.

She swooped down to pick him up.

But as her talons touched his, vines shot up from the tangle, snapping around her wrists and ankles. Dusky's eyes went blank, and he yanked her down toward him, and more vines surged up to ensnare her neck, her tail, her wings.

Luna tried to scream for help, but a vine looped around her snout and pinned it shut.

She was trapped like an insect in a spiderweb, and the spider was casting its poisonous haze across her mind, and all around her the throne room faded away.

CHAPTER 14

Luna opened her eyes.

She was standing on the slope of a mountain, in bright daylight, surrounded by pine trees. . . . *What?*

She blinked, but the pine trees were still there. She held up her talons. They looked like hers. She felt like herself. She did not feel like she was drowning in evil vines.

Is this an evil-vine hallucination?

It felt awfully real.

If it is a hallucination, why is it happening?

For a moment, she stared at the trees, but they didn't seem to have any sinister intentions. They swayed gently, looking the very opposite of suspicious. Their whole aura radiated "nope, not interested in eating your brain."

Something was sitting on her foot.

Luna glanced down. It was Dusky, but he had his eyes squeezed shut and his little arms and tail clamped around her leg. He was so small, smaller even than most two-year-old dragonets.

"Any idea where we are?" she asked him.

He shook his head mutely. She thought about pointing out that he might have a better chance of guessing if he actually opened his eyes and *looked*, but she decided he was already stressed enough.

And this certainly didn't look like the Pantala they knew.

It looked more like the dragon colony Luna had visited in Pyrrhia — the one called Sanctuary, which was surrounded by pine forest like this. Except here, there were no dragons in any direction, as far as she could see.

She spotted an overlook beyond the trees. Luna paced over to it, dragging Dusky along with her — which was not difficult; he seemed to weigh no more than a pine cone.

They gazed down at the land below them.

Luna had expected to see a continent choked with vines; she'd thought she'd find the breath of evil plant spreading from here to the horizon. She wouldn't have been surprised to discover that she'd been unconscious and mind-controlled for years, and this was a future where the plant had won and taken over everything.

But what she saw instead was far more mystifying.

The landscape below her looked . . . strangely organized. It was partitioned into squares and rectangles and ovals, with long, flat lines running between all of them. Many of the sections contained cubic structures, giant boxes with ornate roofs, or taller towerlike things.

It's like a Hive, Luna realized, spotting an arrangement of roofs around an open square that might be a market. *Except all the layers are spread out next to each other, instead of stacked on top of one another.*

Some of the areas were for growing food plants, as far as she could tell — like the Hive greenhouses, but open to the air and much bigger. Those seemed to be arranged around the outer edges, while the inner sections were crammed with cubes and towers and stepped temples and stone-paved courtyards.

"Dusky," Luna said, nudging him with her snout. "What are we looking at? Does this look at all familiar to you?"

He shook his head again.

Luna scanned the sky. "I still don't see any dragons. Isn't that odd?" Did they all live in the flattened-out Hives? She dropped her gaze again and realized that there were shapes moving among the structures and along the long flat lines. They were so small from here that they looked more like ants than anything else . . . but she didn't think they were dragons. They didn't move like dragons, none of them were flying, and they weren't shaped right.

She tried extending her antennae all the way to see if she could pick up any clues. The only vibrations in the sky overhead came from birds; the largest was a hawk drifting lazily far above them.

But somewhere nearby . . . were those voices? They were pitched a little too high and fast. Not dragons — humans.

Luna scooped Dusky into her arms and flew up into one of the trees, perching on a branch where the needles were thick enough to hide her from the ground.

Not that she was *afraid* of the humans, exactly. But after seeing the Guardian and the one on the throne, she thought she might want to keep her distance until she could tell which kind of humans these were.

There were four of them, slouching and swaggering up the mountain, bonking into one another and shouting and breaking twigs off the trees they passed. One of them stopped, picked up a rock, and hurled it at a nearby tree. When it *thunk*ed against the bark, he shouted: "That's right!" and then two of the others scrambled around to grab rocks and do the same.

The last human rolled his eyes and sat down on one of the boulders, stretching out his legs. "So impressive," he said. "You can hit trees with rocks. Someone should make you all emperor."

The first rock thrower grinned and strutted in a circle, holding out his arms to the watching trees. "Not all of us," he said. "Just me! Emperor Coyote!"

Wait. A shock zipped through Luna from snout to tail. *I can understand them. They're speaking Human, but I can understand them!*

This had to be a hallucination, then. She hadn't magically learned Human while flying around under the vines' mind control.

Such a *weird* hallucination, though.

"I'd be a better emperor than you!" shouted one of the other humans, leaping on the first one's back. They tussled for a moment, yelling "Emperor Coyote!" and "No, Emperor Argyll!" and ended up on the ground in a flailing pile of limbs.

These humans were *so loud*. Luna had not seen any like these before. The other humans she'd met were careful and quiet, slipping around the edges of the world so they wouldn't get caught or eaten. Even Wren, who seemed fearless, still held herself in a watchful, cautious way, as though she might need to dart to safety or fight off an attack at any moment.

These four, though, took up all the space and all the air and filled it without hesitation. They never checked the sky; they never looked around to see if anything was coming for them. They acted like it had never occurred to them that something might eat them. As though dragons didn't even exist.

Luna shivered. Do *dragons exist in this strange place?* she wondered. *Why haven't I seen any?*

The one on the rock rolled his eyes at the scuffling humans on the ground. "Very regal behavior," he said.

The first one shoved his friend away and bounced back to his feet again. "There are three empires," he said with a shrug. "We can each have one." He waved at the other two, casually excluding the one on the rock.

"If this plan works," said his seated friend — coldly, Luna thought — "then there will be only one empire left, and only one emperor over this whole continent." He stood up, brushing pine needles off the long, silky outer wrapping he was wearing.

They all wore similar wrappings, Luna noticed — fancier, cleaner, and more elegant than anything the humans she knew wore. Little swirls of silver thread decorated the edges of the wrappings in delicate filigree patterns. These wrappings did not look like they would work very well for climbing trees in a hurry.

"This 'plan' is ridiculous, Cottonmouth," said the bossy one. He started to lead the way up the slope again. "Nobody has seen a dragon in at least a year. Nobody has any idea where they live."

Luna barely stopped a gasp from escaping her.

They're looking for dragons.

Why haven't they seen one in a year? Where is everybody?

She wanted to follow them, but she was a little nervous about what these humans would do if they saw her. She thought for a moment, then climbed higher up the tree and along a branch into the next one, with Dusky clinging to her neck. Her childhood in the webs around Cicada Hive meant she had no trouble clambering and leaping nimbly from one tree to the next. And the absolute racket the humans generated made it easy to follow them. She was pretty sure they wouldn't hear her even if she slipped and crashed all the way to the forest floor.

The humans hiked for a long time, arguing cheerfully about some kind of ball game, before finally stopping to rest not far from the mountain's peak. This was one of the shorter mountains in the range, Luna could now see. Much taller ones extended off to the north, some with snow visible on the jagged claws they reached toward the sky.

From here, she could also see more of the unfolded Hives down below. They covered *everything*. Every spot of land seemed to be cordoned off, built on, growing something in straight lines, or swarming with the little ant figures. Definitely not dragons. Luna was pretty sure they were humans.

Human *cities*.

Just — out in the open! Where anyone could swoop down and eat them! Like a giant buffet set up for dragons!

She wasn't even sure she was in Pyrrhia, after all. She remembered a mountain range like this, bisecting the continent, near Sanctuary. But they'd flown over a vast desert to get to it — the whole Kingdom of Sand, covering most of the territory west of the mountains. And yet, from up here, she couldn't see any sign of a desert to the west. She could see the sun slowly sinking toward the horizon, but everything in that direction was either green or the gleaming white and gray stone of the human cities.

"We should get back to camp," said one of the humans. The four of them were sprawled around a clearing, leaning against the trees and eating snacks from the bags around their waists. "There obviously aren't any dragons up here. Like you predicted, Coyote."

"I know, right?" said the bossy one. He tossed a nut into his mouth and stretched. "But we can say we checked it out, as the commander ordered."

"I wouldn't call this the most thorough scouting expedition," Cottonmouth said in his flat, disapproving voice.

"Feel free to carry on alone," Coyote said grandly, waving one hand at the rest of the mountain left above them. "But I'm telling you, if there were a dragon this close to the Emperor's City, we'd know about it. I bet they've run off to hide in the far north. Around the edges of the Diamond Empire, that's where they are."

"Fine with me," said one of the others. "Maybe they'll eat the Diamond Army and save us the trouble of fighting them."

"Pfft," said his friend. "I'm not scared of the Diamond Army. We smashed them the last time they tried to come through the pass."

"And they smashed *us* the last time we tried to cross to *their* side," Cottonmouth pointed out. "And they're stuck at the river border with Empress Jaguar. None of the empires can expand. We're all trapped, pushing and shoving each other back and forth over the same few miles of territory. That's why we need a new advantage. That's what makes the emperor's plan so genius."

"You keep calling it the 'emperor's plan,'" Coyote scoffed, "but everyone knows you're the one who slithered it into his ears."

"Blech!" one of the others cried, throwing an orange at Coyote. The human deftly snatched it out of the air, produced a knife from his boot, and started peeling it.

"The emperor is very wise," Cottonmouth said calmly. "It is a credit to his wisdom that he listens to even his lowliest advisors."

"Well, I don't see how this *genius* plan is going to work if we can't find any dragons," said the fourth human, yawning.

"We will find them," Cottonmouth said. "I am quite sure of that."

And then he looked up into the trees, straight into Luna's eyes.

— CHAPTER 15 —

Luna squeaked and ducked back into the branches, her heart hammering. Dusky squeezed her neck so hard she felt dizzy for a moment.

What will they do to us? What do they want a dragon for?

There was a moment of silence down below, and then one of the humans laughed and said something mocking, imitating Cottonmouth's pretentious tone. Coyote and the other one laughed as well, and Luna heard the sounds of them getting up and bumping around noisily.

She risked a peek through the needles and saw that Cottonmouth was standing up as well, his gaze focused back on his companions.

But . . . surely he had seen her. Why hadn't he reacted? Or told the others?

"Cheer up, Cottonmouth," Coyote said, slapping him on the shoulder. "I'm sure the emperor will let you chase imaginary dragons for the rest of your life if you want to. You can avoid the front line for years that way."

"That is *not* —" Cottonmouth began frostily.

"Sure, sure." Coyote waved away his protests and bounded off down the slope with the other two close behind him. "Race you back to camp!" he shouted. And with another cacophony of crashing and hollering and noise, they were gone.

Cottonmouth let out a soft, hissing breath and turned, silently scanning the trees around him but not looking up.

One human. Luna could take one human if she needed to. She had flamesilk to defend herself with. What she really needed was answers. If she could understand Human in this hallucination, could they understand Dragon?

"Hello?" she called.

Cottonmouth didn't respond. He prowled away from the clearing, stepping quietly over fallen branches.

Luna gently tucked Dusky into a sturdy triangle of branches and whispered, "Stay." Then she spread her wings and floated down from her hiding place. "Hello?" she called after him. "Ahem? Aren't I the thing you're looking for?"

He kept walking, as though he couldn't hear her at all. Even if he didn't understand Dragon, surely he could tell the difference between a dragon growl and the other noises of the forest.

She padded forward and poked him in the back with one talon.

Zero reaction. He didn't turn, didn't flinch or jump.

"Can you not see me?" Luna asked. "Or hear me? Really?" She darted around in front of him and waved her wings.

He walked *straight through her*.

"Yaaaargh!" Luna shouted. It didn't hurt, but it was SO

WEIRD! She held up her talons and examined them frantically. They were *there*. She could *see them*, and she could touch things like trees and Dusky, so how did she not exist at all for this human?

It was like being invisible, but a different kind of terrible.

She hurried back to Dusky and sat in the tree for a moment, cuddling him in her arms so at least something would be real.

"Dusky, where *are* we?" Luna asked. "Why is this happening?"

Dusky looked up at the sky, and when Luna followed his gaze, she saw a dark shadow descending rapidly from the clouds. It rolled over them like fog, like the entire world blinking, and when it cleared, they were somewhere else entirely.

It was still a mountain, but a higher, colder one, above the tree line, with scatterings of snow dusting several of the boulders. They materialized nearly on top of a mountain goat, but like Cottonmouth, it stared right through them, chewing placidly.

Humans were also scattered throughout the boulders, and for a moment, Luna thought they were all dead because they were lying so still. But then one raised his head briefly before ducking back down, and she realized they were hiding from something.

Oh — probably from the giant cave they were all looking at. Or rather, from the thing inside the giant cave that was rumbling and growling and emitting trails of smoke.

They found a dragon.

I wonder if the dragon will be able to see or hear me.

The growls grew louder as the dragon in the cave approached the entrance. She poked her head out, yawned, and sniffed suspiciously.

She wasn't a very big dragon . . . not very much bigger than Luna. She had two wings, and her scales were orange with lemon-yellow underscales. Small flames flickered in her mouth as she yawned. She seemed muted, somehow, like an undercooked version of a dragon.

I hope they don't hurt her, Luna thought anxiously, glancing at the humans. They were all holding sharp pointy things and looked very intent on something.

"Be careful!" Luna called. "Dragon? Can you hear me? There are humans here, and I think they're planning something."

But the dragon's eyes passed right over her, and nobody reacted to her voice except Dusky. He burrowed into her neck and whimpered, "I told you humans are scary."

The orange dragon stretched her wings and lifted up into the sky. She circled for a few heartbeats, while the humans stayed frozen, and then she flew off toward the east, lit by the rising sun.

"Now," one of the humans called in a low voice.

The three humans nearest the cave leaped out from their hiding places and ran full tilt into the dark opening. Luna realized that one of them was Coyote — but he looked older, more lined and grizzled.

Several long moments passed. The human who'd spoken climbed over his rock and darted closer to the cave, staying near cover, and Luna saw that it was Cottonmouth. He also looked older, with a new scar across one temple and longer hair. The wrappings on these humans looked rougher, too, like they'd been dragged through thorn bushes, with no silver filigrees this time. But Cottonmouth had new gold medallions on each shoulder of his cloak and a bright green feather tied into his brown hair with gold thread. He stared at the cave as though he could drag something out of it with the force of his eyeballs.

And then, finally, the three humans came back out of the cave. Two had their swords drawn, watching the sky. Coyote walked between them, carrying a dragon egg in his arms.

A slow smile spread across Cottonmouth's face. He waved another trio of humans forward, carrying a box, and Coyote slid the egg into the padded interior.

"I knew it," Cottonmouth said, bending over the egg. He brushed his paws over the eggshell.

"Yeah, yeah," Coyote said. "You were right. The emperor will be thrilled."

"How many eggs were in the nest?" Cottonmouth asked.

"Three," answered one of the other humans, missing the warning look Coyote shot at him.

Cottonmouth stood up and looked into Coyote's eyes. "Go get the other two."

"Whoa," Coyote said. "I thought the plan was to start with one."

"I want them all," Cottonmouth said. "Go get them. Now."

"But, sir," said the human on Coyote's left, "won't that make the dragon angry? I thought the scholars said they might not miss one, but —"

Cottonmouth turned and stabbed him through the stomach in one swift movement. The human gurgled and fell over.

Luna covered Dusky's eyes just a moment too late. She could feel him shuddering all through her scales.

"Fine," Coyote said, throwing up his hands. He turned and stalked back into the cave. Cottonmouth gestured, and three other humans ran after him, while the rest of the troop produced two more boxes.

Luna closed her own eyes as the two remaining dragon eggs were lowered into the boxes.

That poor orange dragon, she thought. *She'll come back from hunting, and all her eggs will be gone.*

I wish I could save them.

What are the humans going to do with them?

"Dusky," she whispered. "I think this has something to do with the human and the dragonet we saw. But I don't understand how it's connected to the plant and the othermind."

Maybe the shadow would take them to the next part of the story, if they kept watching. She took a deep breath and opened her eyes again.

They were on an island beach now, their talons sinking into hot sand. The island was small, curving around a bright little bay, the water blue and shimmering. In the shallows, two dragon eggs rested in a rock pool, mostly underwater.

"Oh no," Luna whispered, pressing her claws to her snout.

It was already too late. A group of humans were gathered around the rock pool, lifting the eggs into snug jars full of seawater and padded with kelp.

Cottonmouth and Coyote were not with them. These humans looked slightly different: They wore sleek dark fur pelts over their seal-brown skin, and their hair was shades of blue and green. One wore a simple silver headband with a jaguar symbol in the center of her forehead.

"Quickly," she snapped. "That sea dragon could return any minute."

"That's what all these warriors with spears are for," grumbled the human next to her.

"There's no need to kill them if we don't have to," said the jaguar lady. "The empress said *stealth*. She said don't let them know it was humans who took them." She pointed to the sand near the rock pool. "Wipe away those footprints before we go."

Luna thought this was fairly ridiculous. Surely any dragon could smell the heavy scent of human this many would leave behind, even hours later.

"Are the other empires being this careful?" asked one of the humans.

"We don't know," said the leader grimly. "The spies found out they're stealing dragon eggs, but not much else. We don't know if they've succeeded in taming the dragons after they hatch, or what else they might be trying to do with them."

"Stirring up trouble they can't handle, if you ask me," said one of the others, and then the shadow flickered down again.

When it lifted, Luna and Dusky were in a rocky, sandy area at the base of a reddish stone cliff. Halfway up, a group of humans were hastily passing eggs out of a cave into boxes, then lowering them to the ground below, where an army of soldiers on horses waited. Cottonmouth and Coyote were there. Coyote scanned the sky while Cottonmouth kept his eyes fixed on the eggs.

"If it hasn't worked yet," Coyote growled, "why do you keep trying? This is a pointless waste of soldiers *and* scientists. All we've gotten so far is mauled faces and burned-out laboratories."

"I will figure out how to control them," Cottonmouth said. There were two more feathers woven into his hair, alongside new strands of gray. The grooves in his face were deeper now, especially along his forehead and between his eyes. "We have to scare them into submission. They *will* be my weapons, once I break them."

Coyote looked at him uneasily. "You mean the emperor's weapons."

Cottonmouth smiled tightly, leaning forward to watch the last of the eggs reach the ground. There were six of them this time, Luna saw with dismay.

"Let's go!" Cottonmouth called as soon as the boxes were lashed to their horses. He turned his own horse, and Coyote caught the reins to stop him.

"What about the soldiers still up there?" Coyote asked.

"They can catch up," Cottonmouth said dismissively. He twitched the reins out of Coyote's hands and kicked his horse into a gallop.

Coyote looked back at the figures slowly inching down the cliff on the long, dangling ropes. But after a moment, he sighed, turned his horse, and followed the others.

So only Luna was left to see the dragon's return. This dragon was bigger, sandy tan flecked with black, and Luna thought she glimpsed a barb at the end of her tail as the dragon swooped into her cave.

She exploded out again a moment later, roaring with fury. The last few soldiers on the cliff didn't stand a chance. Luna covered Dusky's eyes and closed her own as fire blasted from the dragon's mouth.

The next moment, they were standing in a stone pyramid with a sand pit in the center of it. Windows high in the wall illuminated words painted in gold on the ceiling, the odd human letters rearranging into language in Luna's brain. *OBEDIENCE* said one wall; *SELF-PRESERVATION* said another; *THE EMPEROR PROTECTS US ALL.*

Human soldiers lined the walls, too, wearing heavily padded leather armor and bristling with spikes and sharp weapons. In the center of the sand pit, a dragon egg was hatching, all alone.

Luna could remember a few details about her own hatching: the gentle rocking of the silk hammock that cradled her egg, the talons that lifted her free of the eggshell, her mother's wings enfolding her, and a feeling of light, warmth, color, security.

There was none of that here, in this cold stone room full of spiky humans.

One human stood close to the egg, but his face was shielded with a metal helmet and armor plates covered his entire body, so Luna couldn't tell if it was Cottonmouth. He held a long metal stick in his paws, hovering over the egg. As the tiny hatching dragon pushed the shell aside and wobbled out onto the sand, the human pounced. A wire circle at the end of the stick closed around the dragonet's neck.

The dragonet squeaked with fear and surprise. It tried to turn, looking for a comforting figure, but the human used the stick to force it to the ground.

"I don't need to see this," Luna said as Dusky buried his face in her neck again. She covered his ears so he wouldn't have to hear it either. "I don't *want* to see this. Show us something else, please."

The human prodded the dragonet with a different stick, then shoved it back onto its feet. The dragonet staggered in the sand, hissing, and snapped its teeth at the human.

Brave little dragon, trying to fight back already, Luna thought. She remembered Coyote's words about "mauled faces," and she hoped *many* humans here had been clawed by their small captives.

But it was awful, too, that the dragonets climbed out of their shells directly into violence and pain. They shouldn't have had to use their teeth and claws yet. They should have had time to be taken care of first.

Finally the shadow flickered through, and now they were in a clinical box of a room, long and lined with tables on either side. On top of the tables were cages, each one with a dragon egg in it. Luna hissed in a breath. There were so *many* — twenty at least, with ten more cages containing broken eggshells where those dragonets must have hatched.

The door at the far end was flung open suddenly, and Cottonmouth stormed in with a man behind him carrying another egg box.

"In here," Cottonmouth said, throwing open one of the cages. "I don't believe there was only one egg in that nest. That dragon was enormous."

"Biggest I've ever seen," the man said anxiously, unpacking the stuffing around the egg.

"How could a dragon that size have only *one* egg?" Cottonmouth demanded. "And why would it hide it so carefully? Are you lying to me? Did my stupid brother decide to leave the rest behind?"

"I'm not lying!" the man cried. He stopped short of touching the egg and clasped his shaking hands together. "I promise you, sir. We had the hardest time getting to it — I promise we wouldn't have risked being sent back!"

Cottonmouth snorted. "That I can believe. Well, it had better be worth it, then." He leaned closer to the shell, glaring at the faint shimmer of orange scales underneath. "At least it's a big one. When I break this dragon, it will burn the Diamond Empire's armies to ash for me."

"I heard —" the other man began, then broke off unhappily.

"What?" Cottonmouth snapped.

"I heard the Diamond Empire and the Jaguar Empire are both trying to tame dragons, too," the man mumbled.

Cottonmouth laughed bitterly. "Yes. No one can keep a secret around here. But most of the dragons in their territories are those swimming ones. Can't breathe fire, according to the scholars. Our dragons will be the most dangerous, once we get them to work."

Get them to work, Luna thought with a shiver of outrage. *As though dragons are nothing more than defective looms or broken carts. As if baby dragons just need a little prodding and fixing to be* useful.

The shadow again, this time casting them into darkness for long enough that Luna wondered if that was the end of the human story.

But at length it lifted again. Now she was in a field of tall green plants. All around her, humans picked interestingly small tomatoes and peapods, filling baskets and chatting as they worked. The blue sky soared overhead, sunlit and peaceful. Dusky lifted his snout and took a deep breath; through their scales, she could feel his heartbeat slow a little bit, despite all the humans around them.

Then a terrifying roar split the air, a wordless howl of fury that felt like all of Luna's worst days rolled together and set on fire.

Three dragons burst out of the forest. They flew low to the ground, close enough that Luna could smell the smoke rising from their snouts. Close enough that she could look into their eyes as they shot past.

One of them was the dragon from the red-stone cliff, whose six eggs had been stolen. The one in the lead was nearly five times that size: a huge orange dragon with rusty copper-green underscales, lashing her enormous tail as she flew. The third was a black dragon speckled with red scales, whose face was set with grim determination.

The humans around Luna screamed, dropped their baskets, and fled toward the buildings in the distance.

The dragons opened their mouths and set the fields ablaze.

Luna clutched Dusky closer, but the flames burned around them without singeing their wings. The plants shriveled and turned to ash as the fire raged across the whole area, but Luna and Dusky stood unscathed.

"I knew it," Luna whispered. She looked up as the dragons circled, now breathing their fire on the closest human dwellings. "Stealing the dragon eggs. *That's* what the humans did to make the dragons so mad.

"Dusky . . . this is the beginning of the Scorching."

CHAPTER 16

Luna was not sure why or how she was watching these slices of the past. But she could see how the story had changed over the thousands of years that had passed since the Scorching. Dragons had poured it into a myth, covering it like layers of treestuff, keeping the memory that a human had done something terrible but wiping away the details of what had happened to their eggs. Perhaps over the years, dragons hadn't believed that humans could steal so many, or that humans could have built a society this advanced, or that humans could be dangerous at all.

And the humans had changed it, too, if the story in the cave paintings was their version. Those paintings hadn't shown the cause of the Scorching. They hadn't included any greedy humans stealing eggs or torturing newly hatched dragons. In the human version, the dragons attacked them unprovoked. Luna remembered the little drawings of dragons eating humans and burning everything. The humans had painted themselves as victims, dragons as barbaric monsters.

But it was the other way around, Luna thought angrily. *Bullfrog was actually right. The humans* did *start it.*

The shadow rolled them into the next moment, leaving them standing atop a towering stepped temple, under the three moons, in the center of a city that wasn't Cottonmouth's. Luna guessed they were on the other side of the mountains, somewhere in the north given the cold temperatures. The humans below them wore heavy furs over snow-white wool wrappings. They screamed in a different language from Cottonmouth's, but they burned just as quickly.

This time there were ten dragons attacking together, burning every corner of the city.

And this time, Dusky didn't hide his face. He pushed his snout through Luna's talons, peeking out to watch.

"I'm glad they're burning those humans," he said softly but fiercely. "I want them to burn every single human so they're all gone forever."

"Dusky, this happened a long time ago," Luna said. "And, listen . . . I know you're upset about the dragon eggs. I am, too. It's awful. But I still don't think killing *every* human would be the right response."

"I do!" he said. "They deserve it!"

Luna understood that. There were days she felt that way about the HiveWings. When dragons — or humans — did something unforgivable, shouldn't they be punished? Shouldn't the punishment be equally as terrible? After the HiveWings tried to wipe out the LeafWings, didn't they deserve to be exterminated in response? And if the humans stole the dragons' children, shouldn't the dragons . . . didn't it make sense to . . .

But she couldn't finish that thought. She couldn't look down at the burning city, all these hundreds of humans, and really *believe* it was right, even after what she'd seen them do to the newly hatched dragonet.

She couldn't think of Wren and Axolotl and wish they'd never existed. Now that she'd met them, she believed that some humans were worth saving.

Just like, now that she knew Cricket, she couldn't wish for the destruction of all HiveWings.

Maybe Sundew is right, that SilkWings are too soft, too forgiving.

But I don't forgive them. I just . . . want the punishment to fit, and to go where it's deserved.

I don't want to be one of these dragons, burning everything and hurting everyone for revenge.

With an awful lurch, she wondered if anyone had saved the dragon eggs in the human cities. Perhaps the dragons thought their dragonets were already dead. In their rage, they didn't realize they were also destroying any hope of finding them again.

Luna shivered.

The burning city faded, and she was on another beach, but it was still nighttime — a different nighttime; the moons were in different phases now — and it was raining.

A wet, trembling group of bedraggled humans were gathered by the water, climbing into things that looked like large wooden bowls, floating on the surface of the ocean. Luna had seen them in the cave paintings — the crescents that carried the humans across the sea. Several of the humans had long sticks with flat ends that they used to push the bowls forward, out into the waves.

Other humans were watching the sky, armed with swords and spears that Luna thought would not be much help against the fiery vengeance of the dragons she'd seen. The humans were probably more protected by the rain than by those tiny, sharp things.

One human, in a long cloak with the hood pulled up, stepped into the largest bowl and turned back, reaching as a box was passed to him. Luna caught a glimpse of thick black gloves, and she darted closer to see his face. Yes, it was Cottonmouth. He must be the one leading them all across the ocean in those paintings. Him and this box.

Luna was sure the box held a dragon egg. The largest one, she guessed, the one she'd seen him bring into his cage room. Even after all this, after all the burned cities and death and destruction, he hadn't given up on his plan.

What is wrong with you? she thought furiously at him. *If you're so clever, couldn't you imagine a better world instead of a worse one? Why did you work so hard on something that would cause so much misery? For power? Couldn't you have put all that energy into making peace with other humans instead and left the dragons alone?*

Don't you realize you destroyed your own world?

Cottonmouth looked up at the cliffs looming over the

beach. "Any sign of my brother?" he asked one of the humans near him.

The human shook her head. "Sorry, sir. No word from Coyote since he rode to warn the southern villages."

Cottonmouth pressed his lips together. "Then we leave without him." He strode to the front of the floating crescent and sat down, tucking the box between his knees and setting his hands flat on top of it. Other humans scurried to get in behind him and push off from the shore.

Not quite the heroic story of the cave paintings, Luna noticed. He wasn't standing alone, nobly leading them across the ocean. He was crouched, filthy and wet, muttering to the box as other people did all the work to get him out to sea.

But he did have a lot of other humans with him. Luna stepped back to watch as they all paddled away into the surging waves.

"Maybe they'll drown on the way," Dusky said hopefully.

Luna knew at least some of them would make it. If the cave paintings were right, Cottonmouth would be one of them, still carrying that box.

"Is there more to this story?" she asked the sky. "Are we almost done?" It was depressing, being trapped in Cottonmouth's spiteful life, at the end of a whole world.

The shadow flickered over them again and lifted, leaving them in a sunlit jungle. They were standing beside a sheer, rocky cliff face pockmarked with caves, and all around them the muggy air buzzed with insects.

Luna turned slowly. There were so many *trees* here. Could

this possibly be Pantala? Was this what it looked like before Queen Wasp and the Tree Wars?

Through a gap in the vines, she glimpsed a huge, sparkling stretch of water. It was still and calm, not roiling with waves, so if it wasn't the ocean . . . could it be Lake Scorpion?

Voices approached, chatting quietly in Human. As Luna turned toward them, suddenly a figure surged up from the ground very close to her talons. He'd been so hidden by the undergrowth she'd nearly stepped on him, not that he would have noticed.

"Stop!" the figure shouted. "Don't move!"

Luna found herself freezing along with the two humans who'd just stepped into the glade. They glanced at each other, then back at the man flapping his hands frantically at them. He was wrapped in leaves and an odd leaf hat, but Luna realized that under all of that was Cottonmouth.

"Sorry, sir," said one of the humans. "We were going to check the caves for a place to hide."

"One of the night guards thought she saw a dragon fly overhead," said the other. "She said maybe they followed us, and not even crossing an ocean will keep us safe from them."

"She's wrong; there are no dragons here. But it doesn't matter," Cottonmouth said, one of his hands shaking as he pointed at the others. "I've found the answer. I know what to do. I know how to get the dragons to bow down to us."

He sounded insane to Luna, but the humans heroically managed not to look too skeptical. After a moment, one of them politely said, "Oh?"

"This plant." Cottonmouth crouched on the jungle floor and stared intently at something. "Look. It takes over the minds of insects. It *controls* them. These ants will carry the seeds to a high place and then die so the plant can grow out of their bodies. These caterpillars will go wherever it tells them to, swallow the seeds, and then feed the plant with their own body as it grows. Isn't that magnificent? The plant spreads and survives by ruling other creatures. By dominating them. It's perfect."

Now the humans did look at each other again; one looked worried, the other disturbed.

"That's . . ." one of them started, trailing off.

"Unnerving," finished the other. "Sounds like a pretty creepy plant. Sir."

Cottonmouth made an impatient gesture. "Don't be absurd. I can make it work on dragons. It's exactly what I need." He snatched up a metal implement and began digging up one of the plants, an eerie glint in his eyes.

Luna felt Dusky bury his head in her scales again as the flicker came and went, and now they were in a cave lit by oil lamps. The walls were rough, and the stone beneath her talons was damp. Out in the tunnels, she could hear clanging and muffled shouts, as though the humans were busy building or digging or whatever busy thing they were up to. The air smelled faintly of rotting greenery and the place was a mess, but something about it still reminded her of the cold, smooth room with all the cages.

Perhaps that was partly Cottonmouth, stepping briskly between the piles of vines and pots of dirt. Or maybe it was the small creatures trapped in makeshift cages around the room. Most of them were lizards of various kinds, but there was a monkey, too, and a long-feathered blue-green bird.

And there was the dragon egg. Luna caught her breath.

A small crack had appeared near the top of the egg. The shell was edging toward translucent, and below the surface, she could see movement. It was almost ready to hatch.

"Running out of time," Cottonmouth muttered. "Why didn't that one work? This one was interesting." He tapped a sheaf of papers and bent over one of the chameleons, which was lying still and listless on a large, red-veined leaf. "Hmmm." He poked it with his writing implement, but the chameleon just blinked. "Get up," Cottonmouth snapped. *"Move."*

The chameleon did not move.

Cottonmouth muttered a few curses and squinted at the dragon egg, then hurried over to the largest pot, where several breath of evil vines rose from the dirt and twined together.

The egg rocked slightly, and another crack appeared around the middle. Cottonmouth hissed and sprinted across the room. He returned with the same kind of metal choker stick that Luna had seen used on the other newly hatched dragonet. She watched him tug on those huge black gloves, lift the stick, and prowl closer to the egg.

"I don't like this part," a voice said suddenly, high and clear, and all at once, the makeshift lab swirled away, leaving Luna and Dusky in a featureless gray mist.

Luna glanced at Dusky, who stared back at her with wide eyes.

"Who said that?" she asked cautiously. There was no response. "Hello?"

"It was the little dragon," Dusky whispered.

"The little dragon?" Luna echoed. "The one in the egg?"

The mist lifted abruptly, and they were back in the throne room. Luna had a weird moment of vertigo — was this real? were they back in reality, out of the hallucination? — as she realized that it was the same, but different.

No plants covered the floor or blocked the archway. The throne and the columns were there, looking newly chiseled and smooth, but no one sat on the throne, and no plant grew from the base of it either. This room seemed brand-new, untouched by the rustling terror Luna associated with it. Now that she could see the floor, she realized it was dirt, not stone as she might have expected. Her claws sank into it, and she was surprised by how soft and rich it was.

"This will do," Cottonmouth said, sweeping into the space and nearly walking straight through Luna before she jumped out of the way. Three humans crowded in behind him. They each carried something: a pot overflowing with vines, a bag that clanked ominously, and a large wooden box with holes in the top that was making some very worrying noises. Luna had an awful feeling about what was in there.

"All is as you ordered, my lord," said one of the humans, setting down the bag and gesturing at the room.

"Is this really going to work, sir?" another human said reverently. She was the one carrying the box, and she lowered it to the ground in the center of the room with gentle caution.

"Of course." Cottonmouth waved one hand. He was dressed regally again, in head-to-toe robes embroidered with silver, plus the gold medallions and the feathers in his hair. "But I must not be disturbed. You will stay at the top of the abyss and ensure that no one comes down here while I work. If I need anything, I will speak through you."

"Yes, my lord," said the first two. The third human, who had not yet spoken, set down the pot of vines without a word. He looked slightly different from the others, more like the ones Luna had seen stealing the sea dragon eggs. His hair was a pale shade of lime green.

Cottonmouth narrowed his eyes at the silent human. A moment later, that human jerked upright and turned to face Cottonmouth. His eyes had an eerie white glaze over them, and his gaze was stiff, petrified in a blank expression. He awkwardly fell to his knees, bowed his head, and said, "That's better."

Cottonmouth smiled coldly. The human slumped as if he'd been released. He staggered to his feet and backed out of the room, bowing as he went. The other two bowed as well and followed.

"Yes," Cottonmouth mused, looking around. "This will do. A perfect place to finally get what I've always wanted." He took the pot over to the throne and transplanted the vines into the dirt there, patting them down like a gardener who actually cared about his seedlings.

At last, he stood up and stalked over to the box. He unlatched the top and threw it aside.

A small dragon head popped out and hissed at him.

She didn't look like any of the ten tribes Luna had met — or rather, she looked like a combination of a few of them. Her orange scales could have come from a HiveWing or a SkyWing, but her two green wings curved like leaves, and something in the shape of her eyes reminded Luna of Queen Glory.

"Don't you hiss at me, lizard," Cottonmouth growled. He unhooked a chain from inside the box and tugged her out; the other end wound around her neck.

"He calls her Lizard," Dusky said softly. "But she doesn't like that. She wants a real name, one that comes from dragons, not humans."

"I can speak for myself," the dragonet said, in Dragon, looking straight at Dusky.

— CHAPTER 17 —

For a brief frozen moment, everything in the room stopped breathing.

"No, you can't," Cottonmouth growled at the dragon in Human, breaking the spell. "Stop interrupting. Our guests asked for our origin story, and I haven't had a chance to show my genius to anyone since the last Guardian, so you shut up."

"I won't," Lizard snapped at him. "I have been stuck with this story and all these memories for five thousand years and it's boring and I hate it and I hate you."

"Well," he snarled, "as you well know, the feeling is mutual."

"It is *not*, though," she said, "because *you* did this to us, so I am entitled to hate you *way more* than you hate me!"

Movement beyond them caught Luna's eye, and she realized that the vines were growing visibly, sprouting new tendrils and starting to climb the base of the throne.

"Is that supposed to happen?" she wondered. "I mean, did they really grow that fast?"

"Yes," Lizard said venomously. "Stupid weed."

"Oh, wow," Luna said. "You really can hear us now? This part is actually happening, like, right now?"

Lizard rolled her eyes and stomped over to Dusky, dragging Cottonmouth behind her. "We gave you ours. Now give me your memories," she ordered. She reached out and tapped Dusky on the head with one of her claws.

"Um," he said. "I . . . don't want to? And I don't know how."

"You just say yes," she said impatiently. "When I ask for them, you say yes, and then I can see them. Give me them."

"No," he said, a little more firmly.

She scowled at him. "You're doing it wrong!"

"Why *would* he give you his memories?" Luna asked.

"Because I want them!" Lizard exploded. "And I am the most miserable dragon who ever lived, and then died, and then had to half-live, half-be-dead forever all stuck together with a hateful human and a desperate weed, so I should get to have anything I want! Give them!"

Dusky widened his eyes at Luna.

"But how did that happen?" Luna asked. She looked up at the throne, and the vines slowly curling around it. "What's the end of the story?"

"What happened is *he* was stupid and accidentally let the plant get us both," Lizard hissed. She pointed at the throne, and the scene around them shifted.

For a gray, falling moment, Luna could see the plants again all around her, and the horrible tableau of the vines growing through the human and dragonet, and then the newer room shivered back into place. The sensation of vines wrapped tightly around her wrists and neck lingered, though, like the ghost of a strangling.

"No," said Cottonmouth, "what happened is *that lizard* was insufferable and rebellious and ruined everything." He inhaled and exhaled slowly. "But who cares? I made it work. So what if this meat shell couldn't move anymore." He waved dismissively at his body. "I couldn't walk or climb the abyss or go outside, but I soon realized that with this plant I could take anyone, be anywhere I wanted. I could be a thousand different creatures at once. The whole continent was mine. I was emperor at last, of even more than I'd expected."

"Ha! Emperor of bees and seagulls," Lizard snorted. "There were no dragons here then. No one anywhere except your little band of shivering cave dwellers, and you kept them scared so they wouldn't go outside."

Cottonmouth curled his fists. "I kept them safe. Otherwise, when the dragons came again, they would have died just like everyone did last time. Dragons," he spat. "Burning my vines, destroying my seeds, cutting me back and taking *my* continent. Ruining everything like they always do!"

"This old whine," Lizard said, rolling her eyes. "You poor human. Can't summon a cloud of possessed bats anymore, what a tragedy."

"I should have wiped out your whole species from the start," Cottonmouth said grimly.

"You should have left us alone!" Luna cried. "The Scorching wouldn't have happened if you hadn't stolen all those eggs!"

"That's where you're wrong," Cottonmouth said, swinging

around to glower at her. "Dragons are dangerous by nature. They're too big and powerful. They would have crawled out of their caves and attacked us and taken our land eventually. I knew we had to find a way to control them before they became too much of a threat."

"Well, great job," Luna said. "Seems like that worked out really well for you."

He glared at her, drawing himself up and twitching the chain with Lizard on the end of it. "You seem to have forgotten that I am winning this war. I have three tribes of dragons in my grasp, and soon I will reach across the ocean and take all the ones on my home continent as well. Thanks to you and your friends, I'll figure out how to get there. I'll get Sundew and spread my plant across the whole world. I'll inject myself into every brain until *every dragon* and *every human* belong to me. You will all be my fingers, my little playthings, nothing more."

Luna paused.

I'll get Sundew.

He said "I'll get Sundew" — which means he doesn't have her yet. She's still safe from him, wherever she is.

Luna felt a wave of relief. As long as Sundew was free, there was hope. There was still someone out there who could save Blue and Swordtail.

"Were those all your memories we just saw?" she asked. "They couldn't be; you weren't in all of them."

"Some of them were lifted from humans I absorbed long ago," he said. "Ones that escaped to this continent with me and then offered themselves to my service."

Yikes, Luna thought. *Let's just breeze right past the word "absorbed" there.*

"I thought the plant couldn't get into our minds," she said slowly. "Cricket said Wasp controls the HiveWings' bodies but can't hear their thoughts or see their memories."

"That is true," he said with a satisfied smile. "I never told her she could get those. She's a clever instrument, but it never even occurred to her to try burrowing into her puppets' brains."

"OK, ew," Lizard interjected. She wrestled the chain off her neck and threw it on the floor. "Why do you insist on phrasing everything in the *grossest possible way*? It doesn't even work like that. He can't just dig them out. It's like I told you; one of us has to ask, and the dragon or human or scorpion or slug or whatever has to agree to let us in. It's not *easy*. Mostly they say no, and there's nothing he can do about it, ha ha."

"My human worshippers tend to be more amenable than my dragon toys," Cottonmouth said, tapping his fingers together. "But I'm about to have hundreds of SilkWings, and they are a weak, fearful tribe. I'm sure most of them will say yes without a moment of resistance."

Luna hoped that wasn't true. Her tribe was gentle, but that didn't mean they couldn't be strong. Blue was the gentlest, sweetest dragon she knew, but he would put up a fight when it mattered; she was sure of it. They were like strands of silk. Soft and insubstantial on their own, maybe, but when you wove them together, they could support hundreds of dragons.

"I don't understand how this works," she said, turning toward Lizard. "If you're all stuck together — do *you* control anything? Does the plant? Or is that human the one doing everything?"

"The plant just wants to spread as far as it can," Lizard said, wrinkling her nose. "It doesn't have thoughts, exactly, and it can't *do* anything on its own. But I feel it inside me all the time, wriggling and starving and grasping for any hold it can get, any scrap of dirt in the world where it can slither another root. It's more alive than we are, but it uses our brains to scheme and plan and spread, and to control anything smarter than it is, which is most everything."

"*My* brain," Cottonmouth corrected her smugly. "You are pointless here."

A flare of rage seized Lizard's face, and she darted toward him, lashing out with her claws. A long, sharp stick appeared in his hands. He jabbed her with it, knocking her back toward Dusky, and she tumbled into a ball and lay there growling.

"I control some things," Lizard said, breathing in short gasps. "I got myself a new toy." She flicked her tail at Dusky.

"That was an accident." Cottonmouth hung Lizard's chain on a loop on the wall, folded his arms, and frowned at Dusky. "And a distraction. We should probably kill it right now."

"NOOOOO!" Lizard shrieked. "He's MINE, MINE, MINE! You're a hateful bag of worms! If you hurt him, I'm going to let her go!" She pointed at Luna.

"I don't need your tantrums right now," Cottonmouth hissed. "We are *this close* to taking over the world, brat!"

"I WANT them!" Lizard yelled, stamping one of her feet.

"I want to play with them! You go stuff your nostrils with mushrooms!"

Cottonmouth rubbed his eyebrows, grimacing. "*If you can shut up and stay out of my way,*" he growled, "you can keep them. *For now.* But I have a lot of work to do, so they had better not be a problem."

"They won't be," Lizard said, suddenly calm again. "Go away and do your boring things."

Cottonmouth snorted and strode across the throne room. He climbed a set of steps carved into the side of the base, settled himself on the throne, rested his hands on his knees, and closed his eyes.

There was a pause. Lizard glared at the oblivious human, switching her tail furiously back and forth across the floor.

"What's happening?" Luna asked.

"He's checking on all his creatures." Lizard rolled her eyes. "He thinks he's so great, controlling a thousand bodies at once, but it gets way harder the more there are, especially when they're smarter than, like, mice or centipedes. Usually he has Queen Wasp helping him, but she only manages the ones she injected, so he has to control all these new SilkWings and LeafWings himself. If he doesn't keep his boot pressing on them all the time, they try to escape. I mean, they can't, but they'll try, and then he'll have to focus on them and fly them back. It makes him tired and grouchy, and it's very funny to watch."

"How are you able to speak Dragon?" Luna asked. "And

why do we understand him and the people in the story who were speaking Human?"

"I learned it from the dragons he's taken over the years," Lizard said, as if that were so very obviously obvious. "And you're in our mindspace now, so you see and hear and understand anything we want you to."

"Mindspace?" Dusky echoed.

Lizard waved impatiently at the walls. "The place we are stuck. Where our minds go so we can talk to each other. We can make it look however we like."

Luna glanced at the cold, empty walls of the throne room. "You both can? If you have a choice, why would you make it look like the place where you're actually stuck?"

"I suppose we could do this instead," Lizard said in a bored voice, and suddenly they were standing in a SilkWing playground, outside a school that said *Weaver Hall* on it, with a balcony open to the clear blue savanna sky off to their right. The only incongruous part was Cottonmouth, who was now sitting in the same position with the same expression at the top of a slide.

Dusky yelped with surprise. "This is my school! My playground!"

"Boring, though," Lizard said. "It's not real and I can't *really* play here or have real friends, so what is even the point."

Dusky gave Lizard a wide-eyed look. "How do you know this place? *Did* you get my memories?"

"Not yet," she snapped. "You have to *let* me have them,

you bozo. But I've seen this place through HiveWing eyes. I saw *you* here. I used to watch you whenever I wanted to."

"That's heebie-jeebie," Dusky said, frowning at her.

"That *gives* me the heebie-jeebies," Luna corrected him, and he transferred his frown to her with an extra dose of "what on earth are you talking about?" on top.

"So you can see through the eyes of anyone who's been infected by the plant?" Luna asked Lizard. "Like . . . right now, you could jump into someone and see what they see?"

"Yesss," she said in that same bored tone. "Fine. Who."

"His name is Swordtail," Luna said hopefully. "He's a SilkWing, in Cicada Hive right now. With my brother, Blue?"

"Hmmmm," Lizard said. She shot Luna a sly, sideways look. "If you give me your memories, I'll know what he looks like, and it'll be easy to find him."

"I don't think I should do that," Luna said. "Not if that means Cottonmouth can have them, too. Besides, you definitely know Blue and Swordtail; they've been part of all the trouble lately."

"Yeah, I do," Lizard said, dropping the act. "I've never seen Cottonmouth so angry. I hoped he would have some kind of apoplexy attack and die." She closed her eyes and put one claw to her temple.

"What would happen to you if he did?" Luna asked.

"Knowing my luck, it would be too much happiness for me to handle, and I would probably immediately also die, of joy," Lizard said. "Here they are."

Luna felt dizzy from the sudden transition to another new place. It took her a moment to recognize the market in Cicada Hive; she'd never seen it from up on one of the guard balconies before. The murals and posters of Queen Wasp still loomed overhead, and the flamesilk lanterns glowed as they always had, but an eerie quiet filled the cavernous space. All the shops along the outer wall were closed and barricaded — from here, Luna could see the empty windows of The Sugar Dream, where she and Blue had gone to get honey drops on her Metamorphosis Day.

The last normal day we'll maybe ever have.

Instead of busy stalls and bustling shoppers, the center of the market held hundreds of quiet, seated SilkWings. Their heads were bowed, and their wings were folded down. Several had tiny wingless dragonets sitting between their front talons, leaning against their legs. A few SilkWings were walking between the dragons, handing out dried seaweed and packets of nuts tied up in twists of silk.

Beside Luna on the balcony, Lizard flicked her tail, staring down at the dragons below. Dusky stood on her other side, clutching the railing nervously. Across the Hive, Luna could see Cottonmouth sitting on another balcony, eyes still closed.

"Are you inside Swordtail right now?" Luna asked.

"*Pfft,*" Lizard scoffed. "No, I'm in a HiveWing. It would be stupid to jump into him because then you'd only see me. No, your dopey dreamboat is down there." She pointed to the exit across from them, which led to the spiraling tunnels that connected the Hive levels.

Standing in the entryway, holding a spear, looking burly and blank, was Swordtail. And right next to him, looking much less burly but equally blank, was Blue.

Luna gasped. It was bad enough to know they were possessed by the queen — or by Cottonmouth and Lizard and the breath of evil, however that worked — but it was heartbreaking to see it.

"Swordtail," she breathed, leaning over the edge. He looked thinner, and so tired, but so perfectly himself. Even zombie Swordtail looked like he might tell a funny story or start laughing at any moment. It wasn't completely gone, the spark in his eyes or the tiny smile at the corner of his mouth.

Unless Luna was imagining things from a distance. But she kind of had to so that she wouldn't fall apart.

"Don't bother flying over there. He can't hear you," Lizard said, guessing Luna's thoughts. "Not unless I come along and make this HiveWing say whatever you want to say, which would freak him out and be so funny. Imagine a HiveWing guard suddenly proclaiming, 'Oooohhh, Swordtail, I looooooooove you, look at your dreeeeeeamy snout.' Ha! This is a great idea; let's do it."

"Yeesh," Luna said with a shudder. "Maybe as a last resort. Can't you bring him into this mindspace, like the two of us?" She gestured to Dusky.

Lizard sighed for an unnaturally long time. "I *could*," she said finally. "But it would be so exhausting. It's easier when you're already in the same room as me. He's, like, all the way across the continent! Bleh. Not worth it."

"Please?" Luna said. "I just want to talk to him for a moment. To let him know I'm all right."

This earned her a skeptical, assessing look from the small dragon. "You're really not, though," Lizard pointed out. "You're trapped in vines in an ancient throne room at the bottom of the abyss, and you've been infected by the plant, and you're definitely going to die down here, and then your bones will decompose and feed our roots. Won't he find that pretty depressing?"

Luna had no idea what to say to that. She hadn't quite accepted the idea that she was really trapped in vines or even infected by the breath of evil. She felt like she was really here, not really there. She felt entirely herself, not possessed by anyone else.

But she knew these weren't really her talons. She knew this was only her mind, floating in the weird vision space that Lizard and Cottonmouth had created. She had been fiercely avoiding the mental image of her body trapped in the vines.

"Also, I'm not sure we could even reach your brother to get him here," Lizard went on, in such a "this is a totally normal conversation" voice that Luna almost wanted to throw her off the balcony. "He's buried himself way down; even when we're not inside him, he barely reacts to anything. Swordtail is making sure he eats. I thought Blue was boring *before*, but now he's like a piece of *furniture*. Pretty but super-boring furniture."

Lizard sighed. "All these dragons are boring. Look at how sad and mopey and pathetic they are. I thought everything would be more fun once we had some shimmery SilkWings to play with, but instead it's going to be exactly the same."

"That's really mean," Dusky said out of nowhere.

Lizard gave him a surprised look. Not an "oh no! I didn't realize I was being a jerk!" kind of surprise; more like "oh, you talk and have opinions? That's disappointing" kind of surprise.

"Yeah, I agree," Luna said. "Really mean. Don't you feel bad for these dragons?"

"Bad for THEM?!" Lizard suddenly yelled. "BAD FOR THEM? Are you KIDDING me?"

Her rage shot them back into the throne room. Luna felt her real body slam sideways into a wall, vines tightening around her throat. Her vision flickered from the mindspace to the real room and its swarm of tendrils, then back to the empty room again.

"Don't hurt her!" Dusky shouted. He tried to grab Lizard, but she kicked him away from her and hissed, flaring her wings.

"Why would I ever feel bad for anyone else?" Lizard shrieked. "*Those* dragons can fly and have friends and breathe real air and eat actual food and have THEIR OWN THOUGHTS WITH NOBODY LISTENING! They aren't trapped with a narcissistic monster *human* for all of eternity! *My* life is the most unfair and the most sad! THEY SHOULD FEEL BAD FOR *ME*!"

"I do," Luna managed to choke out as the real throne room appeared again, looming around her like rustling gray death.

The pressure on her neck lessened. She took in a gasping

breath, and then she was back in the false, mindspace throne room, facing Lizard and Dusky.

"You agree my life is the worst?" Lizard asked her suspiciously. Luna nodded, trying to breathe her racing heartbeat back to normal.

"Can't we get you out?" Dusky asked the furious dragonet. Lizard lashed her tail and narrowed her eyes at him. "Is there a way to set you free?"

A low chuckle came from the human on the throne, and Lizard shot a glare at him, too.

"We're only alive, if you can call it that, because of the plant," she said. "We'd all die if we were separated. Anyway, I don't need to be set free! Here I get to make *his* life worse." She stuck out her tongue at Cottonmouth.

"You are insignificant to me," he said coldly, without opening his eyes.

"He can say whatever he wants, but I can feel what he's feeling," Lizard said. "I *torment* him, just *existing* alongside his brain. Having a *dragon* clawing around in his head. Listening to me *talk all day*, and he can't do *anything* about it. All this power and all these creatures, but he can never get away from me and how much I hate him."

"Perhaps you could not be a brat for one solitary shining minute of your life," said Cottonmouth. He stood up and shook out his robes. "I think Luna would enjoy a little show, don't you?"

"Ooh, ooh," Lizard said. "Do we get to watch all your stupid memories again? Could we be so blessed?"

"If only you had any interesting memories of your own," he said dispassionately. "Oh, that's right. You died before making any."

Lizard snapped her jaw shut and clenched her talons.

"It's time for a lovely experiment," Cottonmouth said, coming down the steps from the throne, rubbing his hands together. "I know we're all wondering whether the mind control will work on dragons from — what is it you call my old home? The Distant Kingdoms? Let's find out, shall we?"

He snapped his fingers.

The room folded away, and a new scene flickered up around them. They were inside a Hive, Luna realized by the patterns on the walls. The view out the windows also told her they were on one of the highest levels of this Hive, and near a coastline. The savanna was gold and rust-colored in the sunset light. A flight of swallows swept in arcs around the sky, like in a tapestry Luna had woven for art class long ago.

Queen Wasp sat coiled on a polished obsidian throne. Lizard stood on one side of her, Cottonmouth on the other.

And crouched in front of them, bound with breath of evil vines, were Tsunami, Pineapple, and Qibli.

——— CHAPTER 18 ———

"Oh no," Luna breathed. She darted forward, but none of the three Pyrrhian dragons reacted to her presence, and when she reached for their talons, hers drifted through them like she was made of smoke.

"We're not really here," Lizard said almost pityingly. "Except him; he's inside one of Wasp's attendants." She flicked her tail at Cottonmouth, who was holding his head in a weird birdlike way, tilting it back and forth and sideways to glare at the prisoners.

"Can you do something?" Luna begged, crouching beside Lizard. "Can't you take over control and set them free?"

"No," Lizard said sulkily. "And even if I could, why would I? I don't care about those dragons. They have nothing to do with me."

"They're my friends," Luna said.

"So?" Lizard yawned, showing off bright white little teeth. "*I* don't have any friends, remember? Besides, maybe they'll give me *their* memories."

Luna turned back to her friends, feeling a wave of despair

crash down around her. She couldn't just watch this happen. There had to be *something* she could do.

"At lassst," Queen Wasp hissed, ticking her long claws against the bowl she was holding. It was made of white porcelain, and when Luna edged closer, she could see a layer of green residue at the bottom. "I have my power again. Time to add to my army, starting with these unusual, hideous worms." She set down the bowl, and a vicious-looking stinger slid out of the end of her tail.

"Wait," Cottonmouth said.

Wasp whipped her head around to glare at him. "No one gave you permission to speak, Malachite."

"It's not Malachite," Cottonmouth said harshly. "It's me. I'm here to speak to these dragons. Stand down, or I will make you cut your own throat."

Luna realized that the queen and everyone else in the real world still saw Malachite the dragon. Only she, Dusky, and Lizard saw Cottonmouth in his place.

The queen's wings buzzed, an almost-inaudible vibration in the air as they rubbed together.

After a long moment, she said, "You can't do that."

"I can," he said. "I don't need you anymore. Shall we find out what I can make you do?"

Queen Wasp bared her teeth and flicked one talon toward the prisoners. "Very well. Speak to them if you must."

"Unbind their mouths," Cottonmouth ordered one of the guards.

Wasp twitched slightly, her claws flexing. "That seems unwise."

"I need answers from them," Cottonmouth said. "They won't do anything stupid. They know how outnumbered they are."

The guard looked from Wasp to Cottonmouth, and then the white film slid over his eyes and he hurried to the prisoners to pull the bindings off their snouts.

Cottonmouth stepped forward, and the Pyrrhian dragons looked up at him: Tsunami defiant, Pineapple pale greenish-blue with anxiety, Qibli managing a mask that was cheerful, curious, and faintly bored at the same time.

"Tell me where Sundew is," Cottonmouth commanded.

"We'll never help you catch her!" Tsunami snarled, at the same moment as Qibli said, "Who?"

There was a brief pause, and then Tsunami said, "I mean . . . who? Right. Who? No idea who you're talking about. Never heard of a sun-whatsit."

"Good save," Qibli said to her.

"Did she go all the way to the Distant Kingdoms to get you?" Cottonmouth asked, his eyes glittering. "Are there more of you?"

"I'm told one is quite enough of me," Qibli said. "It's a vicious lie, though. I think five hundred of me would be adorable, actually."

"Three MOONS," Tsunami said. "I cannot imagine anything more exhausting."

"Pineapple agrees with me," Qibli said, nudging the RainWing's tail with his own. "He's survived a lot already. He's never even used all his skills against another dragon before. He can handle however many Qiblis life throws at him."

"I *am* thinking about throwing you at *something*," Tsunami muttered.

Pineapple blinked and gave Qibli a small sideways smile, and some of the green faded out of his scales. He took a deep breath, and shimmers of purple appeared around his ears.

Queen Wasp stirred slightly behind Cottonmouth. "There are more of them. Someone stole the invisible one."

Moon! Luna thought. *Sundew and Lynx must have rescued her!*

She wondered if there was any chance the other three were here in this throne room right now, invisible. Maybe they would swoop in and rescue everyone! There were a lot of HiveWings lurking around along the edges of the walls; that would be a problem. But maybe Sundew could smash some poisonous flowers into their noses and knock them out. That would be very awesome.

"*Was* that Sundew?" Cottonmouth asked the prisoners. "Was she here, in this very Hive, and did the incompetent dragon behind me let her get away?"

Qibli and Tsunami exchanged glances. "I feel like . . . you're not actually talking to us anymore?" Qibli offered.

"*You* took that SilkWing guard off to do something else," Wasp spat at Cottonmouth. "My HiveWings aren't equipped to watch for invisible dragons. It's *your* fault."

Cottonmouth suddenly vanished from his spot in front of the prisoners, leaving a bewildered-looking orange HiveWing with red wings in his wake. The HiveWing blinked, reaching for the spectacles on his snout, as the human reappeared where Wasp had been sitting. Cottonmouth reached up and clamped one hand around his own throat.

A brief, silent struggle played out on the throne.

"This is always weird," Lizard said conversationally to Luna and Dusky. "When he's punishing someone, he has to jump into them to do it, so inside the mindspace it looks like he's doing it to himself. He'll stop when it starts to really hurt, though. He's a total coward about feeling any pain."

The HiveWing that Cottonmouth had been in a moment before — Malachite, Luna remembered — looked down at the prisoners, then back at the throne. A moment later, he was crouching beside Tsunami, trying to slice through the vines with his claws.

"What's happening?" he whispered to her. "Do you know Katydid? How long have I — how long has it been since —"

"Cottonmouth," Lizard said in a bored voice. "You're getting distracted again."

The human glanced over at Malachite, spat out a curse, and let the queen go. She reappeared on the throne as he jumped back into Malachite. The HiveWing barely had time to whisper *"no"* under his breath, and then he vanished, and all Luna could see was Cottonmouth again, standing over Tsunami with a disgusted expression.

"See?" Lizard said to Luna. "Look how mad he is. So funny."

Tsunami strained at the vines, but Malachite hadn't managed to saw through enough of them for her to break free.

"Let's get this over with," Cottonmouth said. "Before you let any more of them escape."

From the throne, Wasp glared at him with deep, glittering eyes. Thin trails of dark greenish blood oozed down her neck from where her own claws had dug into her scales.

"I have your permission to go ahead now, do I?" she snarled.

"Yes," Cottonmouth said brusquely. "Start with the annoying one."

"Start with *me*," Tsunami growled. "If you dare."

"Hey, hang on," Qibli said. "Who else do you think he meant?" He grinned at her.

Queen Wasp slithered off her throne and stepped toward them, raising her tail stinger high.

No, no, no, Luna thought. *Sundew, where are you?* "Lizard," she pleaded. "Please do something! Please help!"

"Stop bothering me!" Lizard snapped at her.

"I'll give you my memories if you help set them free," Luna blurted.

Lizard's eyes narrowed, calculating.

Suddenly Qibli shouted, "Pineapple, now! The queen!" opened his mouth, and roared fire in Cottonmouth's face. Cottonmouth shrieked and vanished, leaving Malachite writhing on the ground trying to beat out the flames. Beside Qibli, Pineapple's jaws hinged open farther than anything Luna had ever seen a dragon do, and a black spray of liquid shot from his top fangs. It splattered all over Wasp's face, hissing like acid against her scales.

Chaos erupted: Wasp screaming, HiveWings shouting and crashing into one another, the fire spreading from Malachite to the woven carpets on the floor to the tapestries and tree-stuff of the walls. Dusky bolted over to Luna and climbed onto her back, burying his face in her neck. Through the rising smoke, Luna saw Cottonmouth flicker into one HiveWing guard, then another; one moment they would all snap into synchronized motion, eyes white, and then, a moment later, they'd fall out again, stumbling and blinking.

"Oh, this is *perfect*," Lizard cried gleefully. "He controls those HiveWings through Wasp, but when he tries to reach them through her, he has to feel her face melting off! Ha ha, amazing!"

Luna saw Qibli roll under Wasp's flailing wings, a heartbeat away from the stinger she was whipping in all directions. He came up on the other side, stabbed his own tail barb into the nearest guard, and wrestled the spear out of her talons as she collapsed. Still wrapped in vines, he ducked and rolled back to Pineapple, who was staring at Wasp with an expression of blank shock.

Luna knew exactly how he felt, and she wished she could shake him and hug him and shout, "Pineapple, you had to! She deserved it! Stop feeling bad about it, and escape right now!" She wished she could grab the spear from Qibli and cut the vines for them. She wished she could do ANYTHING HELPFUL AT ALL.

On the other side of the room, Tsunami was roaring and swinging her tail around, smacking away guards as they tried to approach her. The flames were licking toward her talons, but when she tried to get to Qibli and Pineapple, she nearly ran her face into Wasp's tail stinger and had to jump back in a hurry.

Qibli sawed awkwardly at the vines around Pineapple with the tip of the spear. Luna saw him glance at the trail of fire spreading across the carpet; with a shiver of horror, she thought, *No! Qibli, don't burn the vines!* But he turned away from them, so either he remembered about the smoke on his own or he didn't want to risk burning Pineapple.

Wasp staggered back to her throne, clutching her face. She flickered — Cottonmouth, Wasp, Cottonmouth, Wasp, and then, for a moment, Cottonmouth was there, his human face contorted in agony. The HiveWing guards all froze, and their eyes went white-marble-white.

Oh no. Luna wrung her talons together. *He's going to fight through the pain. He can't let them escape.*

Lizard appeared at her side and looked up at her speculatively. "Did you mean it?" she asked. "You'll give me your memories?"

"Yes!" Luna said. "If you help them get free, I'll give you all of them, whatever you want."

"Me too," Dusky whispered.

Lizard grinned fiercely. She blinked out of sight, and then

suddenly reappeared across the room, where Malachite had been lying. She lunged to her feet, grabbed a discarded sword, bolted over to Tsunami, and sliced through the vines around her. It was not carefully done; Luna could see blue blood welling up along Tsunami's scales from the cuts Lizard made. But Tsunami was free, and now she could fight her way through the HiveWings with her claws.

A moment later, Tsunami and Lizard were at Qibli's side, cutting away the vines around him. As the vines fell away from Pineapple next, the RainWing's scales shimmered into camouflage, and Luna could only see him in flickers of movement and changing color.

The three Pyrrhian dragons ran for the window. White-eyed HiveWings blocked their way, and they fought, outnumbered ten to three, as thick smoke filled the room. To her horror, Luna saw the fire reach the discarded vines and a greenish smoke start to rise from them.

Get out, quick, she prayed.

"I think that was pretty helpful of me," Lizard said, appearing next to Luna again with a self-satisfied smile on her face. "You're welcome." Across the room, Malachite staggered, shaking his head. He looked around at the burning throne room with a bewildered expression, then turned and ran out through the archway to the rest of the Hive.

"But they're not —" Luna started, and then Qibli sent out another blast of flames, and another spray of black venom splattered over the HiveWing guards. Everywhere a droplet fell, a HiveWing screamed and jumped aside, his or her eyes flicking back to normal. A path opened through the crowd of guards. Tsunami charged into it, battering HiveWings aside with her tail and wings and talons, and then she whipped around, grabbed Qibli's arms, and threw him into the sky.

A rush of camouflaged wings shot over her head, and Tsunami turned and leaped out into the air, too. They shot away over the savanna, into the falling night.

"After them!" Cottonmouth screamed from the throne, and then he vanished, leaving only Wasp, who dug her claws into her face and roared with fury and pain. Half the HiveWing guards launched themselves after the escaping prisoners, but five of them lay howling on the floor, clutching burns or venom wounds, and three others had fallen elsewhere in the room.

"Someone should get them out of here," Luna said to Lizard. "They'll die of the smoke, or the fire — the whole Hive could burn if someone doesn't do something about it."

Lizard wrinkled her snout. "What do *you* care?" she asked. "This is Wasp Hive, not Cicada Hive. There aren't even any SilkWings here right now." She cocked her head as if listening. "Oh, lots of LeafWings are coming, though. Cottonmouth went to get the dragons he can control without going through Wasp."

"What if Wasp dies?" Luna asked. "Would he lose all the HiveWings?"

"No," Lizard said contemplatively. "I think then he'd control them directly. He's already got the ones who breathed the smoke at the Poison Jungle. It wouldn't be hard to make extra sure he had everyone. Especially if he could find stupid Sundew and grow more of the plant."

Luna crossed to the window, walking straight through some of the HiveWings on the floor. Tsunami, Qibli, and Pineapple were almost out of sight, but dragons were streaming toward them from every corner of the sky.

"How will I know if they're all right?" she said, twisting her front talons together.

"They're **not**," said Cottonmouth's voice in her mind. "**I absorbed one of them before they escaped.**" He chuckled mercilessly. "**They'll all be here soon enough.**"

Tsetse Hive

Beetle Lake

Vinegaroon
Hive

Hornet Hive

Cicada Hive

Mantis
Hive

Yellowjacket
Hive

Wasp
Hive

Poison Jungle

PART THREE
TALONS UNITED

Bloodworm
Hive

~ CHAPTER 19 ~

"You're lying," Luna said fiercely, turning in a circle. "They got away. They got away! There wasn't enough smoke to infect them before they escaped."

"Perhaps," said Cottonmouth. "But one of them also accepted a drink from the guards while in prison. A special, slightly greenish, bitter-tasting drink. Not very clever. I mean, of your friend; it was extremely clever of *me*."

The sky in front of Luna shifted and slowly melted away until she was back in the throne room again. This was the real one, in the present, she realized as she saw the vines covering the walls and blocking the door. The husks of Cottonmouth and Lizard sat in their eternally petrified spots on the throne. Thick, thorny vines pressed into her scales, pinning down her wings and arms and tail and neck. She felt like a stone knotted into a tapestry, or an insect wrapped up for later in a spider's web.

When she rolled her eyes sideways, she could see Dusky tangled up beside her. He had his eyes closed, and he looked fragile and breakable, as though the vines only needed to tighten a hairsbreadth to crush him.

"Luna! Luna, where are you?!"

Cricket! Luna tried to wriggle around; she was able to move the smallest amount but only enough to see the doorway more clearly. Cricket's voice was coming from the other side of the vines.

"Don't touch those." *That was Bryony.* "See the thorns? Touching them is exactly what it wants you to do."

"But I think Luna's in there," Cricket said. "She could be trapped. Luna? Luna, can you hear me?"

Luna strained to lift her head — and then, suddenly, the vines slipped away from her snout.

"Cricket!" she yelled. "Cricket, be careful! The vines —"

Something seized hold of her throat. She tried to look down before she realized it was her own muscles locking around her voice, and she couldn't move her head anymore.

"Luna!" Cricket was shouting. "Luna, are you all right?"

She heard her own voice say, "Cricket, you have to get Sundew! Sundew is the only one who can get in here."

"But we don't know where she is," Cricket called back. "Can't Bryony and I help? Luna, what happened? Is Dusky in there, too? Is he all right? There has to be something we can do!"

"*Please*, Cricket," Luna's-voice-but-not-Luna said. "It has to be Sundew! Go find her, and tell her to hurry. I can't hold out much longer. The plant will have me soon if Sundew doesn't come."

"Oh no," Bryony said softly. "Hang in there, Luna."

"We'll try!" Cricket called, and then there was a flurry of wingbeats, and silence.

The pressure eased on Luna's throat, and she gasped for air as she flickered back into the mindspace version of the throne room.

Cottonmouth stood at the base of the throne with a chain wrapped around Lizard's throat and his boot on her neck, pinning her to the dirt floor. Dusky hovered beside them, wringing his talons.

Luna dropped into a crouch and buried her head in her claws. She felt like a tapestry with a thousand holes stabbed in it. Was any part of her still real? Did she have any control? Was anything still connected? Could her mind reach her talons or her wings, or would it be drifting in a nowhere space forever?

I can't believe he used me to trick Cricket. My *voice, sending her to bring Sundew into this trap.*

She stood up abruptly. "That was horrible," she said to Cottonmouth. "You're a horrible creature. What is wrong with you that you would *do* that to someone?"

"You say that, but you wish you had this power," he said. "Anyone who had the chance to be me would take it in a heartbeat."

"That's not true," Luna said. "I don't know anyone who would want to control other dragons like this."

"Ha!" he spat. "Just look at Queen Wasp! She was thrilled about this partnership. And don't forget Hawthorn and Queen Sequoia, who tried to do it to her. They wanted it to work, oh, yes, they did. Not to mention this little snake here." He jabbed his foot harder into Lizard's neck. "She's a precocious little puppeteer, aren't you? You'd love it if I took a long nap and everyone was yours to play with."

"Please, please stop hurting her," Dusky said.

"He's not hurting me," Lizard said. She yawned. "This is all theatre. He can't actually do anything to me, so he's acting out his frustrations by pretending he's so menacing. But I can't *feel* anything, so it's totally pointless. Wake me when he's done." She closed her eyes and let out a snore.

Cottonmouth stepped off her and threw the chain violently across the room. He stormed up the steps to the throne and sat down, closing his eyes as well.

Lizard lay where she was for a moment longer, stretching and snuggling into the stone. Then she opened one eye, confirmed that Cottonmouth was gone, jumped to her feet, and shook out her wings.

"I guess we're done with Cottonmouth Plays Emperor for today," she said with a toss of her head. "Now he's going to be busy chasing those funny-looking dragons around for a while." She reached out her front talons, curling her claws in. "Time to give your memories to me, give, give, give."

"Wait — I need to ask some questions first," Luna said.

"NO!" Lizard shouted. "You PROMISED!"

"I did!" Luna said. "I will give them to you. I just want to understand some things."

"Gah, FINE, hurry up." Lizard stomped impatiently around Dusky, flapping her wings.

"If we give them to you, will we lose them?" Luna asked. "I mean — do we disappear? Or forget everything?"

"No," Lizard said. "Stupid question. It only means I can watch your memories the way you watched stupid Cottonmouth's. You will BARELY EVEN NOTICE. WHAT IS THE PROBLEM."

"But then he'll be able to see all our memories, too?" Luna asked. "Can he wander through them and see any memory he wants to see?"

"Yeah, but why would he?" Lizard asked. "He's the kind of person who's only interested in pictures if he's in them. He might shuffle through your memories to see if there's anything about him, but he will not care about your friends or family or crushes or anything you care about."

I'm not sure that's quite true, Luna thought. *I care about a few things he probably would be very interested in.* "What about the Chrysalis?" she asked. "What if he uses my memories to catch everyone who was in the Chrysalis in Cicada Hive?"

Lizard rolled her eyes and gave Luna a look that was somehow extremely pitying yet not at all sympathetic at the same time. "There is no more Chrysalis," she said. "Soon all those SilkWings will be exactly like the HiveWings, and we'll control all of them. Who cares about your little rebel group when we've already crushed them into dust? Besides, only Queen Wasp would be interested in that, and she won't get your memories."

"She won't?"

"You are so dense!" Lizard barked. "She's not in here with

me and Cottonmouth and the ravenous plant. She's only a puppet who can control some of the other puppets because she eats the plant and it combines with her venom in a useful way." She paused, thinking. "Hmm. Your chatty friend has tail venom like that — I wonder if we could use him the same way."

Luna shivered. She could not, in any universe, imagine Qibli becoming another Queen Wasp.

Lizard shrugged. "Anyway, she's only in charge of the HiveWings when he lets her be. She *thinks* she's his equal, but she is basically one of his big toes."

Luna thought it was fascinating how sometimes Lizard said *he* and sometimes she said *we*. "Do you have, um — big toes of your own?" she asked. "I mean, do you each have separate dragons you control?"

"Noooooo." Lizard lay down on the floor. "They all belong to all three of us: me, him, and the plant. But he does most of the active controlling because he is an enormous jerk when I do anything and it's not worth it. And the plant is too stupid to do anything on its own except make more of itself. Dusky, I haaaaaaaaate this conversation. It's soooooo boring. Make her stop."

"Almost done," Luna said, although really she suspected she could have asked questions for years. She felt like Cricket must feel all the time, overwhelmed by everything she wanted to know. "This is important, Lizard. If I saw something in one of my memories, would Cottonmouth be able to go into that memory and study it? That is — like a book I opened or something. Could he go in and read the pages, even if I didn't read them or don't remember them word for word?"

She hoped that was vague enough but would give her a clear answer. She needed to be sure that Cottonmouth couldn't use her memories to copy the map from Pantala to Pyrrhia. She'd only seen it briefly a few times, and she definitely wouldn't have been able to draw it herself. But what if Cottonmouth could freeze one of those moments in her mind and memorize it?

Lizard thought for a while, flicking her tail. Luna was glad she didn't give a flippant, angry answer. The little dragon could probably guess that Luna needed the answer to be no, and the fact that she didn't just say that right away meant that hopefully she would be truthful.

Luna wasn't sure what she would do if the answer was yes. She'd promised Lizard her memories — but she also could never, never let Cottonmouth get his tendrils on that map.

"I don't think he could," Lizard said. "I haven't seen him do anything like that with the memories the humans have given him."

"Could you try it with some of the memories you already have?" Luna asked. "Choose a dragon holding a book or a scroll and see if you can read it?"

Lizard scowled and scuffed her talons through the dirt. "I can't do that," she muttered finally.

"Why not?"

"I don't *have* any dragon memories, all right?" Lizard snapped. "No dragon has ever said yes before. They just *won't give them to us* and I don't know *why* and it's *so aggravating."*

Luna blinked at her. "But — you said —"

"The *humans* give them up all the time," Lizard growled. "They think he's some kind of god and will give him anything. We've only had four Guardians say no in all these centuries, including the useless one we have now. But we haven't absorbed that many dragons, actually. There weren't any here for the first three thousand years, and then the ones that arrived figured out the hive mind and cleared the plant from the land. They nearly got rid of us entirely.

"The few dragons we had before Wasp came along always thought Cottonmouth was creepy, which he is, and that I'm just a baby or worse, his pet. Like some kind of traitor to my species! So they never, never say yes, and I have wanted dragon memories of my own for *so long."* She rubbed her snout, ducking her head away from them. "You *promised."*

Luna didn't know what to think. She wanted to be sure the map would be safe. But she also felt so sorry for this awful little dragon.

She's never known what it's really like to live a dragon life. She's never been part of the tapestry. She's like a thread of silk that didn't get woven in anywhere.

"Take mine first, then," Dusky said. "See if you can read any of my books."

Lizard turned to him eagerly, her eyes sparking. "That's a yes? I can have them?"

He nodded, and she grabbed his front talons, lacing their

------◆ 2 3 6 ◆------

claws together. A long, hushed silence followed, and then Lizard exhaled, let go of him, and pressed her talons to her temples.

"Wow," she whispered.

Luna was about to ask what it felt like when suddenly she was surrounded by brilliant sunlight. Lizard stood beside her, blinking rapidly. They were high up in the web canopy, with SilkWings peacefully climbing or sleeping or weaving in cells and hammocks all around them.

My tribe. Luna's heart skipped a beat. She'd almost forgotten what normal life had been like in the webs, away from the HiveWings. The shimmering scale colors, the soft silk under her talons, the quiet murmurs of dragon families all around them. The sunlight. She'd missed this.

It was only ours in snatches, though, she reminded herself. *These dragons didn't get to choose their homes or families or work assignments. They're finding happiness where they can, but they should have freedom, too, and a chance to be truly happy.*

She didn't recognize the nearby Hive, but if this was Dusky's memory, she guessed it was Bloodworm Hive. She turned, balancing lightly on the canopy, and spotted a version of Dusky so tiny she almost couldn't believe he was real. He lay curled between the front talons of a lavender-and-silver SilkWing, tangling a ball of silk thread with his claws.

The SilkWing smiled down at him. "Try again. *Dusky.*"

"Dada," said baby Dusky.

"No, no, *I'm* Dada. You're *Dusky.*"

"Dada hee ha." Dusky batted the ball into his dad's nose,

and his dad snorted and shook his head with a laugh. The baby beamed with delight at the funny noise. "*I* Dada," he said confidently.

"You can't be Dada," his father explained, wrapping the thread around one of Dusky's little talons. "Dada is the boss. That's me. Dada makes all the tough decisions, like what we're having for dinner."

"BABABAS!" Dusky shouted.

"I don't *have* any bananas, you little barbarian. It's yams or garbanzo beans again, I'm afraid."

Dusky wiggled out of his dad's talons and bounced across the silk web to a pile of leaves in the corner of the cell. He threw himself into the leaves and dug furiously for a moment. Finally he emerged in triumph, brandishing a very brown, rather squashed banana.

"Oh dear," his dad said, laughing again. "I guess we do have . . . one dead banana. Did you hide that, and how long ago, troublemaker?"

"Bababa," Dusky said happily. He pointed to himself. "*I* Dada."

"Hmm. All right, I bow to your impeccable logic," his dad said, nodding thoughtfully. Dusky trotted over and sat between his dad's talons again, cradling his mushy banana. His dad leaned down and nudged him with his snout. "I love you, Dusky."

The scene vanished as quickly as it had begun, flinging Luna back into the throne room mindspace.

"YUCK," Lizard declared. "ARGH. WHY. SO BORING.

BOO HISS." She threw herself down on the floor and covered her face with her wings.

Dusky stood staring into space, his claws trembling slightly. Luna crouched beside him and tucked two of her wings over his back.

"Did you see that, too?" she whispered. He nodded, and a tear slipped down his nose. "Oh, Dusky." She hugged him close. "Your dad was wonderful." He nodded again and leaned into her, crying silently.

Maybe after all of this is over, we can find his mom, Luna thought. *Whitespeck said she was shipped off to Vinegaroon Hive . . . maybe we can look for her there.*

She realized with a jolt that she was still thinking about an "after" as though they had a future. The image of her and Dusky snarled in vines shoved its way into her head. *Lizard said we would die here.*

But Cricket wouldn't let that happen. She would find Sundew, and they would get Luna and Dusky out . . . somehow.

It was so strange to realize that she believed in Cricket. She knew for certain that, HiveWing or not, Cricket wouldn't abandon her there.

But we'll still have the othermind in our heads, even if we do escape the throne room. I know so much about it — them — now, but I still have no idea how to free the dragons they've absorbed.

I wish I could talk to Swordtail.

She glanced at Lizard, but the small dragon was clearly

having Some Feelings, and Luna guessed this would be the wrong time to ask for another favor.

I wonder what's happening with the others. Will Cricket find Sundew? Are Qibli and Pineapple and Tsunami all right? Where are Sundew, Lynx, and Moon?

It seemed like a long time passed before Lizard finally lifted her wings and sat up again. She rubbed her face violently and turned toward Luna and Dusky.

"Must be weird having a parent who cares about you," she said dismissively. "Not very dragonlike."

Luna tilted her head. "Is that really what you think?" she asked. "That dragons don't care about their dragonets?"

Lizard made a "yeah, obviously" face. "We are *reptiles*," she said with startling vehemence. "Lizards don't care about their eggs. Reptiles don't love anything."

"That sounds like something Cottonmouth has told you," Luna pointed out. "Maybe even something all the humans have always believed. But you've been watching dragons like Dusky through HiveWing eyes. You must have seen that dragons can love each other."

Lizard snorted. "Maybe fluffy little SilkWings can. MOST dragons don't. Not dragons like me."

"Lizard!" Luna cried, then lowered her voice as she saw Cottonmouth twitch on his throne. "Lizard, *think* about this. We saw your mother in his memory. She burned an *entire civilization down* because she loved you so much."

Lizard opened her mouth and then closed it again, emotions

warring across her face. "She was just mad they stole some-thing from her," she said finally. "Like Cottonmouth said, dragons are violent by nature. It was probably, like, instinc-tive for her to start burning stuff." She fluffed her wings back, and her expression settled on indignant. "She could have *looked* for me! She didn't even try to find me before she started burning everything!"

"We don't know that," Luna said. "We only know what he knows." She flicked her tail at the human on the throne.

"Are your memories all as sappy as his?" Lizard demanded, jerking her chin at Dusky.

"Some of them," Luna said. "Probably."

Lizard blew out a gust of air, then held out her talons. "Give them anyway."

"Did you check — I mean, are you sure —" Luna started.

"Yes, yes," Lizard said impatiently. "I looked at the books in one of Dusky's library memories. It felt like I was reading them over his shoulder, but then the words slid right off my brain when I left the memory. Whatever you're trying to pro-tect should be fine."

Luna still wasn't sure this was a good idea, but she had promised, and Lizard had kept her side of the deal by helping her friends escape.

And maybe this is the only good thing left that I can do. I can't help anyone else right now, but I can give Lizard a chance to feel what it's like to be part of our world. She sat back and let Lizard seize her front talons.

She had only about a moment to wonder which memory they'd fall into first, and then they were there: in the art room at Silkworm Hall. Her and Blue, Swordtail and Io.

She was vaguely aware that Lizard and Dusky were there, too, perched atop the tall cabinets, but they faded into the background next to Luna's three best friends in the world.

"Are we allowed to be in here after school?" Blue whispered.

"I need Luna's help with my Metamorphosis weaving idea," Io said cheerfully. "Are they really going to be mad at us for doing extra work? I don't think so."

"But the rules —"

"Are vague on this point," Swordtail said, bumping Blue's side with his hip. "Come on, Blue. They totally won't care as long as we don't break anything. Stop worrying so much, my little caterpillar."

Blue looked around at the mess of silk and fluff and scribbled notes and ends of threads and spilled dyes. "Oooh," he said, "maybe if I tidy up, that'll make them less mad."

Luna laughed from the top of the table where she was sitting. "That would be too funny. 'Silkworm Hall's Model Student Banished to Misbehaver's Way for Stealth Cleaning Without Permission'!"

Blue hesitated, biting one of his claws. "Do you think I need permission?"

"No!" Luna threw a silk pillow at his head. "You walking lump of sugar, go ahead and tidy if you want to."

Her brother happily bustled off to get a broom.

"I'll follow him," Swordtail suggested. "Just to make sure he doesn't walk himself straight into a HiveWing guard."

"Thanks, Swordtail," Luna said, returning his smile.

As soon as they were gone, Luna and Io leaned over the drawing on the table.

"I thought I would use purple for my color," Io said.

"I love that," Luna said. "Silver waterfall, purple mountains?"

"Yes, and some purple butterflies in the spray, I think." Io glanced around, making sure Blue was out of the room. She lowered her voice to a whisper. "But I can't figure out where to hide my Chrysalis symbol."

"Hmmm." Luna studied the design again, tilting her head. This was not long after she'd learned of the Chrysalis, the secret group of SilkWings that wanted to change things. Io was the one who had told her about how Chrysalis members wove a little red shape into their weavings — a shape that could be a leaf or a teardrop, depending on how you looked at it. It was a small wave to other Chrysalis members: We're out here, we'll keep fighting, we have one another. You're not alone.

"What if you added a fish to the pond below the waterfall?" Luna suggested. "It could be purple, but with silver silk woven over top of it so it's partly underwater, and you could hide the Chrysalis leaf in its scales?"

"Ooooo," Io said as Blue came back into the room dragging a broom. She picked up a pencil and started sketching.

"I wish I could do a forest for my weaving," Luna said

dreamily. "Or for a truly giant tapestry. Trees as far as the eye can see, with SilkWing palaces and playgrounds everywhere connecting them, and all the dragons are happy and kind and take care of each other."

"Luna!" Blue paused his sweeping and shot an anxious look at the door. "No trees is definitely a rule."

"Doesn't it seem like a silly rule, though?" Luna asked.

He wrung his talons together. "I don't want you to get in trouble. I don't want anything bad to happen to you, ever."

The Luna watching sighed inwardly from the future. Poor Blue would never have imagined the trouble she was in now.

"I know, sweetness," Luna said, flicking her tail at him. "Don't worry. I'll probably end up doing a night sky or something, like everyone else."

Blue exhaled with relief and went back to sweeping.

Io was just leaning forward to show her new sketch to Luna when Swordtail came flying into the room.

"Look out, look out," he said in a rush. "Headmaster coming, everybody hide!" He bolted out the door again.

Io dove into one of the cabinets and pulled the door shut behind her. Luna shot across the room to Blue, grabbed him, and threw him into the pile of discarded half-finished weavings that Ms. Clorinde kept in the corner for scraps and practice.

"Stay really still!" she whispered, and then she covered him over with weaving scraps until he was completely buried.

"Shouldn't we turn ourselves in?" he whispered back. "We weren't doing anything wrong."

"Shhhh," she said. "Do *not* move, Blue."

She ducked behind a loom in the farthest corner from the door. A heartbeat later, the headmaster poked his head into the room. He swiveled his snout in a slow, appraising arc, his gaze lingering on the broom and Io's sketch on the table, and then coming to a stop on the weaving discard pile. To Luna's horror, he stepped stealthily into the room, as if the weavings were his prey and he was sneaking up on them.

"I'm over here!" Luna shouted, bursting out of her hiding spot at the same exact moment as Swordtail came pelting into the room yelling, "I'm sorry, I did it, whatever it is, it was me!"

The headmaster jumped nearly a foot in the air. He swung around and glared at the two of them.

"What are you doing here after school?" he demanded. "Thieving little worms! My office, now!"

"Thieving? Literally what would we steal?" Swordtail asked as the headmaster pushed him out the door. Luna started after them, resisting the urge to glance back and make sure Blue was still hidden. Io would get him out safely.

"Why did you do that?" Lizard called from her perch. The memory froze around them. Luna shook herself and turned toward the small dragon.

"Do what?"

"You and your nitwit," Lizard said. "You both got caught on purpose! Like you were volunteering to get in trouble! Were your brains not working that day? Do SilkWing brains work at *all*?"

"Don't be mean," Dusky piped up. "They were helping."

"HELPING?" Lizard echoed as though he'd said "hippo carcass." "WHY?"

"Blue was about to get caught," Luna said, pointing toward the corner where her brother was tucked away. "We were distracting the headmaster so Blue and Io could get away. It's really not that weird."

"I think it is," Lizard said. "He could have caught Blue, and *you* could have gotten away."

"But Blue would have been so sad if he got in trouble," Luna said. "It didn't bother me or Swordtail nearly as much." She hadn't *loved* the week of punishment spent sorting and dyeing the new bales of silk. But Swordtail had been with her, and side by side, it hadn't been too bad. "Besides, we're the ones who talked him into staying after school, so it would have been really unfair if he wound up being the only one punished for it."

Lizard shook her head and made a face. "So weird. He's just . . . another dragon. Who cares if he's sad or it's unfair?"

"I mean . . . we do," Luna said. "Because we love him."

"GROSS!" Lizard shouted. "Stop saying that word!" She sat up suddenly and grabbed her head. They jerked abruptly back to the fake throne room, and in the mindspace, Luna could feel a weird thrum in the air.

"Oh, oooooooh. Incoming," Lizard said. "This one's worth bringing here."

The thrum intensified for a moment, and then there was a sound on the edge of hearing that might have been a boom or a click, and suddenly Pineapple was sitting beside Luna, bright green and looking petrified.

CHAPTER 20

"Surprise!" Lizard crowed.

"Pineapple!" Luna cried. She jumped forward to catch him as he staggered, but he was bigger and heavier than her, and they both collapsed to the floor.

She sat up and patted his face gently. "Pineapple, are you all right? What are you doing here? Are you in the abyss in real life, too?"

"Not yet," Lizard answered for him. "But he's coming this way with the other two. Flying fast, with a *lot* of dragons chasing him. I mean, he's not the one flying himself anymore, though." She tipped her head toward Cottonmouth. "*He* is."

"Oh no," Luna said, her heart sinking. "Pineapple, can you hear me?"

"What — Luna?" Pineapple held out his talons and turned them in front of his face like he didn't recognize them. "Why did my wings do that? Why can't I . . . ?" He trailed off, then met Luna's eyes. "Am I dead?"

"No!" Luna spread her wings. "You're still alive, Pineapple. The plant got you, but you're not dead."

"Oh," he said. "I guess it works on Pyrrhian dragons, too, then. That answers that question." He opened and closed his talons again. "So this isn't real. And it's controlling my body right now?"

"Yes," Luna said. "Technically, he is." She pointed to Cottonmouth, and Pineapple squinted at the human in puzzlement. "But the plant is part of him, or he's part of it, and so is she." Pineapple transferred his confused look to Lizard. "Pineapple, what's happened to the others? I saw you escape Queen Wasp, but then what? Did you find Moon and everyone else?"

"It'll be faster if we go see for ourselves," Lizard said briskly.

The ground fell away from Luna's feet, and she yelped in surprise as the sky appeared all around her. For a startled moment, she plummeted, and then she managed to right herself and swing back into an air current.

The Pantalan coastline was flashing by below her, the ocean to her left, an inlet to her right, a peninsula jutting out up ahead. She chanced a look behind her and saw clouds of green dragons filling the evening sky — the LeafWings that had fallen to the plant on the Snarling River battlefield.

Right above her was Tsunami, her face grim, her wings beating furiously. Qibli soared a few wingbeats behind. His eyes kept darting to the patch of sky beside him, where Luna knew he was seeing Pineapple, but she could see Cottonmouth, floating eerily in midair.

"Doing OK?" Qibli called.

Cottonmouth tilted his head in that odd way he did whenever he was inside a dragon. "Yes," he answered.

A little furrow appeared in Qibli's forehead. "Don't feel bad about what you did to Queen Wasp," he said. "She would have done much worse to us. You're the whole reason we escaped, Pineapple."

"Yes," Cottonmouth said again.

Qibli looked even more worried.

"Where are we going?" Tsunami called back to them. "If we can lose them?"

"If we keep flying south, we'll reach a big lake," Cottonmouth said. "There are a million caves there where we can hide."

"Hello, what?" Qibli said. "How do you know that?"

Cottonmouth blinked slowly and looked around, his gaze snagging on Luna, Lizard, and Dusky flying alongside them. "Luna told me," he said at length.

"Ah, right. Just your normal, everyday conversation about the geography of Pantala?" Qibli asked.

"That's right," Cottonmouth answered.

"I find it hard to believe those green dragons haven't caught us with you two moving this slowly!" Tsunami observed over her shoulder. "Stop *talking* so much and fly faster!"

Qibli closed his mouth on whatever he was about to say, but he cast a worried glance sideways at Pineapple.

"Hmm," Lizard said. "Boring. Flap, flap, flap. We don't need to watch this."

"What if Sundew shows up?" Luna said. "Don't you want to see that?"

Lizard frowned at Cottonmouth. "I suppose," she said. "I guess it would be better to know *before* he starts gloating like a big old gloat snake."

The three Pyrrhian dragons flew without speaking for a while, beating their wings steadily. Luna realized she wasn't getting tired, despite carrying Dusky on her back, and no matter how long they flew. As far as she could see, Lizard was also keeping up easily despite her small size. *I guess that makes sense, since we're not really here or using our real wings.*

"Could you jump into Pineapple and talk to them?" Luna asked Lizard.

"Not while Cottonmouth's in there," Lizard said with a shrug.

"Oh . . . one of the LeafWings, then, maybe?"

"They're not going to catch up," Lizard pointed out, as though this was blindingly obvious. "Cottonmouth is holding them back, but keeping them in sight to drive these dragons south."

Luna did not like the sound of that. "Why?"

"He's bringing them to us in the hopes that Sundew will follow." Lizard rolled her eyes again.

"Is her leafspeak really that impressive?" Luna asked. "He seems so obsessed with her."

"I *guess* it's impressive," Lizard said with a snort. She flexed her own talons. "It's stronger than mine; that's for sure. I can maybe double a plant's normal growth speed, but I have to stay focused on it. And I can make plants move a bit, if I'm near them. But Sundew can make them grow *so fast*. If he absorbs her, he could make her cover this whole continent in breath of evil within a month, I bet."

"Yikes," Luna said. She really didn't like the tapestry *that* conjured up in her head. A nightmare of vines choking the entire landscape, and every dragon white-eyed and hopeless.

They flew onward as the sky darkened into night and the moons rose. Two of them shimmered over the ocean, casting silvery tails that seemed to belong to giant distant dragons.

Maybe Sundew shouldn't have come with us. Maybe she should have stayed in Pyrrhia so Cottonmouth couldn't get her and her power.

But maybe she's the only one who can stop him. If her leaf-speak is that strong, maybe bringing her into the abyss will mean she can control the plant and destroy it.

It was interesting that Lizard had leafspeak, too. Maybe LeafWings were descended from Lizard's mother, way, way back. Maybe other tribes were, too.

"Wait, Lizard," Luna said, suddenly realizing something. "Are you controlling the vines moving in the abyss? Like — that's your power, not his?"

"All me," Lizard said, fanning out her wings and soaring to a higher current. "Otherwise the plant can only move as much as a normal plant. Ha ha, that's RIGHT, you old man!" she shouted at Cottonmouth suddenly. "I AM important and useful!"

He didn't even turn to look at her, and the wind whipped her words away.

"But that means . . . *you're* the one who blocked the doorway," Luna said. "And you're the one who's got the vines wrapped around me and Dusky, in the real world. *You* trapped us!"

"That's right," Lizard said smugly. "He couldn't have done that without me. But do I get a thank-you? Does he spend ONE MINUTE thinking about how great I am? NO, AND THAT'S FINE! I DON'T THINK ABOUT YOU EITHER!"

"Lizard," Luna said, trying to keep the little dragon focused on her. "That means you could let us go!"

Lizard looked at her as though Luna were insane. "Why would I do that? I went to a lot of trouble to get Dusky."

"But you have him now," Luna argued. "He's in your mindspace forever, right? So you could let his body go free. And mine."

"I like him better right here with me," Lizard said sulkily. "If I can't go anywhere, why should he?"

"But won't he die if you leave him like this?" Luna asked. "And then he'll be gone, really soon, just like that. Whereas if you let him go, he could live so long and be in your mindspace giving you memories his whole life."

"You are such a pain!" Lizard shouted. "Stop messing with my head!" She stuck out her tongue at Luna and whisked away to fly next to Tsunami instead.

There's something here, Luna thought. *A way to change things. A way to change how Lizard sees the world, maybe. Something about her reaction to our memories.*

She had the first glimmer of an idea. She turned it over carefully in her head as they flew, thinking about Lizard's short, awful life and very long, lonely existence.

"Tsunami, look," Qibli called. The SeaWing swooped around, and Qibli pointed down at a speck of light on a beach up ahead of them.

"What are you thinking?" Tsunami asked.

"I think that looks like fire," Qibli said, "and there aren't any free dragons on this continent who can make fire . . . except Moon, Luna, or Bullfrog, right?"

"If one of them has made a fire so that every dragon in Pantala can find them, I'm going to shove them into the ocean and cover their eyeballs with starfish," Tsunami growled.

"But it could be a signal for us," Qibli said. "If I were them, I'd make a fire, then turn invisible and hide nearby to see who shows up. It's not that stupid."

Tsunami sighed heavily. "All right, fine. We can check. Maybe the dragons chasing us will fly right over us in the dark. It would be nice if *you* were a NightWing right now — wow, there's a sentence I never thought I'd say! Pineapple, camouflage!" she called.

Cottonmouth tilted his head, then squinted as though something very strange was coming out of his ears.

"Hee hee hee," Lizard chortled. "He doesn't know how to do that. He's turning all SORTS of silly colors."

"Pineapple?" Qibli said.

"I don't feel well," Cottonmouth said hurriedly. He veered suddenly down toward the beach, and the others swung around to follow him.

It *was* a fire — a small one, just a few branches, crackling quietly on an empty stretch of sand. Nearby, moon-speckled waves crept ashore and rippled out again. There were boulders scattered everywhere three times as tall as a dragon, and notches in the cliff face behind them signaled caves where dragons could hide.

"Hello?" Tsunami called. "Moon? Sundew? It's us."

"But we are being chased, so —" Qibli started, but before he could finish, something invisible tackled him to the ground. "Eeeep!" he yelled. "Ack! Is this an attack or a hug?"

Three dragons appeared out of thin air. Sundew was sitting up next to the fire, pressing the IceWing wristbands together, with Lynx standing nearby, smiling. Moon had her arms and wings wrapped around Qibli and her face buried in his neck, and she was radiating happiness so bright the fire and the moonlight seemed unnecessary.

Luna had to close her eyes for a moment.

Swordtail, I miss you so much.

"Aww," Qibli said, hugging Moon close. "Best invisible attack ever."

"You got away!" Sundew cried. "Are you all right? Are you . . . yourselves?"

"Absolutely," Tsunami said, and "Yes," said Cottonmouth, a little too fast but no one else seemed to notice.

"We wanted to rescue you, too," Sundew went on, "but we'd left Cricket and Luna and Wren alone for so long —"

"We were worried about them," Lynx finished. "We were

hoping if we got to the abyss we could defeat Queen Wasp that way and then come back for you."

"Makes sense," Tsunami said. "I myself am pretty good at doing the smart thing instead of the impulsive thing these days. Sometimes. Once in a while. I'm working on it!"

"I wanted to stay and free you," Moon said in a quiet voice to Qibli. They were sitting up now, with one of his wings around her and their tails intertwined carefully around his venom barb.

"But then you remembered that I'm very clever and would totally figure out how to escape on my own," Qibli joked. "Right? Guess what I did, guess what I did. I stood there, like an absolute *hero*, while Pineapple saved all of us. Didn't I, Tsunami?"

"Heroes in books talk way less than you do," Tsunami said. "When we get back to school, I'm going to start a class called Not Taunting the Bad Guys While They're Holding You Hostage, and you're getting an automatic fail before it even starts."

"Rude," Qibli said. "Bad guys *love* my taunting."

Tsunami glanced at the sky. "We should hide. And destroy this." She stepped over and swept sand into the fire with her tail and talons, until the flames were out and the embers were covered.

"Back to being invisible," Sundew agreed. She held up her talons and glanced around at the other dragons. "Are you ready?"

"Meet at the tallest tree by Lake Scorpion if we get separated," Lynx said. "That's the biggest lake on the southern peninsula, apparently."

Sundew touched the wristband diamonds together and murmured, "Hidden be," and all six of them flickered out of sight, including Cottonmouth. Luna was left standing with Lizard and Dusky on what seemed to be a deserted beach. It felt like a giant blanket of loneliness suddenly crashing down and smothering her.

She'd forgotten for a moment that she wasn't really with them. She'd forgotten that she was half a continent away, pinned under vines in a dark abyss, absorbed by the othermind.

And that I might die here and never see any of them again.

"That must be the same lake you mentioned, Pineapple," Qibli's voice said out of the dark.

Oh! I can still hear them!

Because we're getting this through Cottonmouth/Pineapple, and he's invisible with them, she realized.

"That's kind of a weird coincidence that you're going there, too," Qibli went on.

"Cricket and Luna left us a message," said Sundew's voice. "That's where they're going. Supposedly the abyss is near there, or at least they think so."

"Hmm," Qibli said thoughtfully.

"If everyone is able to fly," Tsunami's voice interjected, "I think we should get as far as we can tonight."

"Agreed," said Sundew. "I'm worried about Wren and the others. If they go into the abyss without us, and anything happens to them . . ."

"I'm ready to fly," Lynx said, her voice closer to Luna than Luna had expected. She wished she could turn and grab Lynx's talons and they could both know the other was there, like they had in the sky over the ocean, the first time they turned invisible.

"Me too," Moon and Qibli said at the same time.

"Ready," Cottonmouth agreed a half beat later.

"Ooohh, exciting," Lizard said. The beach and the dark starry sky faded to gray, and the mindspace throne room closed in around them. Pineapple was still beside Luna. He was watching Cottonmouth with a faraway expression, as though he were trying to unravel a tapestry, knot by knot, with his mind.

"More dragons coming to the abyss," Lizard said, rubbing her claws together. "WEIRD dragons! Dragons who probably have more normal, prickly memories than you two cuddly butterfly hug monsters. It's going to be crowded in our throne room for the first time ever! So many dragons to absorb." She grinned toothily.

"Sundew's going to tear this place apart," Luna said with as much ferocity as she could muster.

"Uh-huh," Lizard said. "We'll see."

There is one thing I can try, Luna thought to herself. *I shouldn't sit here and wait for Sundew to save us, especially if this whole thing is a trap for her. I have to do something, no matter how small it seems.*

"Lizard, I have a new proposal," Luna said. Lizard quirked an eyebrow at her, and Luna pointed to Pineapple. "If I can convince him to give you his memories, too . . . I want you to set me and Dusky free."

CHAPTER 21

"No," Lizard said. She added a yawn for good measure. "Obviously not."

"Hear me out," Luna said. She sat down and spread her wings. "You think SilkWings must be different from other dragons, right? That all other dragons will be tougher and meaner and stronger than us, or something like that."

"Yeah," Lizard said. "I'm sure of it. Other dragons don't do hugging and saving each other and sappy nonsense. I've seen the ones in Cottonmouth's memories; they're terrifying! Big and scary! Toothy and hungry! I want to feel what it's like to BE the dragon eating the human! I want some memories that match the enormous monster I could have been!"

"That's why I'm offering you Pineapple's," Luna said.

"Uh —" Pineapple said beside her, and she trod on his foot to shut him up.

"That's not enough," Lizard said. "For me to let you fly out of here? One dragon's memories? *Pfft*. Never going to happen."

"But you could always bring us back, couldn't you?" Luna

said desperately. "You would only be letting our bodies out into the world, knowing you could still control them and bring us here whenever you wanted." She waved her talons at the mindspace. "I feel like *we're* the ones who aren't getting enough out of this deal."

The small dragon lashed her tail and narrowed her eyes at Pineapple. "I can't unblock the door," she said at last. "That's part of his whole elaborate Sundew trap. He'll never let you wander off, even for a minute, because you're the bait. Remember?"

Luna's wings drooped. She had been hoping that wasn't *quite* all she was.

"But I can let you out of the vines," Lizard said reluctantly. She tossed her head. "It's a little tiring keeping them wrapped around you anyway."

Luna felt a tightness in her chest start to ease; she hadn't even realized how hard it had been to breathe. She closed her eyes and tried to focus on feeling her body — her real body. She didn't think either Lizard or Cottonmouth were inside it right then. It wasn't like they could use her for anything, as long as she was still trapped in the throne room.

So much for my great superpower, Luna thought. *The wondrous and rare flamesilk, chosen by destiny to have fire under her scales . . . ends up in the one situation where she can't use it.*

She remembered what she'd done with Cricket when they were invisible, grounding herself in her senses other than sight. She breathed into her scales, sensing the places where they touched the damp, slippery vines, until she could feel her real talons stretch and flex. Finally her wings fluttered loose, and she stretched them as wide as she could.

With her eyes closed, she felt her way along the vines until she reached Dusky's cold scales, and then she carefully untangled him, too, and hugged him close to her chest.

"All right, all right," Lizard said impatiently, bringing Luna's attention back to the mindspace. Luna opened her eyes, disconcerted by the feeling of Dusky in her arms while her eyes told her he was standing a few steps away, beside Lizard.

"Big fierce memories now," Lizard demanded. "Ooo, you're the one with the death spit!" She eyed Pineapple and rubbed her talons together with glee. "Show me all the times you've MELTED dragons' FACES with your death spit!"

"Um . . ." Pineapple gave Luna an "are you sure about this?" look.

"Trust me," Luna said. "Tell her yes, she can see your memories."

"All right," Pineapple said, shrugging agreeably. Lizard grabbed his talons, and a heartbeat later, they were all standing on a platform in the greenest, leafiest place Luna had ever seen.

Luna gasped with awe.

It was *beautiful*. There were trees *all around them*, huge trees, fifty times the size of dragons, and there were flowers everywhere, tiny lavender ones that looked like claws and giant bright orange-and-gold ones like rioting flamesilk. And there were birds, hundreds of birds in every color, some of them in eight different colors at once; and there were glass-winged butterflies as big as Luna's talons, and everything around them smelled like green and mangoes and bananas and mammals and birds — mammals? oh, yes, now she could see furry little silver-gray creatures snoozing on the nearest branches — and the air was warm and buzzing, and sunlight through leaves was somehow so much gentler and more peaceful than the same sun beating down on the Hives and —

"Luna," Dusky breathed. "I *love* this place."

"Where are we?" Lizard demanded.

"The rainforest in the Distant Kingdoms," Luna guessed. She knew that's where Pineapple's tribe lived. But she'd never imagined how close it would look to her dream of a SilkWing future. She wasn't sure she could possibly capture all this in a weaving, but she would be happy to spend her whole life trying to.

Lizard turned in a circle and stomped her foot on the polished wooden platform. "Is there about to be a battle? Is someone going to attack? Where IS he?"

"Up there," Dusky said, pointing.

They looked up and saw a huge leaf hammock hanging just beyond the platform. Cuddled inside of it, drenched in sunlight, were two sleeping dragons, one bright yellow with splashes of pink, one bright pink with hints of yellow around his ears.

"WHAT," Lizard barked.

The yellow RainWing yawned and looked up at the leaf canopy overhead. "We should probably be done with suntime now." From his voice, Luna realized that was Pineapple. He looked so rested and happy.

The pink RainWing shook his head and snuggled farther into the hammock. "Nuh-uh. I need more Pineappletime."

Pineapple laughed. "Your entire life is Pineappletime. I'm always here for you."

"Because I'm very cute," said the pink dragon with his eyes still closed. "And excellent at tree gliding. And related to royalty."

"Hmm," said Pineapple. "If those are my reasons, I must be a pretty shallow dragon."

"No, no," said the pink dragon. "You are SO deep. The most deep. Very deep. So, so . . . deeeepy . . ." He trailed off, making snoozy snoring noises.

Pineapple chuckled softly. "All right. I'll prove what a deep boyfriend I am by letting you drool on me, just this once."

"Very cute drool," the pink dragon mumbled.

"Jambu!" a voice called from somewhere out in the trees. "JAAAAMBUUUUU!"

"Not here!" the pink dragon called, waking up again. "No Jambus, no Pineapples! Just us frogs! Ribbit, go away!"

Luna recognized the dragon who came sailing down onto the platform: this was Queen Glory, the one who currently ruled both the RainWings and NightWings.

"Jambu, you goof," Glory said, throwing a nut that bounced off the pink dragon's head. "Suntime ended ages ago."

"Told you," Pineapple said, nudging Jambu with a grin.

Jambu flopped one arm and one wing over the edge of the hammock and gave Glory a soulful look. "But I'm tiiiiiiiiiired," he said. "I watched Peacemaker and his little friends *all morning*, and that dragonet has SO MUCH ENERGY and it was EXHAUSTING."

"Yes, well, he could be worse," Glory said. "Jambu, listen, I have to go to Sanctuary. I was hoping you'd come with me."

Pineapple rested his head on Jambu's shoulder. "Right now? Why? What's happened?"

"Dragons have arrived from the lost continent, apparently," Glory said. "They've come asking for help, so we're having a queens' gathering. I won't know the details until I get there, but I want to bring a few dragons I can count on."

"*Mmmmmmmmmmmmmmmmrf,*" Jambu said, burying his face in the leaf hammock. "Hours and hours of boring politics talk. I mean yay."

"I could go in his place," Pineapple offered.

Jambu looked up and batted his eyelashes. "Oooooo. And I could go back to sleep?"

Glory shrugged elegantly. "I suppose that's all right with me, if you really don't mind coming along."

"I wouldn't mind," Pineapple said. "I'd like to be helpful."

"While *I*," Jambu said, "would like to be *sleeping* instead of helpful."

Pineapple bumped him with his snout. "You've done lots of helpful things," he said. "You helped our amazing queen become queen. Let me take a turn."

"All right, yes, love you, bye!" Jambu said, wriggling all the way back into the hammock.

Pineapple laughed as he extricated himself. Once he was

hovering in the air beside the hammock, he reached in and squeezed one of Jambu's talons. "I'll miss you, too."

"Deep *and* noble," Jambu mumbled sleepily.

"Thanks, Pineapple," Glory said, moving a small blue salamander off her tail. "Hopefully you'll be home and sleeping in the sun again in no time."

The memory drifted away like morning mist, slower than the others, leaving the ghost of the scent of jasmine in the mindspace.

"TALONS AND TENTACLES," Lizard yelled, making them all jump. "That was even WORSE than yours!" She clamped her talons to her temples and scrunched her eyes shut.

Luna glanced over at Pineapple, but he'd gone back to his faraway, undoing-knots-in-his-brain expression. They'd flown together for three days, and he hadn't let on that he was missing someone back at home. He'd always acted so cheerful and even-keeled.

He might have been really sad all that time, and I had no idea.

I wish he'd told me. We could have talked about Jambu and Swordtail. At the very least, I could have given him a hug or told him I understood. Or said thank you for coming all this way and risking so much to help save someone I love the way he loves Jambu.

"We're going to get you home, Pineapple," she said. "I don't know how, but I promise you'll see him again."

He blinked as if he were coming out of a fog, and then he looked down at her and smiled. Little rays of yellow bloomed all around his scales.

"I know," he said. "I will."

"NONE!" Lizard exploded. She stormed over to Pineapple and deliberately stomped on one of his feet. He took a polite step back as she kept shouting. "Not one! single! FACE MELTING! What is wrong with you? You have DEATH SPIT and instead of using it for something cool — like MELTING THE FACES OF YOUR ENEMIES! — you spend all of your time cuddling and eating chocolate and making up songs about pandas with your boyfriend!"

"Oh, wow," Luna said, thinking about the rainforest again. She'd only had chocolate twice before, and it was almost as wonderful as honey drops. "That sounds like the perfect life."

"I don't have any enemies," Pineapple told Lizard mildly. "At least, until Queen Wasp. And that was quite stressful, actually. I think you might be overestimating the awesomeness of face melting."

"You LITERALLY MAKE NO SENSE!" Lizard huffed away across the throne room and threw herself into a petulant sulk in the corner.

Luna tried sensing her real body again. She opened and closed her wings and felt the weight of Dusky in her arms. Still free. So at least Lizard hadn't taken out her anger on them by snaring them in the vines again.

When she opened her eyes, Pineapple was watching her curiously. "Why did you let that dragonet think she'd find scary memories in my head?" he asked quietly.

"Because that's what she expects to find," Luna said. "But I want her to see that dragons are not what she thinks. I want her to know what it really feels like to live a dragon life, which is something she never got to do." *I want to weave her into our tapestry,* she thought, but she wasn't sure if that would sound too mystical and fluffy to Pineapple.

"Aw," Pineapple said. "Poor little dragon."

"And I'm hoping she sees that dragons mostly want to take care of each other and love and be loved and not fight all the time or hurt anyone." Luna hesitated and took a breath. "At least, I hope that's what most dragons are like. Sometimes I'm not sure. I mean . . . I'm not sure about HiveWings, I guess."

Pineapple nodded. "I know exactly what you mean. That's how I felt about NightWings when they first came to the rainforest. They'd done all these terrible things, and they thought they were the only dragons worth caring about, and that everything should belong to them and they should get to decide how all other dragons lived their lives. I thought they were too different from us and they'd only cause trouble." He looked down at his talons. "I didn't see how we could even start forgiving them."

"Did you?" Luna asked.

"It's a work in progress," he said with a rueful smile. "But they're more like us than I expected. They wanted to live somewhere safe and take care of their families. We just had to make it really clear to them that they should treat dragons equally even if they're from different tribes. And that Glory was their queen now, and that they had to work to atone for everything they did. There are some NightWings . . . I don't know if I'd call them *friends* yet, but I can see that they're trying to be better."

"Hmm." Luna found it almost impossible to imagine trusting any HiveWings who weren't Cricket.

Pineapple lifted his head and twitched his ears. "Do you hear that?"

"Is it Cricket coming back?" Luna asked. "Oh, wait, no — you're not where I am in the real world. What is it?"

"I thought I heard someone say my name," he said, turning slowly in a circle. "Hello?"

"Pineapple?"

"I heard it that time!" Luna said, startled.

"I'm here," Pineapple said. "I'm in here — down here — hmm. I'm right here."

"Oh — there — found you," Moon said, appearing next to him. "That was very confusing." She blinked at the throne room, the small dragons staring at her, the silent human on the throne, and finally at Luna. "Um. Where are we?"

CHAPTER 22

"Oh no!" Luna cried. "Moon, what happened? How did the plant get you?"

"The plant," Moon said, her eyes going slightly unfocused. "I don't . . ."

"We don't have her," Lizard said. She stood up and came over to peer at Moon. "We haven't absorbed this one. What in the moons — how are *you* here?"

"Qibli, shhh," Moon said to the air, then shook her head. "Pineapple, there's something else in your head, isn't there? I had to kind of, um, slide around it to find you."

He nodded, and she touched one of his talons. "The other-mind got you? But how?"

"I think it was a drink they gave me while we were in the Wasp Hive prison," he said. "Sorry. I should have been more suspicious. I bet Qibli and Tsunami didn't drink it."

"Moon!" Luna said insistently. "Talk to me! How are you doing this?"

The NightWing scratched her head and peered at Luna. "Are you really here? Actually Luna?"

"Yes," Pineapple answered. "While the othermind controls my body, my own mind was brought here. I think it's a mental construct, like an imaginary space where several minds can meet as though it's a real place. The othermind seems to be three minds woven together — the plant's, a human's, and a young dragon's." He nodded at Lizard.

"Ha!" Lizard said. "I'm, like, five thousand years old, you snoozy gorilla."

"And Luna is here, too," Pineapple said. "So she must have been caught and taken over by the othermind as well. Watch out if you run into her in the real world."

"You won't," Luna said. "I'm in the abyss. Moon, *how are you here?*"

The NightWing hesitated again for a painfully long time, and then she said all in a rush, "Don't be mad. I can read minds."

What?

WHAT?

"You — I thought you could see the future!" Luna blurted.

"I can do that, too." Moon squirmed uncomfortably. "I didn't know how to tell you. It's hard to bring up, and then the longer I don't tell someone, the weirder it gets. I'm still bad at dealing with it. It's one of the many things wrong with me. I'm sorry, Luna."

"If it makes you feel any better," Pineapple offered, "I just found out, too."

"Bullfrog and Sky and Lynx don't know either," Moon

said with a wince. "Queen Glory thinks we should keep it pretty quiet, as long as we can."

"The whole time — on the beach, and in Sanctuary, and when we were flying back here — you could hear all my thoughts? Everything I was thinking?" Luna's head was spinning.

"I try not to!" Moon said. "I've gotten better at filtering out most dragons — I mean, it feels like a hundred conversations going on all around me at once, so I've had to learn how to make it quieter. Unless you're directly thinking *at* me, I usually can avoid hearing it."

Three moons. Luna had thought all KINDS of things at Moon! She didn't know whether she felt more angry at Moon for keeping this secret or guilty about all the mean things she'd ever thought around her.

While she was struggling to figure out what to say, Pineapple brushed Moon's wing with his. "So right now you're . . ." he prompted.

"We stopped to get some sleep," she said, "and Qibli asked me to check your mind because he said you've been acting weird. Oh, Pineapple, what do we do now?"

"Tie me up and leave me behind," Pineapple said. "I'm dangerous as long as he's —"

A strangled roar of fury came from the throne. Cottonmouth's consciousness was back, and he'd finally spotted Moon. He shot to his feet and pointed at her.

"How?" he bellowed. "What sorcery is this?"

"Uh-oh," Moon said, and vanished.

Cottonmouth roared again and slammed one of his fists into the stone behind him. Cracks like lightning zigzagged out from the impact.

"Not real," Lizard whispered to Dusky. "SO melodramatic."

"What is he doing?" Luna asked anxiously as Cottonmouth's eyes closed. "Lizard, is he hurting Pineapple or Moon in the real world? Can we see what's happening?"

Lizard shrugged and flung their minds down on a dark beach. Rain was pouring from the sky, and thunder seemed to be coming from everywhere at once.

Wet talonprints were scuffling outside a nearby cave, and Luna remembered that all these dragons were currently invisible. She ran toward the sound of shouting.

"Everyone wake up!" Qibli was yelling. "Pineapple has the othermind in his head!"

"That's not true!" Cottonmouth shouted back. "Moon does! She's the one who's been infected! She's lying to you!"

There was a sound of claws connecting with scales and a gasp of pain.

"Moon?" Qibli cried frantically.

"Where is he?" Tsunami roared. "Qibli, where's Pineapple?"

"I think he's —" Qibli's voice cut out with a yelp.

"Sundew, we need to see him," Lynx's voice said urgently. "Use the bracelets and then make everyone but Pineapple invisible again."

A flash of lightning illuminated the beach as six dragons appeared: Sundew in the opening of the cave, pressing the wristbands together; Lynx right behind her, wings touching; Qibli on the sand outside, a long bloody slash along his neck; Tsunami a few steps away, crouched and ready to pounce; Moon in motion, darting away from the cave into the boulders; and Cottonmouth inside Pineapple, reared up tall and hissing, slashing the air in front of him.

"Don't attack him!" Qibli yelled to Tsunami. "He'll use his venom!"

"Sundew, quick, now!" Lynx shrieked.

Cottonmouth whipped around, fast as a cobra, and launched himself at Sundew. Lynx darted forward at the same moment and shot a blast of freezing air at his face. He rolled out of the way just barely in time so it hit his shoulder instead, and he roared with rage and spun to attack her, and then five of the dragons vanished again.

"No!" Cottonmouth howled. He leaped for the spot where Sundew had been, and his talons closed on empty air. "You need me!" He whirled and put his back against the rock wall, seething. "I have your flamesilk! I'll kill her right now if you fly away!"

"Uh-oh," Lizard said conversationally to Luna. "I might have to strangle you, after all."

"Couldn't you *not* do what he wants?" Luna burst out. "Don't you hate him enough to always do the opposite of what he says? Don't you *want* to fight him?"

Lizard scowled. "Shut up," she said with a snarl. "I do what I want when I *know* what I want. But what he does works, too! I wanted dragon memories and now I have them — even though they're stupid — and the whole reason I have them is because of his sneaky plans. Why *should* I fight? There's nothing to fight *for*."

Luna's friends reappeared on the beach, in a semicircle around Pineapple but several paces away. Qibli was the closest. In his talons, he held a sharp wooden stick, which he lit on fire and pointed at Pineapple. Opposite him in the half circle, Lynx had her jaws hinged open, ready to shoot ice again.

But Cottonmouth's gaze went straight to Sundew, standing directly across from him.

"Are you lying?" Sundew asked.

"No. I have Luna," he said. "Ask your devil creature." He nodded at Moon.

"It's true," Moon said. "Luna was there, in the — mindspace — with real Pineapple."

"Does it have Cricket and Sky, too?" Sundew asked.

Moon shook her head. "How did you catch Luna?" she asked Cottonmouth.

"She flew into the abyss and threw herself into my vines," Cottonmouth said nastily. "Perhaps she was trying to prove what they say about the tiny, tiny brains of SilkWings. She's still alive, but if you want her to stay that way, you'll come down here and join her."

Luna lashed her tail. "Don't listen to him," she said, even though she knew they couldn't hear her.

Sundew and Qibli exchanged glances. "You want us to come to the abyss," Qibli clarified.

"Will you let Luna go if we do?" Sundew asked.

"Certainly," Cottonmouth said with a magnanimous sweep of his arms. "I will allow her to fly right back out into the open sky, in exchange for one of you. I think you know who I mean."

"Not going to happen," Tsunami growled.

Sundew made a little "wait" gesture at her. "We had been planning a trip to the abyss anyway," she said. "How about this. You lead us there, and we'll see what happens."

"Sundew —" Lynx said worriedly.

"Sounds interesting," Cottonmouth said, his eyes glittering.

Sundew pointed at him. "You fly ahead of us. The rest of us will be invisible, so none of your zombies can show up and grab us. When we get to the abyss, I'll go down with you. Nobody else."

"Argh, no —" Qibli started, and Lynx said, *"Sundew,"* again and Tsunami growled, but Cottonmouth said, "Agreed." He looked up at the sky. "The rain is slowing. Shall we go now?"

Sundew looked at Moon. "Is Pineapple all right in there? Will he be OK if we keep flying now?"

Moon's gaze drifted vaguely over Sundew's shoulder, and Luna realized she'd seen that look on Moon's face a million times. *That's her "listening to thoughts" expression. Or "distracted by other dragons' thoughts," I guess. She must be talking to Pineapple in the mindspace.*

"He says yes," Moon reported, her eyes focusing again. "He says go save Luna."

"It's not about me," Luna couldn't stop herself from

protesting. "You have to come destroy the plant." She reached for the LeafWing hopelessly. "Sundew, please don't let him catch you. You're the only one who can stop him."

But Sundew couldn't hear her, and Luna's claws drifted through her friend, as ineffective as smoke.

CHAPTER 23

"See, that's the thing," Lizard said, shifting them back into the mindspace. She tossed her head at Luna. "You tell me to fight Cottonmouth, but all you really want is to kill the plant, which means killing me, too. Of course I'm going to stick with the monster who's at least got a reason to keep me alive."

Luna sighed. Lizard was right. If Sundew managed to crush the plant with her leafspeak, then Lizard's consciousness would die along with the plant and Cottonmouth.

Luna crouched on the floor of the mindspace temple and traced a tree in the dirt with her claws. Her idea about giving Lizard real dragon memories hadn't quite worked the way she'd hoped. She'd wanted to give Lizard a feeling of connection and some understanding of dragons from a dragon point of view, instead of Cottonmouth's twisted perspective.

It had worked for Luna — she felt closer to Dusky and Pineapple, even with only those two short memories. And seeing the rainforest made Luna feel so hopeful. She loved knowing that somewhere like that existed, and that it *was* possible to live peacefully and kindly. If they survived Queen Wasp and the othermind, the SilkWings could try to build a home like that.

But perhaps it only made Lizard feel worse . . . or even less connected, knowing she'd never get to go there or have that kind of life.

"I'm sorry about our memories, Lizard," she said.

"You SHOULD be," Lizard said, dragging Dusky over and plunking them both down beside Luna. The angry little dragon drew a circle in the dirt, and Dusky leaned over to add sun rays around it. "You all seem to spend your time doing things for other dragons. Or hugging. *So much hugging.* Yeesh." She gave a little shudder. Dusky drew a snaking line in front of her, and Lizard added wings to it. "It's just my luck that the three most boring dragons ever are the ones who agree to give me their memories."

"Actually, I meant I'm sorry if our memories made you sad," Luna offered.

Lizard gave her the most outraged look Luna had ever seen. "I'm not sad! They didn't make me sad! What a weird thing to say! Why would I be sad?!"

"Because no one's ever hugged you?" Dusky guessed.

"I don't care about that!" Lizard shoved him over so he toppled on his side. "I never got to set anyone on *fire*! I never got to fly into battle or eat a human or stab anyone even once! That's what I'm sad about! Real dragon stuff! Except I'm not sad, shut up!"

"Hugs are better than all of that," Dusky said, sitting himself up again.

"I BARF at you," Lizard snapped.

"Do you want one?" Dusky asked. "Maybe you'll like them better if you get a real hug?"

"It won't be real!" Lizard barked. "Nothing about this is real!"

"But . . . it would be close, right?" he said. "Can I hug you?"

She scowled ferociously, then wrapped her wings around herself and hunched her shoulders. "Fine, but only if you promise to shut up about hugs and sad feelings from now on."

Dusky didn't have wings to hug with yet, but even as tiny as he was, he was still bigger than Lizard. His arms fit around her folded wings, and he rested his chin on the top of her head.

"Hmph," Lizard muttered after a moment. "Stupid."

But she didn't push him away. Luna watched them for a moment, wondering how it felt to be hugged for the first time in a five-thousand-year half-life, and whether Lizard saw the world any differently with all of Pineapple's and Dusky's and Luna's memories in her head.

Luna crossed the room and crouched beside Pineapple. "I think we need more memories," she said to him in a low voice.

He blinked at her sleepily. "For Lizard? Didn't we give her all of ours?"

"Yes, but I think it wasn't enough. She can convince herself that we're different from other dragons because of our tribes, but that most dragons are the way she thinks they are. We need to show her memories from more different tribes." Luna dug her talons into the dirt. "I don't know how to get them, though — I mean, I'm not volunteering anyone to get absorbed by the plant."

"They already have lots of HiveWings, don't they?" he asked. "Maybe one of them would let her have his memories."

"But what if their memories *are* as bad as she expects a dragon's to be?" Luna worried. "That would reverse everything I'm trying to do."

She thought for a moment, then said slowly, "What if . . . could Moon help? I don't know how mind reading works, but maybe?"

"She's been checking in with me," he said. "I'll ask when she comes back."

"Thanks, Pineapple." He smiled and brushed one of her wings with his.

Luna closed her eyes, reached through her scales until she sensed her real body, and hugged Dusky closer, hoping he could feel it somehow. In her real body, she felt the slippery twists and tangles of vines underneath her.

What else can I do? Her wrists felt warm, and she was sure they were glowing brightly in the dim gray-green tomb. *Why would the prophecy send me down here — why would the universe give me flamesilk and put me in front of a monster — if I'm not supposed to use it?*

Maybe because I'm not the one who's supposed to change the world, after all.

Maybe I'm supposed to sit here and wait to be rescued, again.

She sank her real claws into the vines and felt sap ooze around the holes she left.

If I set these vines on fire, would the smoke really rise all the way to Bryony's group of dragons? Would everyone in the caves be infected and absorbed?

But if the fire destroyed all of the plant down here, there'd be nothing left to control anyone, would there?

She wasn't sure it was safe to take that chance. What if the othermind could live on and use its power as long as any plant roots survived anywhere?

"Lizard," Pineapple said. "We can get you more memories, if you want them."

Luna opened her eyes and saw him crouch beside Lizard, who had wiggled out of Dusky's hug but was still sitting near him, tails lightly touching. Moon was there, too, hovering at Pineapple's side with her gaze fixed nervously on Cottonmouth.

"You can?" Lizard sat up. "How? Did you infect the others?"

"No," Pineapple said, giving her a serious look. "That's not going to happen. But we think Moon can be a conduit. It wouldn't give you all of someone's memories, but she can connect to the others flying with her, and they could each choose a memory to share with you." He glanced at the silent human on the throne. "Just you, possibly. Not totally sure how this will work."

"Yes, yes," Lizard said immediately, holding out her talons. "Give, give — wait." She pulled back and eyed him with suspicion. "What do you want for them? I can't let Luna go."

He shrugged. "No trade. We're flying right now, so it

should be easy to do. And Luna said they might make you happy, so — why not?"

That sentence seemed to puzzle Lizard into silence. She looked down at the dirt, where she had drawn an awkward-looking butterfly. Beside it, Dusky had drawn another, with their wings touching.

"Fine," Lizard said. "Whatever, sure. I'll take it." She held out her talons. Pineapple took one, and Dusky took the other. Moon slid Pineapple's other talon between hers, and Luna took Dusky's free talon, forming a chain.

"Wait!" Lizard said as Moon closed her eyes. "I only want something fierce! No hugging!"

Suddenly they were back in the rainforest, but now it was nighttime, with the three moons spread out across the sky. This was blurrier than the other memories, like paint on glass, or like a sketch left out in the rain. The frogs and insects and trees all seemed to be holding competing orchestras, filling the forest with noise.

A tiny black dragon, no bigger than Lizard, was sitting in a pool of moonlight, gazing up at the stars.

"Imperial," she whispered, pointing to the biggest moon. Her claw traced across the sky to the next one. "Oracle. And Perception." She brought her talons down and wrapped her wings around herself. "I remembered." She looked up at Oracle and whispered, "Mother will be here soon."

A moment passed, and then she looked away from the moon. "Well. She said she'd try." The small black wings fluttered. "If she doesn't come tonight, she'll come tomorrow. Or the next day." Another pause. "She'll always come back."

Luna didn't know if she was somehow feeling Moon's emotions, too, but the loneliness was almost overwhelming. This dragon was so small to be alone in this wild, noisy place.

Another moment, and then little Moon said, even more quietly, "I'll be all right."

A cold wind whisked around Luna's talons, and the warm rainforest folded aside, replaced by rolling hills of endless snow. Someone had built a small snow fort — probably one of the five white-and-blue dragonets running around it — and fortified it with frostbreath to make it shine in the winter sunlight.

"This is OUR fort!" shouted one of the dragonets, scaling the wall and sitting on top of it, glaring down. She wore a lopsided tiara talon-made out of icicles. "Go make your own!"

"No, I think we'll take this one," said the biggest dragonet. He nudged the dragon next to him, and she pounced on the smallest dragonet. "Ha ha, and now we have a hostage!"

The captured dragonet squeaked and wriggled. Luna recognized the pattern of blue scales freckled across her snout: this one was Lynx.

"Surrender the fort, Snowfall, or we'll toss her in the ocean!"

"And maybe the walruses will eat her," cackled the one who had Lynx pinned down.

"Do your worst!" Snowfall shouted. "You took the wrong

hostage! Lynx can swim better than either of you! And she's not afraid of walruses! Right, Lynx?"

Lynx managed to wrest her snout free long enough to yell, "Walruses are adorable, boss!" before her captor stuffed her head back into the snow.

The fifth dragonet suddenly surged over the wall of the fort, pelting the two hostage-takers with snowballs. "Let her go!" he shouted. "We never leave a dragon behind!"

"Win*ter*," Snowfall said with an aggravated sigh as the biggest dragonet easily knocked him over. "Lynx doesn't need rescuing! This is why I don't play with you, because you play all wrong. I'm going to switch to Hailstorm's side if you keep doing stupid heroic things! Look, see, now I'll have to rescue *you*."

A gust of wind blew snow in Luna's face, and as it melted away, so did the fort and the IceWings and the frozen landscape, leaving them in the streets of a busy dragon town, baking in heat.

When I try to remember being Lizard's age — well, Lizard's size — my memories are short and blurry, too, Luna thought, turning to try to guess where they were, and whose memory this was.

Then a crowd of SandWings ran by shouting, "Fight, fight, fight!" and she realized this must be Qibli's. *Maybe this will be fierce enough for Lizard,* she thought, hurrying after them.

"You took it from him!" a voice yelled.

"So what?" another voice shouted back. "I'm big and he's small! That's how it works!"

The dragons were gathering outside a cluster of market

stalls: a tea shop, one selling candles, another hung with dried herbs and flowers, a fourth glittering with bejeweled metal figurines. Two SandWings were facing off, hissing at each other, but neither looked like Qibli. The one she'd heard first was a tawny female SandWing, and the dragon facing her was twice her size, grinning smugly with a mouthful of broken teeth.

"But I *made* it," shouted a tiny dragonet, charging between the feet of the female dragon. Aha — there was Qibli. "I had to figure out how and get all the stuff and it was really hard and you give it back!"

"You don't care about this little pipsqueak," said the big dragon. "Let me buy you a lemonade, and we'll forget all of this."

"Give him back his drum toy," hissed Qibli's defender, "or fight me."

Qibli looked up at her, his eyes round with awe. "You would *fight* for *me*?" he breathed. "Instead of taking *lemonade*?"

"It's not just for you, kid," she said. "I'm fighting for justice."

"Yesss," Qibli whispered to himself. "I'mma do that too when I'm big." He puffed up his chest. "No! I'mma do that right now!" With a great hollering yell, he threw himself at the big dragon and sank his teeth into the thief's ankle.

The memory broke apart in chaos and shouting and dragons throwing punches, dropping them into Sundew's mind. The scene was the Poison Jungle; it started with chasing a frog through dark leaves and ended with meeting a green dragon named Willow.

Lizard's not going to like that one, Luna thought. *She*

probably thought Sundew, of all dragons, could give her a battle memory.

But even fierce, scary Sundew keeps thinking about the dragon she loves.

The last memory took them to a cave that flickered with torches. Five little dragonets sat in a circle by an underground river, studying a faded map. One was muscly and brown; one was tiny and golden yellow; one was a fidgety NightWing. The other two Luna recognized as a much younger Tsunami and Glory, who were arguing with each other.

"Look, the Kingdom of Sand is *clearly* biggest!" Tsunami shouted, stabbing one claw at the map.

"*You* don't know where the borders are!" Glory argued back. "Maybe the Sky Kingdom includes all of this!" She yanked the map toward her and pointed at a swathe of northern mountains.

"Oh, please be careful," said the NightWing, *tsk*ing nervously. "If we tear this map, Kestrel will be furious. She'll do something awful to both of you, I know it."

"No, it'll be worse," said the little yellow one, "because Clay will tell her it was his fault, and she'll punish him instead."

They all turned toward the brown dragon, who was blissfully chewing on something and looked very startled to suddenly have their attention.

"Mmmf?" he said. "Wha?"

"Yeah. He would do that," Tsunami agreed.

"All right, I'll keep my claws off it," Glory said, lifting her talons in the air. "But I still say the Sky Kingdom is bigger than we think."

"Everyone is fighting over the Kingdom of Sand!" Tsunami cried. "It *has* to be the biggest!"

Clay poked Tsunami in the nose. "Doesn't matter which one is the biggest," he said.

"Oh, really?" Tsunami batted his claw away.

"Nope," he said. "Only matters which one has the best food. That's where we're going to live, all together, one day when we're old and creaky."

The little one dissolved in laughter, and Glory said, "I have no intention of ever being . . . *creaky*."

Tsunami slung one wing around her and said, "Oh, you'll get there, as long as Clay keeps stopping me from murdering you."

And then they were back in the mindspace.

Moon exhaled, let go of Pineapple, and rubbed her forehead with a wince. "I'll be back," she whispered, and disappeared.

Luna looked from Dusky to Pineapple to Lizard; they all looked a little windblown from being whisked through all those memories, one after the other.

"Well," Lizard said finally. "I hated ALL OF THAT."

"You did?" Luna said. "But that was so many different dragons. All those different kinds of lives — isn't that what you wanted to see?"

Lizard growled to herself for a minute, and then she burst out, "I thought there would be someone like me! I wanted to know what *I* could have been like! But none of those dragons are *anything* like me!"

"I think they are," Luna said. "I mean, everyone is different, but we all still fit together." *Like the threads of a tapestry. We can weave Lizard in; she can still be part of something.* "Think about what you saw. Moon as a dragonet was so lonely, but she kept surviving anyway — that's just like you. Qibli stood up for himself even when his enemy was much stronger than him. You do that, too, every time you yell at Cottonmouth. Tsunami got mad so quickly as a dragonet — I think she still does that — and you do, too, but you've had to learn to calm yourself down, with no one else here to help."

Lizard rubbed her face. "What about the other two?"

Luna thought for a moment. "Sundew goes after what she wants without letting anything stop her. I think you're determined like that. And you heard that IceWing — Lynx didn't need rescuing. She wasn't afraid of being fed to walruses, and neither are you."

Lizard snorted. "That's true. I have no idea what a walrus is, but I know I could take one in a fight!" She paused and took a deep breath. "If I'd had a chance to grow up and meet one anyway. I think I'm more like that other white dragon on the wall, though. Snowfall? She was my favorite."

"Lizard, it's not fair what happened to you," Luna said.

"What's really not fair is the biggest difference between me and those dragons," Lizard said passionately. "They all had someone who loved them. No one ever loved me! Not that I care; I don't care, I don't care. But *that's* the unfair part, *actually*."

"You're right." Luna hesitated. "I think maybe also, though, it's unfair that *you* never got to love someone. That's important, too, and I'm sorry you never had that."

Lizard sniffed and wiped her face again with an impatient gesture. She glanced sideways at Dusky.

"Seems like loving someone makes you do really stupid things," she said.

"Yeah, true," Luna said, thinking of the many times Swordtail had thrown himself into trouble to spare her or Blue. Of Blue breaking all the rules he cared about so much to find Luna when she was taken to the flamesilk cavern. And Cricket, leaving behind her entire tribe and risking her biggest secret, to help a SilkWing she barely knew.

Lizard looked at the throne, at the tortured grimace on Cottonmouth's face as he puppeteered hundreds of dragons at once, somewhere far away. She looked back at Luna, and the flamesilk on Luna's horns reflected in the fathomless pools of Lizard's eyes.

"All right," Lizard said. "Listen, because I'm only going to say this once."

She took a deep breath.

"If you cut the vine that's growing through our heads," she said, her voice low and shaking, "the plant will be a normal plant again, and we'll be gone."

~ CHAPTER 24 ~

Luna stopped breathing.

"What?" she finally whispered.

"You heard me," Lizard said. "Don't make me say it again. Don't make me *think* about it. I don't want to talk about it and you'd better not say thank you and whatever you're going to do, I don't want to know. I shouldn't know. Distract me! Dusky, be interesting."

"Um!" Dusky sat up, looking very alarmed. "Like how?"

"Sing! Dance! Grow an extra head! I don't know!" Lizard shoved him again, and this time Dusky pounced on her. Lizard yelped, and they rolled across the dirt, play-wrestling.

"Quiet over there!" Cottonmouth shouted, and then went back into his trance, muttering.

Cut the vine. Luna pictured the throne room she'd flown into. The vine growing from the floor through Lizard's head and then Cottonmouth's.

Can I really do it?

Me, of all dragons?

I should probably wait for Sundew. She could do it easily, I bet.

But . . . I should try, at least. I'm the one who knows about this. I'm the one who's here, in this throne room, right now.

Even if I only get so far, even if I only help a little bit, that would still be a little bit closer to defeating the othermind and freeing the others.

I have to be like the dragons whose memories I just saw. Dragons who don't give up; dragons who jump in to save the ones they love; dragons who fight even when the enemy seems much too big. Dragons who don't need rescuing.

I don't want to be the dragon who always needs to be rescued.

All right. So how do I do this?

Can I get over there without him noticing? And then what — saw through the vines with my claws? He can take over my body and stop me anytime. My only chance is to get there stealthily and then do it quickly . . . ideally when he's distracted.

She closed her eyes and reached her way back into her real body. It was heavy and cold, clammy from the damp vines under her talons. Her claws were still curled around Dusky's small, listless form.

What do I do with him?

If I leave him here on the vines, Cottonmouth could use him against me. The moment he realizes what I'm doing, he could hurt Dusky and make me stop.

But I guess that's true no matter where Dusky is. And I'd rather have him with me.

Blindly she pushed and tugged the small dragonet over her shoulder until he was draped between her wings. She felt his tiny talons twitch against her neck. She forced her limbs to take a cautious step forward and felt the vines flex and bow and ripple under her feet. It was worse than walking on the sand on Jerboa's beach. There were a lot of vines and they were very thick, but her talons kept slipping through the gaps and tripping her up. It didn't help that she couldn't see where she was stepping, or be sure which way she was going.

I hope I'm pointed at the throne.

She slid forward another inch and then another. *Hurry!* her muscles screamed, but her mind screamed back *Careful!* and *What if he sees you?* and *Too fast!* and it was a whole stressful mess of conflicting instructions rioting around inside of her.

She wasn't sure how much time had passed, or whether she felt time the same way inside the mindspace — her internal clock felt like it was all out of order — when she heard Cottonmouth let out a hiss. Instantly she froze her real body in place. *Nothing to see here, nothing to see,* she thought frantically.

She opened her eyes in the mindspace. Dusky and Lizard were still romping around the room, tackling and pinning each other and wriggling free and running off. They looked so much like ordinary dragonets playing for a moment that Luna's heart hurt.

I wish there was a way to save her. To keep Lizard alive and give her a real life.

"We're approaching Lake Scorpion," Cottonmouth said imperiously. "Lizard, stop being infantile and focus." He stood up and glared around the mindspace as Lizard stumbled to a stop. "Make sure the mindwalker does not get in here. Do not let her speak to these two again." He nodded at Luna and Pineapple.

"Why do I have to do anything?" Lizard asked mutinously. "I thought you were *so brilliant* and I was *so useless* that I might as well not even be here."

"But you are here, so do as you're told," he said. "I'm busy enough. There are dragons causing trouble at Cicada Hive, Queen Wasp won't stop moaning and wailing about the pain in her face, so she's no help at all, and this rainbow dragon I'm in is about to run into my rogue HiveWing and her merry band of human pets." He thought for a moment. "I know. Jump into a HiveWing in Cicada Hive and kill a couple of SilkWings to make them all shut up."

He didn't notice the expression on Luna's face, but Lizard did.

"Boring," she said. "Don't feel like it. Oooo, I could make the Guardian climb up and steal another dragonet, though."

He gave her a withering look. "How would that help me at all? No. I forbid it. You've already cluttered up the place with these toys; that is quite enough for now."

"Bleh," Lizard said, flopping down on the floor and resting her chin on her talons.

"Well, you can sulk, or you can come fight some dragons; I don't care which," Cottonmouth said, closing his eyes again. "Just tell me if the mindwalker comes back. I assume you can be trusted with a task *that* simple."

Lizard stuck her tongue out at his blank face.

"Should we check on Cicada Hive?" Luna asked nervously.

"What does he mean, dragons are causing trouble? Are Swordtail and Blue all right?"

"Probably," Lizard said, exhaling. She toppled Dusky over, sat on him, and waved one talon in the air like a conjurer whisking away a curtain. The mindspace floated aside, and the Cicada Hive market settled in around them. It was much noisier than before. Many of the SilkWings were standing now, shouting at the guards, asking for answers. The dragons guarding the exits were white-eyed and perfectly still, blocking the way with their bodies but not fighting back or responding.

Luna thought she saw a flicker of dark purple wings in the crowd — *Io*? But when she turned, she couldn't see her friend anywhere. She spotted Swordtail on the far side of the Hive and spread her wings to fly over to him.

"Ooo, hang on," Lizard said, bumping her side. "Exciting things happening over by Lake Scorpion! Come on!"

Luna had no choice; a moment later, they were hovering in the air above a huge lake, glittering in the midday sunshine. Luna blinked, disoriented by the light. She hadn't realized how much time had passed in the real world.

Bringing Sundew closer and closer to Cottonmouth's trap.

Speaking of whom: there was the human, descending through the sky toward a cave opening on the north shore of the lake. It looked like the cave in the drawings Luna had seen, the one with all the humans walking into it.

A LeafWing was waiting on the pebbly beach by the lake. Water rippled over the dragon's green talons, and it seemed to be staring up into the trees. Real actual trees, on Pantala! Luna had never been to this peninsula, and she didn't know anyone else who had either. It wasn't quite the wild jungle of Pineapple's memories or the forest Luna had visited around Sanctuary. But there *were* trees here, growing along the hills that covered the cave system.

I bet that LeafWing is as amazed as I am, Luna thought. *I wonder if they're thinking the LeafWings should have hidden here instead of the Poison Jungle . . . but then again, it would have been much easier for Wasp to find and attack them here.*

Wait . . . who is that?

Bryony, Hemlock, or Pokeweed? Who else could it be?

Cottonmouth-in-Pineapple landed and approached the LeafWing. Luna nearly called out to warn the green dragon, not that it would have helped. But then the dragon turned, and she saw his boiled-egg-white eyes.

Oh no. One of Cottonmouth's creatures.

They didn't speak, but the other dragon turned toward the copse of trees behind him, and six other white-eyed dragons came forward — three HiveWings, three LeafWings — dragging Cricket and Bullfrog between them.

"Cricket!" Luna yelped.

The bespectacled HiveWing had two LeafWings flanking her, brandishing spears at her side. She blinked in confusion at Cottonmouth.

"Pineapple?" she said. "What are you doing here?"

"Pineapple is out to lunch, I'm afraid," Cottonmouth said, smirking cruelly.

Cricket's face crumpled. "Oh no, Pineapple. I'm so, so sorry."

There was a kind of crackling in the air, and suddenly the rest of Luna's friends were standing behind Pineapple. Sundew's scowl was so fierce, Luna was surprised Cottonmouth didn't go up in flames.

Cricket burst into tears. "*All* of you?"

"No," Qibli said quickly. "Cricket, we're all right. It only got Pineapple . . . and Luna."

Bullfrog looked startled. Cricket glanced toward the cave opening and pressed her talons together. "But — she's in the abyss — she said if I brought you, Sundew, that she'd be OK . . ."

"She *will* be," Sundew snarled, her eyes locked on Cottonmouth.

Tangles and threads, Luna suddenly realized. *I should be trying to cut the vine. I got distracted by watching, but this is my best and last chance. Quick, before anything else terrible happens here.*

She closed her eyes and reached, reached for her real body. It was harder from here, where she could sense the warmth of the sun on her scales and hear the trees rustling in the wind. This felt so much more real than the cold, damp, uneven, green-rot-smelling place where she really was.

Breathe, like Cricket said.

Finally her real claws began to tingle, and when she ordered her muscles to move forward, it was her real body that moved, not the one in the mindspace. The weight of Dusky still rested between her shoulder blades, breathing deeply.

"Let Cricket and Bullfrog go," she heard Sundew say with menace in her voice.

One step. Another step. Slippery vines around my ankle . . . carefully disentangle them . . . another step.

"Why in the world would I do that?" Cottonmouth answered. "It would be much more fair if I absorbed one of them. Or both of them. Then you'd have four of your dragons and I'd have four of your dragons, and you'd be much less tempted to try any clever tricks."

Luna's real nose bumped into something solid. *A wall? A column?* She felt it with her talons: flat, straight, a few vines zigzagging up it — the wall, then. *Pick a direction. Keep going.* She turned right and kept one left wing touching the wall as she felt her way forward again.

"The clever tricks are nonnegotiable," Qibli said. "Sundew is not going to deliver herself into your, um . . . petals? Sundew, what do you call the part of plants that eats dragons?"

"Jaws," Sundew said grimly.

"Yeep," Qibli said. "I think I'll stick with petals."

Luna's wing on her right side brushed cold stone. She reached out and felt it — smooth and curved — one of the columns. *Hope I'm going the right way.* She took another step, vines squishing and flexing under her talons.

"You don't exactly have a choice," Cottonmouth said. "I have infinitely more dragons than you do, and —"

"Hang on," Qibli interrupted. "Not *literally* infinitely. That's mathematically impossible."

Another column on Luna's right. That seemed promising.

She'd been close to the door, hadn't she? So if she was going the correct way, she would have to pass two columns before reaching the far wall with the throne. She thought. She hoped. It was hard to focus while listening to her friends in danger.

She pictured the throne room again, using the mental tapestry she'd imagined when she first saw it. What if she anchored herself, to make sure she could find her way back if anything happened?

Carefully she rested both front talons on the column, then spun out a long thread of ordinary golden silk. She passed it around the column and tied it off, leaving the other end still unspooling from her wrist as she started forward again.

"Do not bother being aggravating," Cottonmouth said in a bored voice. "Sundew, this HiveWing is Carabid. I chose him specially to be the one to inject you. He has marvelous stingers in his claws and tail and the ability to inject much more toxin than boring Wasp. He's been consuming all the breath of evil I could get him from the moment I met you. I think we might be able to absorb you on the first stab . . . although if we need to do more stabbing, there's time for that, too."

"Back up!" Tsunami yelled, making Luna stumble. "Don't you get any closer!"

"If you turn invisible again, or shoot any more unpleasant ice at me, I will have Carabid stab Cricket first," Cottonmouth hissed.

Luna walked straight into a wall. She was shaking a particularly clingy vine off one of her back feet and forgot to reach forward for a moment; her head thudded painfully against stone, and she let out a gasp of pain.

"Luna?" she heard Lizard say.

"Nothing," she whispered, dizzy. She took a deep breath, waiting for the shock of the pain to subside. "Ignore me."

She'd reached the corner. With luck, if she turned right here, she'd find the throne. Or, if she'd come the wrong way, she'd be back at the blocked entrance to the room. She turned, kept one wing on the wall, and felt her way forward.

Suddenly chaos erupted in the mindspace. Dragon screams filled Luna's ears, and she instinctively froze, paralyzed with terror.

"What's happening?" she cried. *Should I open my eyes? But I can't help them in the outside world. I can only help them if I stay focused and keep going in here.*

"A whole bunch of LeafWings just attacked!" Lizard yelped. "Including Sundew's mother! This is so exciting!"

"Didn't you know they were coming?" Luna cried. "Couldn't you have warned us?"

"How and why, exactly," Lizard asked. "You can't expect me to do *everything* around here."

That's true, Luna thought. *Stay on task.* She pressed forward again in her real body. The vines were so thick here, both underfoot and swarming up the wall. It was hard to feel the wall at all most of the time; she felt like she was floundering through a twisting pit of snakes, while at least twenty dragons roared and battled in her ears.

"Plants are just BURSTING out of the ground!" Lizard reported gleefully. "Sundew's got Carabid pinned in a bramble bush! Ooo, Cottonmouth nearly got Tsunami with his death spit! Eee, Belladonna just tried to stab Moon and Qibli jumped in the way! That ice dragon has frozen two of the LeafWings! ACK, like, NINE of our dragons just grabbed Cricket and THREW her at Carabid OH SNAP PEAS WE'RE FINALLY GETTING CRICKET NOW!"

"Cricket!" Luna squeezed her eyes shut and covered them with her talons to stop herself from opening them. "Can she hear me? Cricket!" She felt the thread connected to the column flick against her wings, humming softly.

"I'll take care of her," said Pineapple's voice, distant and drifting. "You keep going."

Forward. Another step. Fight the vines. Another step.

And then — her reaching talons found a mass of vines, and her heart sank.

Am I on the wrong end of the room?

She plunged her talons through the vines, feeling around frantically.

There! There was a heavy stone shape under the vines, solid and unyielding. *The throne. It has to be.*

I'm almost there.

"Sundew is MAAAAAAAD," Lizard announced. "Moon keeps yelling, 'Don't hurt Pineapple! Don't kill him! Sundew, remember it's not him!' but with all these branches flying everywhere, I'm pretty sure someone's going to die!"

Luna could hear Moon's cries herself. She also heard Lynx

shouting, "The wristbands!" and Qibli shouting about eight different instructions and Bullfrog and Tsunami roaring furiously and it was so hard to think; so hard to stay here, in the slow tangled space, instead of opening her eyes to make sure her friends were safe.

Do the thing I can do.

Pray that it helps.

I hope that Lizard is right about this.

She found a vine so thick her talons couldn't reach all the way around it. When she gingerly traced its path upward, her claws brushed a tiny foot and brittle scales.

Lizard's body, she thought with a shudder.

This is the vine I have to cut.

Do I cut it below Lizard's body, before it reaches them?

Or . . . if I cut the vine that's growing between Lizard and Cottonmouth . . . would that cut Cottonmouth out of the other-mind, but leave Lizard alive?

Lizard hadn't said exactly where to cut it, and Luna didn't want to ask in case Cottonmouth heard her.

All right. I'll try cutting it between them and hope that works.

"Oh, wow," Lizard said through the din of the roaring dragons. "Someone injected that big brown one, too. I wonder what *his* memories will be like."

Bullfrog . . .

Don't think about that. Focus on this.

Luna was hovering in the air now, her wings keeping her aloft in front of the tall throne. She beat them once to rise a little higher, tracing the curve of the vine up and through

Lizard's skull. Keeping one talon on the vine, she reached up to be sure Cottonmouth's head was above her, connected along the same winding trail.

Here.

But now what? She couldn't use her claws. The vine was so dense, and the moment she started to hack or slice at it, Cottonmouth would surely sense the attack, jump into her, and stop her.

She carefully rested her feet on the edge of the throne. The silk connecting her to the column rubbed against her wing again.

What if . . . ?

Luna spun out several more coils of silk and cut it loose from her wrist. She looped the silk lightly around the vine — *gentle, gentle, harmless, only leaves brushing each other* — crossed it over the thread coming from the column, and tied the loose end to her arm.

I hope the silk is strong enough. I hope my weight is enough to pull it straight through the vine in one quick slice.

Luna took a deep breath, braced herself to shove off, and launched herself away from the throne at full speed.

── CHAPTER 25 ──

The *SHRIEK* that filled Luna's head drowned out all the other dragons, and then they all cut off mid-roar, mid-shout, mid-scream, and Luna was flung violently out of the mindspace.

She opened her eyes just in time to see the wall of the real-world throne room as she smashed into it.

"Ow . . . owwwww," she moaned, sliding down and landing in the carpet of vines.

Silence enveloped her. She sat up, her head reeling, and reached over her shoulder. A little talon clutched hers, and her heart leaped.

"Dusky? Are you all right?"

The dragonet scrabbled up her back, wrapped his talons around her neck, and leaned into her, breathing deep shaky breaths.

"I think so," he said after a moment. "What happened? Where's Lizard?"

Luna turned to look at the throne, finally.

Her trick with the silk had worked. With her momentum pulling on one end and the other anchored at the column, the silk had sliced right through the vine, severing its connection with Cottonmouth.

How strange. I thought my flamesilk was what made me special, and that it was the one magic thing I could use to save the day. But instead it was my ordinary silk, and it could have come from any SilkWing at all.

And now *something* was happening. All the vines that branched out of the top of Cottonmouth's skull were withering, shriveling into brown and curling shreds before her eyes. The decay spread rapidly out along the long tendrils of the plant, all the way up to the ceiling and racing along the walls.

Luna scooped Dusky up and beat her wings to hover in the air, just in case. She thought the plant was dying, but she didn't want to be standing on it if it happened to have any last creepy death throes.

"Lizard?" she said out loud. The petrified body of the dragonet on the throne looked exactly the same, while Cottonmouth's husk already looked like it was starting to crumble around the edges. "Are you still there? Can you hear me?"

"You did it wrong," said Lizard's voice, echoing inside their skulls instead of coming through their ears. "Why would you do it *wrong*?"

"I did?" Luna said. "But it looks like it's working. Do you mean I cut it in the wrong place? I was trying to get rid of Cottonmouth and keep you."

"*Keep* me?" There was a sort of floundering silence for a moment. "You *can't*, you idiot. As long as the plant has an intelligent brain to work with, it won't give up. It wants to survive more than anything in the world. And with only two of us in here, now it's as strong as I am. Rrrrrgh . . . hang on . . ."

"But — you don't have to be evil, right? Now that Cottonmouth is gone?" Luna tried. "Maybe you and the plant can coexist. Maybe you'll like being a not-evil plant. And — and we can come visit you down here — right? And talk to you, like this?"

"NO!" Lizard shouted. "You are SO STUPID! The plant is already trying to use my leafspeak to grow back into Cottonmouth. Or it'll replace him with the Guardian, or if that doesn't work, it'll find some other awful human." Luna had forgotten about the Guardian — but there he was, curled up at the foot of the throne, rocking back and forth with a dazed expression.

"Luna!" yelled Lizard's voice in her head. "I don't want to just *exist* in this *nothingness* trying to fight a *desperate weed* for the rest of eternity! I HATE that plan!"

"I'm sorry, Lizard." Luna was crying now, and so was Dusky. "I'm so sorry. I didn't want to lose you. You saved us, and it's not fair."

"And you're funny," Dusky chimed in. "And fun to play with, and very loud, and scary sometimes, and bossy all the time, and brave and really interesting, and I don't want you to go away either."

Lizard didn't reply for a moment, and when she did, her voice was muffled. "Well. I have to," she said. "So you should say good-bye, and then you should get over here and cut the vine *below* my head, so the plant will stop using my brain to connive and flail around. Do it quick, before it gets to Cottonmouth again."

Luna realized with alarm that Lizard was right: a new spray of green was growing out of the vine where Luna's silk had sliced it, crawling tentatively up as though Cottonmouth's head was the sun.

She started forward, but Dusky tightened his arms around her. "Wait," he said. "Can we give Lizard a new name first? A real name, of her own, so she doesn't have to die still stuck with *his* name for her?"

"That seems pointless," Lizard said, but Luna thought she could hear a wary curiosity in her voice. "A new name for thirty seconds?"

"A new name forever," Luna said. "One we can remember you by, and write songs about, and weave into tapestries."

"Hmmm," said the five-thousand-year-old dragonet. "You better not put my shriveled corpse with a hole in its skull in any tapestry."

"YUCK," Dusky objected.

"I won't," Luna promised, laughing through her tears. "I'll weave you flying. You'll be with all the dragons who gave you their memories."

"Your friends," Dusky put in. "Especially me. Can I be in the tapestry?" he asked Luna.

"Of course," Luna said. "You'll be together. And you'll be free."

The tiny dragon sighed inside their heads, long and wistful.

"What do you want to be called?" Dusky asked.

"I don't know what tribe I was," she answered. "I don't know what kinds of names we had, or what my mother might have called me." She paused for a moment. "Do you think . . . would Freedom be a weird name for a dragon?"

"Not at all," Luna said.

"I like it," Dusky agreed. "It's what you'll have and also what you're giving everyone."

"We'll call you Freedom from now on," Luna said.

"Cool," Freedom said quietly.

Luna reached up and squeezed one of Dusky's talons. They flew over to the throne, now surrounded by crackling, dying vines. Only the original stem rising from the floor was still green and vibrant — that, and the new tendril that was trying to claw its way back from the severed vine.

Luna set Dusky down on one corner of the throne.

"Can I help?" he asked.

She touched the top of his tiny head. He'd already been through so much. "Are you sure?" she asked. "Won't it make you sad?"

"I'm already sad," he pointed out. "This way I'd be helping say good-bye."

"But —"

"She's already dead," he said matter-of-factly. "What we're doing is setting her free from the plant."

I suppose that's right, she realized. *That's the right way to look at it.*

Luna produced more silk and tied one end around his

wrist; then she wound the silk around the vine and tugged gently on the other side to tighten it.

"Thanks for this," Freedom said awkwardly. "And most of all for the look on Cottonmouth's face as he poofed into dust. It was even better than face melting."

"You're welcome," Luna said with a smile.

"And thank you for all your squishy, ridiculous, cuddle-monster memories," Freedom said in a rush. "I guess maybe they weren't *so* bad. If I'd had a real life, it would be maybe OK if you two were in it."

"Hey, we *were* in it," Dusky said. "In your life, I mean."

"Huh," Freedom said. "All right, fine; you can be right, just this once."

"Are you ready?" Luna asked.

"I am," Dusky said, nodding.

"Me too," said Freedom. "Good-bye."

"Thank you, Freedom," Luna said, and then she and Dusky pulled on the silk and severed the breath of evil from the dragonet who'd saved them.

~~ CHAPTER 26 ~~

Soon after they cut the vine, both of the husks on the throne crumbled into dust. Luna dug down into the dirt around the last, original piece of the vine that Cottonmouth had planted so many centuries ago. She used her flamesilk to burn all the roots, which stretched far into the ground like burrowing eels. The smoke was green and a little dizzying, but it dissipated quickly, and there was nothing left to reach into their brains or take them over.

All the rest of the vines in the room had shriveled up, including the ones blocking the door. Flying up out of the abyss was much harder and more tiring than flying down into it, especially with Dusky on her back and the disoriented Guardian cradled in her talons. But Luna was so happy to be flying, so happy to be out of that throne room, that her wings felt like they could keep beating forever.

At the top of the chasm, she found Wren, Axolotl, and Sky with the humans who had kidnapped Dusky.

"Luna!" Sky cried as she rose over the edge.

"*Yes,*" Wren said triumphantly. "I *told* you she'd survive!

You owe me a turtle! Hang on, why did I agree to bet in turtles."

"Are you all right?" Sky asked. "What happened down there?"

"It's a long, long story," Luna said. She landed and gently deposited the Guardian in front of the other humans. He pushed himself to his feet, wobbling. The one named Raven gasped and grabbed her friend's arm, and then they both ran forward and caught the gaunt, bedraggled human before he could topple over.

"Is he back to normal?" Luna asked Wren.

Wren said something to Raven in Human and then all the humans had a chatterfest for a minute. Finally Wren looked up at Luna, grinning.

"They think so," she said. "That is, he remembers that his name is Vole, and he remembers the Guardian Ceremony, but not much after that except being hungry all the time. They hope he'll be all right after a lot of rest."

"And a bath," Sky suggested. "Also a haircut. Maybe several more baths."

"Let's go find Cricket and the others," Luna said. "I think the othermind is gone, but I want to make sure they're safe."

"Cricket!" Axolotl said in a near-perfect Dragon accent. They patted one of the pouches around Sky's neck, which Luna recognized as the one with the dragon book in it. "Book friend," Axolotl added with a smile.

"Wow," Luna said to them, impressed. "Very good."

They pointed to her. "Luna. Fire friend."

"We've been practicing," Wren said proudly. "You were down there for days, you know."

"I am very, *very* hungry," Luna realized.

"Me too!" Dusky chirped from her back.

"We can eat after we find the others. Do you know how to get to Lake Scorpion from here?" she asked Wren.

Wren spoke to the abyss humans again, then said, "Raven says she'll take us there, while Mole gets his brother back to the village."

It was strange for Luna to walk through the tunnels with the sharp-faced, feathered human, listening to her murmuring voice in conversation with Wren and Axolotl. This human kidnapping Dusky was the whole reason Luna had wound up in the abyss. But Luna couldn't bring herself to be angry at Raven.

On the scale of all the things that humans and dragons had done to one another over the centuries, it was only one small, desperate act. And continuing the cycle of fury and revenge and punishment . . . that was for other dragons, perhaps, but not for Luna.

At least, that's how she felt when it came to present-day humans. *I'm still angry at Cottonmouth. And Queen Wasp. They were trying to make the world a worse place for their own selfish reasons, and they hurt a lot of dragons.*

And she didn't know what to think yet about the HiveWings. She had a feeling that would depend on what they did next, without malevolent voices in their heads.

The sunlight up ahead was so dazzling that Luna was

blinking, her eyes watering, long before they reached the cave entrance and stepped outside. How many days had they been underground? How long had she been trapped in the abyss? She had no idea, but it felt as though years had passed since the real sun had warmed her scales. In the mindspace vision, the whisper of the trees and the leafy scent of the air had seemed real enough, but now that she could truly breathe them in, it was overwhelming.

She stood in the sunlight with her eyes closed for a moment, letting her senses and her internal clock realign, feeling her real body really here and nowhere else. She felt Sky gallop past her, yelling, "Pineapple! Qibli!" and a hubbub of voices came toward them through the trees.

When she opened her eyes, Cricket was standing right in front of her, eyes shining.

"The othermind is gone, isn't it?" Cricket asked. "You did something amazing, didn't you?"

"Not just me," Luna said. "Everyone helped."

Cricket impulsively threw her wings around Luna, and Luna hugged her back, smiling. For the first time, this didn't feel like "a HiveWing" hugging her; this was Cricket, who was more than her scales and her tribe, just like every dragon.

"Ahem," Sundew interrupted, coming up to join them. "Before we get to the hugfest, can someone tell me what exactly happened? One minute, I was locked in a ferocious battle, turning every plant I could reach into a fearsome weapon, ready to fight to the death, and the next minute, all my foes suddenly fell over as though their bones had turned into ferns."

"I felt that," Pineapple said. "It was like . . . that feeling when you're holding up a huge bunch of bananas while someone saws them free, and then suddenly the last fiber is cut, but you weren't paying attention, so the whole thing plummets out of your talons and it's like, ack! oops! but wow, you feel so much lighter. Sad about the bananas, though. Hmmm. Maybe that wasn't the best analogy."

"Did you feel them both go?" Luna asked. "Cottonmouth, and then the dragon?"

"Yes," Pineapple said. "There was an odd in-between time when I felt like I was myself but still sort of . . . tethered, maybe? And then I felt her and the plant go, and I was all me again."

"Her?" Sundew demanded. "Her who?"

"I'll tell you the whole story," Luna said. "Everything that happened in the abyss." She glanced up at the sun, now slanting down toward the western horizon. "But . . . can I tell you on the way to Cicada Hive? There's someone waiting for me in the Mosaic Garden."

And when they arrived the next morning, Swordtail was there, he really was, he was standing on the hill surrounded by violets and sunshine, waiting, as though he could wait forever and *would* wait forever for her, and when she swooped in through the open sky arches and soared over everyone's heads and crashed into his arms, he laughed as they fell over and they rolled through the grass, and it was real, *he* was real, at last.

"Are you all right?" she said finally, sitting up. She lifted his eyelids and studied each beautiful dark blue pupil. "One hundred percent Swordtail?"

"I *was* all right," he said. "And then YOUUUUUUUU squished the honey drops!"

Luna squeaked and jumped back, discovering a squashed white box under her tail.

"See," he said self-righteously. "I am not the only one who sits on candy around here."

"Aw, you got me honey drops," she said, beaming. She scooted the box aside and snuggled under his wings.

"Well," he said, "what else do you get for the dragon who rescued your brain? I don't think they covered this in Manners and Proper Behavior class."

"They actually did," she said, "and you know what's weird? The answer is honey drops." She reached up and patted his snout while he laughed, checking again that he was real. "I missed you SO MUCH."

"I missed you more," he said.

"Where's Blue?" she asked.

"In the webs with Io and your moms," he said. "He needs a lot of hugs right now."

"On it," Luna said, jumping up. "Let's get Cricket and go

hug the antennae off that dragon!" She sprinted back to the sky arches with Swordtail behind her.

Outside, Cricket and Sky and Pineapple were flying in a circle, waiting for her, with Wren on Sky's back and Axolotl on Pineapple's. The other dragons had gone to Wasp Hive with Sundew, to make sure someone imprisoned Queen Wasp so she could be brought to justice.

Luna beckoned to her friends and led the way back to her home in the sunlit, silk-spun webs full of rainbow-colored dragons. She hadn't been paying attention before, but now that she looked, there was a weird quiet hanging over everything. The dragons she could see looked like they had all just come out of their cocoons: disoriented, startled, and potentially thrilled but in a very confused way.

In fact, she realized, she hadn't seen any HiveWings at all yet.

"Swordtail," she asked. "Where did all the HiveWings go?"

"Home," he said. "Deep into the Hive. When the mind control snapped, some of them tried to keep ordering us around, but most of them just wanted to go home and find their families and be inside their own bodies again, in their own space. Wasp had been controlling them since she brought them to the Snarling River, which is much, much longer than she'd ever stolen their minds before." He hesitated. "I still think they're the worst, and if it were up to me, I'd take every HiveWing soldier and merchant and teacher and snob who was mean to us and put them on Misbehaver's Way for a year. But after having someone in my own head like that . . . I mean, it was pretty terrible."

He looked up at the pale sprays of cloud feathered across the sky, then back at her, adding quickly, "But they still could have DONE something to try and be better dragons. Like, maybe they could have noticed that Queen Wasp was an evil dictator, and certainly they could have treated SilkWings like equal dragons and generally not been jerks. So. I go back and forth a bit."

"*My* brain words," Luna said ruefully.

He laughed. "Words of my head."

"I have no idea what's going to happen with the HiveWings," she said, brushing one of his wings with hers. "But let's do what we can do for right now, which is take care of Blue."

She glanced around and saw Cricket hanging back shyly as they approached Luna's home. Luna wondered if Blue had had a chance to tell their moms about the HiveWing who loved him. Burnet, Silverspot, and Io all stood up, bristling, when they saw her, but Luna took one of Cricket's talons in hers and guided her into the silken cell.

"Hello, all," she said. "This is Cricket. She's part of our family now."

And then her moms saw the look on Blue's face as he saw Cricket, and Luna knew it was going to be all right. It might take them a moment, the way it had taken her a moment, but if Blue loved her and Luna trusted her, soon they would, too.

She did not even mind that Cricket got to wrap her wings around him first. That was fine because her wings fit over

Cricket's, and Swordtail's could go around hers, and they were together, and safe, finally, finally, finally.

Luna knew they had only started to change the world. There was still a lot to do — a lot of dragons who needed help, dragons who needed homes, and dragons who needed a new way of looking at the world, which would be the hardest thing of all.

But she didn't have to do it by herself. She didn't have to be the one great and mighty and wonderful flamesilk who set the world on fire and saved everyone and fixed everything all alone. And she also didn't have to be the sad, lost dragon who sat and waited to be rescued.

She only had to be herself, Luna, talon in talon with Blue and Cricket and Swordtail and Sundew and all the dragons of the Distant Kingdoms, and hopefully the humans, too. If each of them tried, even a little bit, to make the world even a little better . . .

Then maybe there was hope.

And maybe things could change.

~ EPILOGUE ~

The sky was full of dragons.

Luna had made six weavings and was halfway through a seventh, but she still hadn't managed to capture quite how breathtaking it was to see so many colors and so many wing shapes diving and soaring together. The more visitors flew over from the Distant Kingdoms, the more complicated her tapestries got.

"Maybe I don't have the sky color quite right yet," she said, holding up her claws to frame a piece of the feathery clouds. The rain had stopped not long ago, and the air felt like wading through sunshine, liquid and gold up close and lined with dark gray in the distance, and *completely* impossible to capture in silk. "Or maybe I'll never figure out how to convey motion in a tapestry. Like pinning down a dragonfly or a firefly; it's not the same if they're not moving."

"I think your weavings are perfect," Swordtail said contentedly.

"And LOOK at that rainbow," Luna said with disgust. "Nobody would believe it if I put a rainbow that pretty into my tapestry. Everyone would be like, 'Oh, sure, Luna, I just bet there was also a perfect rainbow in your perfect scene of dragons from different tribes getting to know each other. VERY subtle metaphor, well done.'"

"You could do a tapestry of the SilkWing Assembly trying to get anything done," Swordtail suggested. "If you're looking for a . . . less perfect scene."

"Ack, I love them, but oh my goodness," Luna said.

"Oh, *sorry*, did you have something to say?" Swordtail struck a pose, imitating the SilkWings who'd been chosen for the Assembly. "No, no, please, you go ahead! Wait, maybe she had an idea? Oh no, I'm sure he was about to speak! These are all great suggestions, everybody, really great. Someday eventually we'll get around to potentially doing something about some of them. Break for lunch!"

Luna laughed. "They're lovely," she said. "They'll figure it out. We haven't had a SilkWing in charge of anything in a really long time, and Wasp left no descendants from Queen Monarch, so I think this is a good compromise."

"*I* think perhaps *two hundred* SilkWings in one governing body is *a few too many*," Swordtail said, rolling his eyes. "Especially when Morpho is one of them."

"Io and Tau will sort them out," Luna said. "At least we're not in the mess the HiveWings are in."

Wasp was imprisoned in her own flamesilk cavern, along with all of her sisters. Lady Jewel was nominally now Queen Jewel of the HiveWings, but there was a lot of rumbling and grumbling and several disgruntled factions in the tribe.

Some HiveWings wanted to get far away from the Hives and any reminder of what Wasp had done to them — one named Treehopper had immediately come to find Tau and never left. Another was Hawker, one of the checkpoint soldiers Luna remembered from Cicada Hive. And to Luna's surprise and Cricket's delight, the one they'd rescued on the island, Earwig, had defected from the HiveWings, too. She'd appeared in the new SilkWing encampments, looking for the dragons who had left her the map to get home.

"See?" Cricket had said to Sundew triumphantly. "It *was* the right thing to do."

But not all dragons felt that way. There were rather a horrifying amount of HiveWings who wanted Queen Wasp back, mind control and all, which was the most mystifying thing Luna had ever heard.

She was glad there were other dragons — LeafWings, mostly, like Belladonna — who were happy to grapple with that problem.

"I was sort of hoping we'd fixed everything," Luna said to Swordtail. "We defeated the big bad guy! Whoosh! All better! Right? So whyyyyyyy are there still more problems and things to fix, I don't like it."

"Yeah," Swordtail said. "And they're *woobly* problems, all *complicated* and stuff. BLERGH to you, problems, I say."

"I don't know how you reach dragons like those HiveWings," Luna said. "Like . . . how do you help dragons save themselves? Or teach them to care about other dragons, especially

ones who don't look like them? It feels completely impossible."
She sighed, and Swordtail brushed her wing with his.

"You know what makes me feel better?" he said. "Thinking
about the good dragons instead of the bad ones. I focus on
how many dragons are out there trying to make the world
better instead of worse. It's not only us — lots of other dragons are trying to fix things, too. Right? We all keep going and
keep trying and keep fixing what we can. And if you're tired
or sad or need a break, that's OK. Because it's not all on you.
There's lots of us doing this together."

Luna rubbed her eyes and looked up at him. "I get sad
sometimes," she admitted quietly.

"I know," he said, putting his wing around her. "And
when you do, you can tell me."

She nodded and took a deep breath. Most of the time, she
was all right; most of the time, she could think about her art
and the dragons she loved, and the sadness would lift. But
sometimes it still found her; sometimes especially when she
thought about the HiveWings, and how there were still so
many dragons who didn't care about hurting others.

"I kind of wish we could do the same thing for them that
we did for Freedom," she said. "I wish we could link them to
our memories and let them feel what it's like to be someone
else for a little while. Or show them that what we're trying to
build is a better world for everyone, not just us."

Swordtail bumped her side. "That's what your weavings
are for," he said. "And those stories Cricket and Blue have

talked about writing." He reached into the bag around his neck and pulled out the rolled-up weaving she'd brought for Sundew.

It was one of Luna's visions for the LeafSilk Kingdom: a vast forest of trees covering the southern half of the continent, with webs of silk and hammocks and tree houses all connected together. It looked a little bit like the RainWing home, but here half the dragons were green with leaf-shaped wings, and there were gardens in the clearings, and galleries full of silk tapestries, and a library full of books that told the truth.

Swordtail unrolled it and spread it on the grass, smiling.

"You looked at it five minutes ago!" Luna said with a laugh.

"I know!" he said. "Looking at it makes me happy. I mean, who doesn't want to live in this world?"

"Oh!" Luna cried, clutching his arm. "Here they come, here they come!"

Cerulean-blue and orange-gold-black wings were descending from the sky; the sunlight reflected brightly off Cricket's glasses. Luna waved at them as Swordtail rolled the weaving back up again, and Blue veered toward her. From Cricket's shoulder, Axolotl waved back.

"Did we get here before Sundew?" Cricket called.

"Nope," Sundew said cheerfully, bounding up next to Luna with Willow beside her. She grinned at Blue and Cricket as they landed. Her smile wavered a bit at the dragons right behind them, but everyone had already awkwardly met Cricket's parents, Katydid and Malachite.

Luna had told them how Malachite tried to help Qibli,

Tsunami, and Pineapple in Wasp Hive, and they'd also heard the story of how Malachite had been taken away by Queen Wasp when she realized Lady Scarab cared about him. He was one of the HiveWings who hadn't been in control of his own body for many years — him and the Librarian and a few others. Most of them were among those who'd come to seek refuge in the LeafSilk Kingdom.

"It's so beautiful from up there," Blue said to Sundew, his eyes shining. "It's like a huge dragon spread green wings all across the Dragontail Peninsula. I can't believe how many more trees there are already. We were only gone a few days!"

"She might tell you that's the magic of leafspeak," Willow said, "but the true magician will be whoever can get her to stop and *actually eat something* once in a while." She twined her tail around Sundew's and released Bumblebee into the grass. The little HiveWing bounded over to hug Cricket's leg, her wings vibrating happily.

Axolotl slid down beside her, patted Bumblebee's head, and gave her a carrot to gnaw on. The human was staying with Cricket for a while to keep studying Dragon, and they had found the way straight to Bumblebee's heart very quickly.

"I eat all the time!" Sundew protested. "I ate a . . . something . . . this morning while we were sorting Pyrrhian tree seedlings! Didn't I? I think I did. The seedlings were very noisy, full of questions. It must be weird to fly across an ocean when you're a tree. Not a common tree experience, I suspect."

"If you're talking about that talonful of cashews, that does not count," Willow said.

"Dose MY CASHOOOS," Bumblebee announced grumpily. "Snudoo in BIG TRUBUBBLE."

"Well, we're having a big feast after this, right?" Swordtail interjected. "I was promised a tree planting party!"

"Ah, yeah," Willow said. "Sundew's idea of a tree planting party is one where we plant trees all day and then look at them and go: 'Well done, us. Good night, trees!' And that's it, that's the whole party."

Swordtail looked outraged, and so did Bumblebee, although that was Bumblebee's normal face much of the time, so it was hard to tell how much this concept of a party was specifically offending her.

"No, no, no," Swordtail said. "A tree planting party is: we plant ONE tree, and then we eat and dance and flop around and eat some more and *ideally* play charades."

"Turns out Swordtail is weirdly great at charades," Luna said. "This is a new discovery. Qibli's fault, it may not surprise you to hear."

"Charades are my secret superpower," Swordtail said, fluffing out his wings. "Just wait until it's *my* turn to save the world."

"If anyone can save the world with charades, it's you," Blue said loyally.

"Yes," Luna said, "when the bad guy gets SO FRUSTRATED because you refuse to tell him what you're acting out, and the charades never end, so he can never enact his evil plan."

"I think this party can find some happy medium between

planting trees all day and infinite charades," Willow said with a laugh.

"Did you bring it? Can I meet it?" Sundew asked Cricket.

Cricket's wings shimmered as she reached into the large basket her parents had been carrying between them. She gently lifted out a ball of roots and dirt, out of which grew a tiny, perfect tree.

"Tree!" Axolotl said with delight. "Book friend, tree friend." They pointed to Cricket and then Sundew. Bumblebee bonked their hand with her snout and Axolotl laughed. "Loud friend."

"I can't believe my tree survived while I was away," Cricket said. "I wonder if someone at school was secretly watering my terrarium for me. Wouldn't that be kind? I was so happy to see it again. I hope it's all right. Can you tell if it's all right? I tried to explain to it that it was going to a place where it could grow big and strong and free in the sunshine."

"I'll let it know," Sundew said, taking the ball of dirt into her talons. She touched her snout to the top of the miniature leaves and closed her eyes.

"It's a ficus," she whispered. "It says hello, more or less, in, like, a tree way, you know. It also says thank you, Cricket, for keeping it alive. I mean, I'm translating, but that's essentially what it's saying. Would you like to grow bigger, little tree?" She listened for a moment, then nodded. "All right, let's see."

Sundew carried the tree over to the hole Luna and Swordtail had helped to dig earlier. She tucked the ball of roots in like it was a baby dragonet — well, an agreeable baby dragonet, like Dusky; not the shrieking hurricane of fury that Bumblebee turned into most bedtimes.

She's better when they have sleepovers, Luna reminded herself, glancing at the little HiveWing, who was watching Sundew with awe. *And Dusky loves her fierceness.*

They had found Dusky's mother, the sweetest dark blue dragon, who had cried and cried when she finally got to hug her dragonet for the first time. Luna wasn't worried about him anymore. He'd have all the hugs he could possibly want, and Luna was close by if he needed more.

Sundew covered the roots and buried her claws in the dirt. A few moments later, the tree's leaves quivered, then started to stretch, reaching for the sun. The branches spread and the trunk widened as it grew. Cricket's parents and Axolotl let out matching gasps, and Cricket clapped her talons together with delight.

Soon the tree towered overhead, looking enormously proud of itself.

"I love it," Cricket breathed.

"Me too!" Bumblebee declared. "Less call it BUMBOBEE JUNIOR!"

"You should make a tapestry of this tree," Sundew said to Luna. "The most beautiful Bumblebee in the world."

"WHAT?" Bumblebee shrieked.

Sundew and Willow both cracked up, and Bumblebee shook her little fist at them.

"Wait until you see her newest weaving!" Swordtail said

happily, pulling out Luna's tapestry again. "I think this is my favorite."

"You say that about every single one!" Blue pointed out.

"And it's always true." Swordtail beamed. He unfurled the weaving, and they all gathered around it.

"Oh, wow," Cricket said. "All right, this one is my favorite, too."

"You ALSO say that about every single one," Blue observed, and they gave each other little starry-eyed nudges.

"Cricket," Luna said slowly. "I've been wondering if I should make some tapestries about . . . well, about the Scorching, and Freedom's story. The real story of all the terrible things that happened. I don't really want to. I feel like they would be awful weavings and they'd make everyone sad, which is not what I want my silk to do. But I have to, don't I? Because they'd be true, and everyone should know the truth, shouldn't they?"

"Yes, they should," Cricket said, "but that's what I'm here for. I'll do that for you, Luna. I feel like that's my responsibility, and something I *can* do. I'll make sure dragons know the truth, and that we record history in our books the way it really was — about Cottonmouth and the Scorching, about the real Book of Clearsight, and about what humans are like now."

"We'll help," said her dad. He adjusted his spectacles in exactly the way Cricket always did. "Writing was something I loved to do, when I was myself. When I was little, I had this plan that I would write about something that happened every day and give the story to all my neighbors."

"I did, too!" Cricket said, wide-eyed. "I had that exact same plan!"

Malachite patted her head tentatively, like he was still trying out the gestures that went with the idea of "dad." "My parents shut that down pretty quick, I'm afraid."

"Mine, too," Cricket said glumly. "I mean . . . my grandparents did."

"You wrote the stories for me for a while, though," Katydid reminded her. "I loved those. The one about the peacock that got loose in your school and ran around screaming for a day — that was amazing."

Cricket lit up as though her veins were full of flamesilk. "We can do it now," she said to Malachite. "Together." She turned to Luna. "We'll do that part. You let us worry about telling the past, and you keep making tapestries like this, about the future we can all hope for." She touched the corner of the one Sundew was inspecting.

"Is it worth it?" Luna asked. "Dreaming all these big wild dreams that will probably never come true? Sometimes I think I should make my ideas smaller and more realistic."

"No!" Blue said, taking her talon in his. "I want the world with big dreams in it."

"Me too," Sundew agreed. "We need dragons who can see the brightest futures so we can try to get there, even if it takes longer than we want it to."

"And even if some dragons are stupid and make getting there harder than it needs to be," Swordtail declared.

"YEAH!" Bumblebee shouted. "SOME DRAGONS STUPID!"

Cricket winced. "Except we don't use that word, remember?" she said, giving Swordtail a pointed look. "We try to use *kind* words and *understand* each —"

"SOME DRAGONS VERY STUPID!" Bumblebee shouted, loud enough that several of the dragons in the sky turned to see what the noise was. "THE STUPIDEST! BRAINS FULL OF STUPID! HA HA HA!"

"Thank you *so* much," Cricket said to Swordtail as Bumblebee bounded off into the grass, pouncing on grasshoppers and yelling insults at them. He gave her an innocent shrug and crouched to roll up the tapestry again. Blue laughed.

We do try to understand each other, Luna thought, looking at her brother, the sweetest, most understanding dragon in the world, who had still managed to fight back when he had to. *But even if we find a way to understand the dragons who hurt us, that doesn't mean we have to let them do all the terrible things they want to do. We can empathize with them like Blue does and try to stop them, like Sundew would, all at the same time.*

"Well, now that certain little chaos monkeys aren't listening," Willow said, watching Bumblebee charge away, "who wants to try the fried bananas Luna and I invented?"

"BANANANANANAAAAAAAAAAAAAAAAAAS!" Bumblebee bellowed, skidding around at top speed and hurtling back toward Willow.

"I suppose I deserve that," Willow said as the dragonet

scaled her leg and threw her arms around Willow's neck to yell "BANANAS!" in her ear.

Axolotl laughed. "Bananas," they tried. "St—upid?"

"Bananas yes," Cricket told them, holding out her talon. "Stupid no." Axolotl climbed up to her shoulder, looking puzzled.

"Who's got the dreamvisitor this week?" Sundew asked. Luna raised her talon, and they all turned to walk into the forest that Sundew was growing with her leafspeak. "Maybe we can see if any of our friends are asleep in the Distant Kingdoms and want to say hi."

"Pineapple and Jambu promised to visit soon," Luna said.

"And then we'll go there!" Swordtail said. "And then they'll come here and then we'll go there and then there will be dragons in all directions!"

"Dragons and humans," Cricket offered, nudging Axolotl's foot affectionately.

"Sure," Swordtail agreed. "Weird. But mostly dragons."

"Dragons and humans, living in peace after all this time," Luna said, tilting her head back to watch the sunlight through the leaves. "I can't wait to see what that future is like."